Wings Over Luckenbach

The Story of Jacob Brodbeck and His 1865 Air Ship

Iris Brodbeck Macek

Illustrations by Molly Macek

Printed in the United States of America

ISBN: 1722090871
ISBN-13: 978-1722090876

Dedication

Wings Over Luckenbach is dedicated to the memory of Hugo and Lolete Brodbeck, loving parents of Rodger Brodbeck, Buddy Brodbeck, Iris Brodbeck Macek, and Danny Brodbeck. Instilling in their children the strength of family life, they provided a foundation for experiencing life's joys and coping with life's struggles. Thank you, Mom and Dad. Thank you to my wonderful brothers; to Rodger's wife, Patsy, and to Danny's wife, Cil, for their love and support all through the years.

Wings Over Luckenbach is also dedicated to the many descendants of Jacob and Christine Brodbeck. The circle of life goes on.

Acknowledgements

I give God praise for the inspiration given to me in writing *Wings Over Luckenbach.* I thank Him for placing the right people in my path and the right research materials in my hands at each crucial turn.

I want to thank the Highland Lakes Writers' Club of Marble Falls, Texas, and all their members who offered me much guidance when I first started writing my book.

At the second meeting, I met Dodie Lemley and LaTrelle Bagwell, who believed in my project from the very start. Thank you, Dodie, for all your writing tips and technical input. Thanks so much, LaTrelle, for listening to my ideas and offering encouragement in getting me started.

I soon joined a critique group associated with the Highland Lakes Writers' Club. Of this group, Bob Allgeier, Roy Henley, Amber Jones, Kay Lee and Louise Heindel all helped me become a better writer. Bob Allgeier steered me in the use of active voice over passive voice in my writing. Many thanks to all of you!

Freedom Writers, a critique group with emphasis on Christian writing, greatly benefitted me. I thank Amber Jones who initiated its beginnings. Tom Chick, the group leader, along with Amber, Lane Chisholm, and Dave Cagley shared their writing skills as we poured over their work and my chapters. Tom suggested certain German words and phrases; later he made the first donation towards getting my book published. Soon, Jamie Greening joined our sessions adding his unique insight and editing techniques. I am very grateful to all of you for your constructive input.

A new direction appeared at the time I needed it when Jamie Greening, already a published author, started a daytime critique group focused on getting manuscripts ready for publishing. Thanks so much, Jamie, for your leadership and literary expertise. Amber Jones came along with her inventive mind. Pat Shaub, a retired helicopter pilot, joined us. I thank all of you for the hours spent helping me edit my manuscript.

God placed Pat Shaub in my path at a critical turn. Writing in vivid detail about his experiences in aviation, he became interested in the story of the early flight of Jacob Brodbeck. His enthusiasm for my book and his experience in getting a book published were invaluable to me. I am so grateful to you, Pat!

Along the way there are others I want to acknowledge. Reta Killingsworth, the current Brodbeck Family Reunion President and a relative, offered early encouragement. Her findings detailing Johann Georg, the brother of Jacob Brodbeck, helped round out his part in the story. Thank you, Reta! And I truly appreciate another relative, Elnora Kneese, for her wonderful watercolor painting on the front cover.

I want to say a special thank you to my talented granddaughter, Molly Macek. She looked at photographs and listened when I explained the story to her. With her intuitive nature, she created the wonderfully expressive illustrations which grace the pages of the book. I appreciate her technical skills with the placement of the illustrations and photographs. Linsay, Molly's mother and my lovely daughter-in-law, helped solve other technical issues. I am so grateful to you both.

I thank my brother, Danny and his wife, Cil for their loving support. In our many discussions about writing, Cil, a published author, helped me understand the process.

And finally, for believing in me and listening to all my ups and downs, my heartfelt thanks go to each of my three dear adult children, Dawna Macek Ferrell, Jody Macek and Jarrett Macek, all accomplished in their own ways. My love and appreciation for each of you is endless. You are the sun, moon and stars of my life.

Introduction

A biographical novel, *Wings Over Luckenbach* tells the story of Jacob Brodbeck and his 1865 airship.

What is a biographical novel?

Irving Stone explains in the forward of *The President's Lady,* based on the lives of Rachel and Andrew Jackson . . .

> *"a biographical novel differs from a historical novel in that it does not introduce fictional characters against a background of history, but instead tells the story through the actual people who lived it and made it happen."*

Wings Over Luckenbach—based on the real-life events of Jacob Brodbeck—takes the reader on a journey of Brodbeck's life-long quest to construct and fly an air ship. As he confronts the obstacles of human flight, he is aided by his loyal brother, Johann.

Being a great-granddaughter of Jacob Brodbeck, throughout my life I was privy to many stories which have been retold through generations of Brodbeck descendants.

Along with family pictures and drawings of the "Air Ship," in the back of the book there is a bibliography of resource materials used in helping to create the background for the Brodbeck story.

Because many pieces of the story are missing, I used common sense and a healthy dose of my imagination to fill in the gaps. Where there was ambiguity in different reports and different family stories in the sequencing of events, I chose sequences which told the best story.

Scavenging through books and online accounts, I investigated the lives of actual people the Brodbeck brothers might have met during their lifetimes. I took the liberty to create experiences and conversations between them. Along the way, a few fictional characters emerged to give flavor to the narrative.

Of significance in *Wings Over Luckenbach* is the background story of how two German immigrants survived the Texas frontier, helped establish towns, schools and governments where none or few had existed, all the while managing to experiment with manned flight.

To be sure, the Wright Brothers encountered many hurdles in the pursuit of flight, but perhaps none as formidable as those faced by Jacob Brodbeck and his brother, Johann, in 1865.

Iris Brodbeck Macek

Prologue

I raised my hand to answer my fifth grade teacher's question.

"My great-grandfather invented the airplane," I announced when my teacher called my name.

Looking rather stern, my teacher asked, "Where did you find this information?"

"I've always known it. My Daddy told me about my great-grandfather's flight and at our Brodbeck reunions, I hear about him a lot. His name was Jacob Brodbeck. He died before I was born."

The teacher continued, "Then why do you suppose your history book clearly states the Wright Brothers invented the airplane?"

"The book just got it wrong," I blurted out quickly.

An uncomfortable stillness permeated the classroom.

What would the teacher say?

She quietly ignored me and said, "Class, let's turn to page 240 and read aloud about the Wright Brothers' invention."

I sank down in my seat and tried to hide my embarrassment.

Upon relaying the incident to my Daddy that night, he explained to me, "Well, mostly the people who live in and around Luckenbach and Fredericksburg know about Jacob Brodbeck's air ship. They say he actually flew a short distance some thirty-eight years before the Wright Brothers. But he was not able to stay in the air like they did. Your Opa Brodbeck was ahead of his time and ahead of the invention of a combustible engine that was needed as a power source for his airplane."

As time passed, it became a hobby of mine to collect articles written about my great-grandfather's attempts at flying an airplane. I found these gems in various Texas magazines. My Dad also saved articles for me whenever they occasionally appeared in the San Antonio or Fredericksburg papers.

Later in college, I started a scrapbook of the articles, clippings, pictures, and anything else I could find about Jacob Brodbeck's air ship. During the years of my teaching career, librarians and other people knowing of Jacob Brodbeck brought me different sources of information. After that, as a Mom, I told my three children about their great, great-grandfather and his flying machine.

Through the years, stories grew into legends about the day that schoolmaster Brodbeck flew over the barn tops near Luckenbach, Texas, in his homemade "air ship." Many articles and research reports continued to keep his story alive.

In 1967, Texas Governor John Connally declared Jacob Brodbeck the Father of American Aviation. Later in 1986, Texas Governor Bill Clements proclaimed May 16, 1986, as Jacob Brodbeck Day at Randolph Air Force Base in San Antonio, Texas. All the descendants of Jacob Brodbeck were invited to come and be honored that day.

It was a wonderful day. The Snowbirds from Canada and the Blue Angels of the United States, both jet precision flying teams, put on an air show dazzling the crowd.

The Randolph Air Force Base Museum was opened and on display were sketches of Jacob Brodbeck's "air ship." Next to them lay the blueprints of the Wright Brothers' airplane. The similarity could not be denied.

Also of significance in 1986, great-granddaughter Anita Tatsch, wrote and published a biography, *Jacob Brodbeck "Reached for the Sky" in Texas*. Aided by her mother, Thekla Staudt, (my aunt on my father's side) they spent years of research attempting to uncover as many of the actual events as possible. I am indebted to them because their research helped lay the foundation for my book.

Intrigued by this biography and the parts of Brodbeck's story still missing, I could not stop thinking about it. It would not go away. How did this man's dreams and the events they spawned come together over time? Of course, no one could know all the unwritten thoughts and words spoken by a man who lived over 150 years ago. One would just have to imagine.

Just imagine how it all began back in the years of 1830 to 1849 during the Great Migration when thousands of German citizens immigrated to a distant land—hoping for a brave new beginning in the fledgling Republic of Texas—just imagine. . .

Main Characters

Jacob Brodbeck
Schoolmaster/Inventor

Johann Brodbeck
Jacob's loyal brother

Katarina Becker
Johann's sweetheart

Christine Behrens Brodbeck
Jacob's wife

Chapter One
A Wondrous Vision

The Atlantic Ocean, 1846, aboard the sailing ship, *The Element*

Jacob hurried to aft deck where he crouched unnoticed behind a bulkhead. He grabbed his notebook and pen from his vest pocket, intent upon capturing the conditions emerging before him. His passion to find answers to the many questions penetrating his mind blinded him to the perils of a storm at sea.

Driven by curiosity, like the driving rain hitting his face, he wanted to know —how do the sailors adjust the sails during a storm?—how does the captain keep the ship on track with high winds tossing her to and fro?—with land so far away, what happens to the sea birds during a storm—the sea birds he had so meticulously studied and drawn during this voyage—the mighty albatrosses, the petrels and shearwaters, or the diving, plunging gannets?

The ship quivered—a sleeping giant awakened.

Jacob grabbed for support as the ship heeled once and then, again. Streaks of lightning split the sky. Shrill vibrations and humming noises penetrated the air as the strong and fierce wind ripped through the lines.

"Shorten sail!" Captain Springer barked through his speaking tube.

Unseen on the aft deck near where the Captain manned the ship's wheel, Jacob heard all the commands shouted to the sailors.

"Stand by to take in the royals and flying jib. Take in mainsail and spanker."

Captivated by the changing sights and sounds around him, Jacob knelt down and clutched his notebook inside his jacket to shield it from the rain. He struggled to write as the wind beat against him. Then something magical happened. He felt as if he were inside a bubble. An undisturbed calm came over him as he watched and jotted down the procedures for furling in some of the sails and changing the directions of others. So absorbed was he in grasping these procedures, he failed to notice the last warning whistle for passengers to go below deck.

*****

Near the center of the ship, crewmen hustled passengers down into steerage where they were boarded. One man resisted, struggling and fighting off the two crewmen as they shoved him backwards down the steep ladder.

"Sir, if we let you search for your brother, we will have two men in danger!" The hatchway door slammed shut as the sailors rushed to secure it tightly with ropes to prevent interior flooding.

Shouting at the top of his voice, Johann pummeled the closed hatch with his fists, "Find my Bruder! Save my Bruder!" He shoved his body against the hatch pushing with fierce animal energy. Then a sudden heave of the ship knocked him off the ladder and he fell to the steerage floor. The fall stunned him. His desperate appeals ceased.

The banging noises caused from the commotion of boxes, luggage, and other unattached possessions sliding back and forth as the ship pitched from side to side, kept anyone from noticing Johann's fall.

Except for Katarina Becker. She glanced across the berths looking for Johann. As the hanging lantern swayed back and forth, she caught a brief glimpse of him lying on the steerage floor. The flickering flame revealed a trickle of blood curling down his temple.

Jumping down from her berth, she reached Johann's side just as the lamp guttered out.

*****

Jacob, half standing now and lost in his own world, watched in fascination at the procedures taking place around him. With one arm, he wiped the pouring rain from his eyes. Completely enthralled, he centered his attention on how changing the sail formation altered the ship's course. Now it sailed *with* the wind. Without thinking, he straightened up to get a better view of the sail pattern.

Looking up, his eyes widened. What he saw electrified him!

The birds—the birds! The birds flew straight into the wind—they flew against the wind. And the rush of the wind under their wings lifted them up, up out of the storm! Birds did not zigzag to catch the wind as ships did in order to move forward. No, they did not spend all that time and energy. They instinctively knew using their wings against the wind lifted them up into the peaceful realm beyond.

What joy if man designed wings that used atmospheric conditions to fly as birds did!

In that moment of epiphany, Jacob sensed God's calling on his life.

Standing with his feet planted wide apart—bracing himself against the whipping wind and rain—he raised one fist to the heavens and declared, "Just as birds know how to rise above the storms, I will search, so help me Gott, even if it takes a lifetime, to develop a new kind of ship for mankind—a ship that soars above the seas when storms threaten or sets down upon the seas if needed. An air ship!"

> *"I bare you on eagles' wings and brought you unto myself." Exodus 19:4*

Chapter 2
Master of the Ship

A slap of cold rain broke Jacob's trance. Before he could brace himself, the wind knocked him off his feet. As he fell, the ship pitched leeward flinging him against the bulwarks.

Catching his breath and his wits, Jacob quickly grabbed and held onto the slippery wood, narrowly avoiding the foaming sea below. Trembling with cold, Jacob wondered how long he could manage to hold his grip. As the ship tilted even further leeward, Jacob saw more of the churning ocean below him than the ship's watery deck.

Forcing his eyes to focus on the bulwarks to which he clung caused him to remember the lines of the beloved Martin Luther hymn of assurance. Whenever they faced a calamity as children, their Mutter taught them to sing this hymn in order to cast their fear aside.

Ein feste Burg ist unser Gott	(A mighty fortress is our God,)
Ein gute Wehr und Waffen	(A bulwark never failing:)
Er hilft uns frei aus aller	(Our helper He, amid the flood)
Die uns jetzt hat betroffen.	(Of mortal ills prevailing.)

Jacob began singing as he had never sung before. The louder the crashes of waves and thunder about him, the louder he sang.

*****

Coming out of the brief stupor from his fall off the ladder to the steerage floor, Johann felt Katarina's soft hands on his head before he heard her panicky voice.

"Johann, are you all right? Johann, speak to me. It is Katarina. It is so dark, you cannot see me. You fell and hit your head. Johann, please say something!"

"Jacob! Jacob! I left Jacob!" Johann crumpled into heaving sobs as his memory returned.

Katarina moved closer to Johann in order to comfort him in her arms, "Johann, nein! Do not say that! There was no time to search for Jacob. You were helping my parents get all the children to safety."

Johann barely heard Katarina's voice above the whimpering, groaning, and occasional screaming coming from the emigrants. He drew in shallow breaths in order to keep from gagging from the suffocating and putrid odors in the darkness all around them. He forced his cloudy mind to focus on the here and now. If he could not help his Bruder, he must help those around him.

Johann pulled himself back a little from Katarina's embrace as more screams of fear penetrated the din of moaning and vomiting. Banging on the walls, one woman's piercing voice rose above the rest, "Help us! Help us! We are sinking! Are we to be buried alive in this watery tomb?"

Johann drew close to Katarina and asked, "Katarina, can you sing?"

"Sing? Did you say sing?

"Ja, sing! Mutter taught us to sing whenever we were in trouble. She read from the book of Acts when Paul and Silas were thrown into prison at midnight. Scripture says they prayed and sang hymns to Gott. The other prisoners were listening. Do you remember what happened next?"

"Ja, of course, there was an earthquake and the prison doors flew open."

"Ja, singing praises to Gott shows our faith in His power to work in our behalf. Mutter taught us to sing "A Mighty Fortress Is Our God" when we needed assurance of Gott's faithfulness. Bitte, sing it with me."

As two lone voices tentatively began singing the old German hymn, a hush fell on the rest of the emigrants as they listened to the familiar strains of the hymn written by Luther. Then, one by one, other voices joined in. Encouraged by their singing, Johann shouted, "Louder! Louder— until we drown out the forces outside with our faith inside!"

*****

No amount of singing drowned out the sounds of *The Element* caught in a battle with nature's stormy blasts. Groans, creaks and shuddering noises emanated throughout the ship as the surging of the great waves beat against the hull. Even the most sea-worthy mate feared the vessel might implode from the pressure pushing from the outside.

Mastering all his strength, Captain Springer shouted into the raging wind, rain, and thunderous lightning, "Heave Ho! Stay your course, you mighty ship. You have not earned your name in vain!" With the rain beating against his face, he clenched the wheel with determination and screamed louder, "You are *The Element*! Fight these warring elements! Render to us your strength!"

Jacob, hugging the bulwark with all his might, needed superhuman strength to keep holding on. His voice, raspy from singing the hymn, fell silent now. He prayed, "Oh, mein Gott, Thou hast brought me this far! Show me what to do next!"

In the next instant, the thought hit him, "Give thanks for your rescue!"

Urgently, he called out, "Vater above, I thank Thee that Thou art bringing us safely to Texas! Vater, Thou art more magnificent than these rolling waves. Vater, Thou art mightier than this raging sea. I thank Thee, mein Gott, for Thou art the Master of this ship!"

Another lurch of the ship, stronger than any before, tore away Jacob's grip slamming him to the other side of the watery deck. Reaching and grabbing wildly for anything to keep him from sliding overboard, Jacob found his hands wrapped around human flesh.

"Achtung! Where did you come from?" said a strange voice."Gut Gott in Himmel, an emigrant!"

Reaching down to the hands grasping his ankles, the sailor hauled Jacob to his feet while the two of them struggled to maintain their balance on the leaning, slippery surface.

Just as startled, Jacob sputtered through the sea water in his mouth, "Danke schön—danke schön, Thank You! Thank You, Gott in Himmel—danke schön."

*****

Below deck, the sudden lurch of the ship in the opposite direction caused a change of commotion as well. Grappling and grasping bunk posts, other people, or anything they could find to keep from slamming into the other side of the ship, the emigrants stopped singing. Indeed, they needed all their strength to keep from being pan-caked on top of one another.

One determined emigrant shouted above the rest, "Praise Gott! Perhaps the wind shift is a sign the storm is soon over! Hold tight! Keep your faith!"

*****

Looking up, Captain Springer noticed the wind change. In the dim light, he saw the clouds moving ever so slowly, but starting to dissipate. The rain slackened; the wind's force diminished.

Both Jacob and the sailor felt the ship righting itself as the sea calmed. Tentative at first, they began to loosen their grip on one another. They looked at each other and at almost the same time, they said, "Is the storm over?"

As the wind lessened, the waves lashing against the hull subsided. Like ants coming from their holes after a rainstorm, the crew of *The Element* scrambled across her deck hastening to heed the boson's barking orders. Some ran hurriedly to unlock the hatch to the steerage to free the emigrants below. They discovered Johann already pounding on the hatch calling to be let out.

In their efforts to check for injuries, the seamen brushed past Johann as he pushed up and out in search of his brother. He only had to turn once to see Jacob coming toward him. The two men bear-hugged, shouting their gratitude in German, "Danke mein Gott! Danke schön!"

With tears of relief streaming down Johann's face, he asked, "Where were you? Did you not hear the warning whistle?"

"Achtung! The birds, Johann, the birds! Do you know what they do during a storm?"

But before Jacob could answer his own question, the rest of the passengers from steerage streamed onto the main deck to the fresh air they needed. Some still retched as they leaned over the rails of the ship. Others with stronger constitutions—Jacob and Johann among them—found buckets to fill with vinegar-water. They went back below to try and scrub away the acrid smells of vomit and other body excretions that did not make their way into pails during the storm.

When most of the upheaval on deck settled down, the youngest of the Becker brood, little Otto, yanked the skirt of his big sister, Katarina. Waving his little finger in wild glee toward the western sky, he called out, "Look! Look at the rainbow . . . look how bright it is!"

Catching the enthusiasm in little Otto's high-pitched voice, the remaining emigrants on main deck, stopped and took time along with the little boy to delight in the resplendent, almost perfect arch of hues extending across the western sky.

Reverend Becker leaned down to his son, "Ja, Otto, this is Gott's way of telling us the storm is over."

"Vater, I think Gott made this rainbow better than any He ever made before because He knew how scared I was."

Busy though he was, when Captain Springer overheard the little boy's words, he smiled and decided to join the conversation. He walked over to where Otto was standing and kneeled down to the child's eye level.

"Young man, when it is evening and the sun is really low in the horizon like it is now, the elements are just right after a rainstorm for there to be a very brilliant rainbow like the one we see now."

After thinking a moment, Otto said in a serious tone, "Ja, I think Gott planned it that way for us today."

Though Captain Springer was not German himself, he smiled and replied, "Ja, I think you may be right."

*****

That evening in their cramped space, Jacob told Johann in hushed tones the incredible moment when he saw the birds and how they escaped the storm. He shared with his Bruder, his very closest friend, the message he believed God spoke to him.

"With Gott's help, I will invent a machine that can fly above the storm like the birds do—or when necessary, land on the water—an air ship!"

Even in the dark of steerage, Johann heard and felt the tremendous excitement in his brother's voice. He had anticipated Jacob had some new project or invention in his head, but nothing like this. He was tongue-tied—almost dumb with disbelief—at Jacob's assertion that he could invent a way to fly like a bird. He could think of no response to say to his brother. He remained silent giving himself time to find the right words to offer.

It didn't matter. Within moments, Jacob, limp with exhaustion, went straight to sleep. In contrast, Johann was wide awake and deep in thought. He pondered how in the world Jacob could accomplish the impossible. But Johann knew better than anyone else, if it could be done, Jacob would find the way. And just as certainly, no matter what it took, he would be right by his brother's side.

Fatigue soon overcame him. Thoughts of the terrifying events of the day faded away as his mind carried him back home—home to Germany and the safety of their solid, stone house—a house not rocking back and forth on its foundation.

While Johann dreamed of stability, Jacob, already in a dream consciousness, drifted back to haunting memories of their Vaterland. Playing before his eyes were images and scenes of two brothers about to be caught up in a world of great conflict . . .

Chapter 3
Unrest in Germany

Three years earlier . . . Stuttgart, Germany

Jacob sat reading the *Stuttgart Zeitung* as he drank his last cup of coffee before leaving to teach his class at the University.

Johann walked in, a cup of coffee in one hand and waving a travel brochure with the other. "This should be better reading than that censored skeleton of a newspaper," chided Johann. He slipped the brochure between the newspaper pages.

"Where did you get this?" asked Jacob.

As Johann slid onto the bench at Jacob's side, he said between sips of hot coffee, "They are everywhere down at the train depot. Posted here and there. Porters handing them out to anyone taking the next train from Stuttgart. You would have to have your head filled with sawdust not to notice. Of course, some people just appear to be dense and unaware of their surroundings because their mind is consumed with visions of contraptions, wires, gears, tinkering noises . . ."

Jacob ignored his brother's jibe about his distracted mind and continued intently reading the brochure.

"I would not want to fight Indians in Texas any more than I want to fight Prussian soldiers here in Germany."

Johann reasoned, "The Indians in Texas are only protecting their own lands, they are not trying to impose their political, economic, and religious beliefs on you. Leave them alone and they leave you alone. Besides, even if there *were* Indians to fight, you would be fighting on your own piece of land; land free from the tyranny and desperate conditions which await us here in Germany.

"How long has it been since the Holy Alliance was signed in 1815? Twenty-seven years? That was before either of us were born. Still the monarchs of Europe have failed to advance Christian principles in opposition to the revolutionary disorder surrounding us.

Johann paused allowing time for those thoughts to settle. Then in a more casual tone, "And say, might I add, that in the grand Republic of Texas, there might be enough room to spread out all those inventions running around in your head!"

Both men's eyes connected as spreading grins suggested the teasing and warm camaraderie existing between them.

Jacob continued, "We could not leave Vater and Mutter as well as the rest of our family."

"Of course not! We take them with us. I will bring more pamphlets and books home. We will all dream and plan together."

"Ha! And I am the one everyone calls the dreamer! But ja, these colorful descriptions on these pages do intrigue me—land of the free and the brave! I wonder how brave I would be if I came face to face with an Indian warrior? I am a man of learning, not one of daring and adventure."

"Ach! We would have protection." Pointing to the lower right hand corner of the brochure, Johann went on to explain, "Notice this. This is the seal of the Society for the Protection of German Immigrants to Texas better known as the Adelsverein. They would not only help us book passage to Texas, but they would guide us all along the way until we were settled on our own land grant."

"Ja, but look closer at the seal. There is a lone star which no doubt represents the Republic of Texas. But here, also, below the star, is a bundle of arrows which must symbolize the presence of Indians. I see no guarantee that the Adelsverein's protection continues once you were on your own land."

"And what guarantee do we have here? These noblemen who organized the Adelsverein believe one way to alleviate Germany's economic problems is to send thousands of willing Germans to Texas. Why wait until conditions improve? We help our country by leaving. We help the fledgling Texas Republic's waning treasury by forging new settlements on the land given to us."

Jacob placed the brochure inside his pocket. He stroked his beard, obviously in thought. The arguments Johann offered were ones he considered himself. Having his younger brother present them gave him a chance to buffer his own reasoning. He already knew he wanted desperately to go, but just as desperately he wanted his decision to be the best one for all the family. Was the timing right? To subject his aging parents and the rest of the family to the treacherous ocean voyage, the hardships and dangers awaiting them, Jacob must call upon all the forces of heaven to bear down on them and guide them.

Did he have that kind of faith?

> *"Commit thy way unto the LORD; trust also in him; and he shall bring it to pass."*
> *Psalm 37:5*

Chapter 4
Decisions

The fateful morning of July 22, 1843, began like any other day for Jacob. In the quiet predawn hours before the rest of the world invaded his mind, he entertained all kinds of exquisite ideas. By candle light, he worked in his cramped basement workshop of the Brodbeck home. Centuries old—the two-story, stone house appeared to have escaped the ravages of time.

Today his mind focused on his latest mechanical idea: a self-winding clock. As he tinkered with the springs he hoped would achieve the automation he desired, another part of his brain actively engaged itself in the last conversation with his brother.

Amazing how Johann had the understanding to grasp the meaning of the cataclysmic political events of the past several decades. Unlike himself, the German educational system steered Johann into trade school and he became a stone mason. Even without the benefit of university training, Johann seemed to comprehend the causes of the upheaval and insecurity currently dominating the mood of their kingdom of Wurttemberg, Germany. In his trade as a mason, Johann talked often to the many older workmen around him. These workers did not have the work they needed to even begin to build a new Germany.

Jacob could not stop the disparagement settling over him. When he thought of Prince Clemens von Metternich, the dominant political figure within the German Confederation and the ways he commandeered policies, he wanted to hammer some sense into him instead of hammering the metal into place.

Ja, Metternich feared another revolutionary uprising like Napoleon's. So to prevent this from happening, his reactionary ideas led him to put in place a system of press censorship. Jacob felt his blood pressure rising when he thought of how Metternich sought regulation of the universities in order to restrict German intellectual life. These actions hindered the publications of writings of free-thinking individuals like himself.

Because of this, he and Johann, both knew that it would take military action to keep these unpopular policies in force. The threat of going into a Prussian war over domestic strife had little appeal to many young men of Wurttemberg.

Healthy, young, and unmarried males with a skill or university training such as themselves much preferred facing the unknown future in a new and far away Republic, such as Texas, instead of fighting in yet, another war. Ja, taking risks in order to forge a way of life with meaning for them and for future generations made much more sense.

But what about the old, the very young or women? What were their chances? Were the odds better to continue living in a country of strife where at least they had some idea of what to expect?

These questions kept pounding in Jacob's head even as he pounded on the small pieces of metal trying to get them to fit into the clock's configuration. His mind's two-fold calculations running parallel now—calculating how to get gear to turn gear—calculating the risks involved in taking aging parents, women and children with them—getting this gear to perfectly match the groove in the bigger gear—agonizing over the thought of leaving their loved ones behind should he and Johann decide to go without them. The probability of never seeing their family again, tormenting—the gears not fitting in place, frustrating.

Soon his perplexing deliberations came to a halt—the next few moments altering life for the entire Brodbeck family.

A piercing, agonizing scream jerked Jacob's attention from his tedious experiment. He scrambled up the flight of stairs instinctively shouting, "Mutter, Mutter! What is wrong?"

"Jacob, come quickly . . . in the kitchen . . . it is Vater! He is not breathing!"

Jacob's eyes skimmed the kitchen. His face paled at the sight before him. Slumped over beside a spilled cup of coffee, sat his white-haired father. His color ashen, he made no sound or movement. Jacob ran to his father's side, "Mein Vater, mein Vater," but even as he cried out to the old man, Jacob knew his beloved Vater was gone.

*****

On a Sabbath morning, one year after his father's death, Jacob's hands glided deftly over the keys of the church organ, playing the composition he composed for his father.

Elizabetha Brodbeck listened to the soaring melody that her son played with masterful skill—celebrating the life of her husband.

She listened, thankful, one more time they still attended the church service of their choice. Bowing her head and closing her eyes, she surrendered herself to the rising strains of the music. Memories flooded her mind of a past and more pleasant time. She saw Jacob at barely three years of age poking and jabbing his chubby little fingers at the organ keys or whatever else he found to poke or prod. She loved all of her children—but Jacob—Jacob was gifted in ways different from the others.

Listening now to his apparent musical talent, she thought, also, of his mechanical genius. His self-winding clock was maybe months or perhaps even weeks from becoming a reality. How soon would the Prussian war take these talented young hands away from their inventions, music and teaching to train them to shoot rifles?

Time would soon run out. She knew soon, very soon, she must encourage Jacob to be on his way across the vast ocean to the freedom-loving Republic of Texas, a place they heard about so often. She also knew she would not be going along. Now, with the loss of her husband, she no longer had the drive to forge a new way of life. Of the ten children she had borne, only four had survived to adulthood. So much loss. Each succeeding death boring a hole in her soul leaving behind canyons of grief. No, she could not go, but Jacob must. And she must find the will to let him go. How could she endure seeing Jacob leave knowing she might never see him again? Her very special Jacob.

As she pondered these matters in her heart, she remembered another mother long ago who knew the grief of giving up a precious Son. Her head bowed, Elizabetha prayed Gott give her the courage to carry out His will.

When Jacob heard his mother express her thoughts of that day, he remembered one moment, in particular, when he played the last refrain. Seeing his mother's gaze upon him, he sensed a turning point in their lives as he touched the keys that brought the composition to its conclusion.

A week later, Jacob came home from the university to find all the Brodbeck clan sprawled about on the living room floor amongst papers, brochures, and maps of all descriptions.

Jacob's older and only sister, Barbara, noticed him first, "Jacob, Jacob . . . we wait for you to come home. Johann brought more brochures and some exciting news."

Johann jumped up from his squatting position, "Bruder of mine, they form a new passenger list for the next voyage to Galveston, Texas. To be on that list, you must be ready. There are papers to get in order—permits you need to leave Germany—you need to build a wooden chest to hold your belongings—you must resign your teaching position from the King . . ."

"Hold on there, little Bruder of mine. I stopped back on the single word "you." Am I the lone Brodbeck being pushed out of this nest?" As Jacob asked this question the gestures of his hands encompassed the room demanding a response from the others as well as Johann.

The solemn faces of their sister, Barbara, and her husband, Michael, turned towards Elizabetha. Johannes, the oldest son, and his wife, Agnes, held hands but cast their eyes down. Even Johann remained quiet. Moments lapsed, and then Elizabetha stood up.

"My son, I encouraged Johann to gather all the information he could about this trip. But it must be your trip and not mine. Since your Vater is gone, I no longer have the wunderlust for this adventure I once had.

Stopping to regain her composure, she went on, "But in your young heart and limbs, this desire reins strong. You must follow your calling. I have prayed about this many times. I know by the peace in my heart you must go. And ja, I also know it will not be easy to leave your family with the thought you might never see us again.

'We have talked about it over and over. We have come to believe the best plan is for you to go and go soon. Perhaps, when you become settled, others can follow."

Jacob's eyes quickly traveled from his mother's pleading ones to rest on Johann's perplexed ones. "And what are your thoughts, little Bruder?" Jacob's voice was low but resonated with an intense, inquiring tone.

"Ach, how can we ask our Mutter to let go of two more sons at one time? As Mutter says, I can follow once you are settled." Johann's voice was barely audible.

An uneasy silence begged to be broken. Johannes let go of his wife's hand and walked over to lay a hand on Jacob's shoulder. "Jacob, we have word that the conscription begins very soon. Your age group is the first to be targeted. Johann is younger and has more time. I am older and not as attractive to the draft. We stay with Mutter as you go and prepare the way. Then maybe time and events will lead us in following behind you." He stopped to emphasize his next words. "Jacob, your ideas and ideals are ones whose time has come. Go now, with your family's blessing."

Jacob saw the resolve in his family's eyes. He motioned to them to kneel beside him. "Then let us come before our heavenly Vater and ask His blessing as well."

> *"And the LORD, he it is that doth go before thee; he will be with thee, he will not fail thee, neither forsake thee: fear not, neither be dismayed." Deuteronomy 31:8*

Chapter 5
Texas Bound

Jacob stared at the tedious paperwork that lay staring back at him—paperwork required to leave Germany. As he penned in his full name, Jacob Frederick Brodbeck, he realized that a name was missing—his younger brother's name, Johann Georg Brodbeck. Restless and unable to concentrate, he pushed his chair back from the table. How could he leave without the close companionship of his best friend?

Deciding to broach the subject again with his brother, he ambled down the stairs to the basement. He found Johann in the middle of measuring planks of wood for Jacob's trunk.

With purposed casual ease, Jacob said, "I want you to build two trunks. Since I have so many instruments, equipment, and books to take along with me, there will be no room for your things."

Johann looked up from his calculations. He rose from his kneeling position. Looking directly into his brother's steady gaze, he took time to form his reply.

"I wondered when you would ask me again to go with you."

"Ja, well, I know the manner in which your mind mulls over things. You need time for matters to settle themselves before you feel satisfied with the outcome."

Jacob's statement brought a curious smile to Johann's face.

"Ach, mein Bruder. That is not my mind. You are the thinker. But I will indulge you. Am I feeling satisfied with my decision to stay behind in Germany while my big Bruder follows his heart to Texas?"

"Nein, you are feeling cheated about missing the adventure your big Bruder is about to take. And a little worried as well. For even though he is your big Bruder, you often feel responsible for him and his absent-minded ways. For instance, reminding him to eat when he forgets because he is in the middle of one of his captivating projects."

Another pause. Then a long look between the two young men.

Finally, Johann sighed, "What would we tell Mutter?"

"Knowing Mutter, instead of sewing one set of clothing for me, she has probably cut the patterns for a second set as well," Jacob replied.

And so it was. Elizabetha Brodbeck prepared for two sons to leave for Texas instead of one.

*****

Antwerp, Belgium—1846

Among the passengers milling around the busy Antwerp harbor this August day, stood the two Brodbeck brothers looking for their vessel, *The Element*. Their eyes roved over the names of the host of ships lined up alongside the cobblestone quay. Like so many geese come back to shore, the myriad vessels with their sails furled down along their masts, rocked back and forth in the choppy waves.

Jacob's stance beside their wooden trunks showed the confidence and anticipation of a twenty-five year-old single man ready to embark on the journey of a lifetime.

The warm August breeze ruffled his thinning sandy hair as he gazed across the dockside looking for their ship.

Johann spotted it first.

"There it is, Bruder. There, next to *The Hamilton.*"

Jacob squinted, "Ja, now I see it. Not as large as I thought, but perhaps we have a modest passenger list. Have you heard?"

Johann—twenty-one and four years younger than his brother—nonetheless, stood two inches taller than Jacob. Lanky as they both were, their homemade clothing hung loosely on their frames. Unlike Jacob's serious eyes, Johann's blue eyes often twinkled with humor and merriment.

Trying to remember anything about their fellow passengers, Johann wiped aside a strand of flaxen hair from his wrinkled brow.

"Ja," he said, "I thought I saw a passenger list attached to some of the papers we received." He fumbled in his inside vest pocket, "Here it is."

He handed the list to Jacob who read, "Ach, I see we are among 170 passengers aboard *The Element* bound for Galveston, Texas. Ja, das ist gut."

Jacob looked up, his eyes fixed on the sea beyond. As he reflected on what he had studied about ships carrying emigrants, he said to Johann, "Most of the emigrant ships with German affiliations do not overbook, usually running from 200 to 250 passengers."

"Why is that?" Johann wanted to know.

"Ja, they heeded the lessons learned from the many overbooked Irish emigrant ships. Many Irishmen and their families sailed to America, desperate to flee the Potato

Famine in their homeland. But many found even worse conditions of malnutrition and disease aboard the crowded ships than what they left behind."

"What happened then?"

"Many emigrants did not survive the long and harsh journey to New York. And worse yet, the emigrants who did survive, were often turned back because American port authorities would not allow ships of diseased passengers to unload on American soil."

Johann said, "Ach, how terrible for those poor folks."

Jacob agreed, "Ja, learning of this tragedy, the German lines were diligent to not overbook in order to offer less crowded conditions."

The Captain's call interrupted their conversation, "All aboard *The Element* for passengers leaving for Galveston, Texas."

"Did you hear that, Johann? That is our ship! We are on our way to Texas!"

In addition to their personal trunks, Jacob and Johann brought another box holding eating utensils and dried foodstuffs their mother packed for their journey. Lugging everything they possessed in this world, they and the other 168 emigrants followed directions down the narrow steps of the ladder to steerage. This was where they would live for the next several months or so of their voyage. It took some minutes before their eyes adjusted from the bright sun on the main deck to the darkness below on the steerage deck.

A fragment of natural light escaped from the open hatch. From the center of the hold of steerage ran the mainmast to the upper deck. A lone flickering lamp hung from the lower part of the mainmast offering the only welcoming light below.

Once their eyes became accustomed to the dimness, they noticed compartments of four berths each lining the walls. There were no portholes. After all, steerage was meant for storage. Most emigrants did not have the money to book first class passage.

The brothers agreed upon two berths located near the entrance—deciding to let the families choose the ones that offered more privacy. They spent the next moments making beds, hanging up tin cups and organizing utensils necessary for eating. Most of the women hung blankets over their berths to give them more privacy.

Jacob looked about their cramped living quarters. Boxes and trunks jammed up against one another provided only a narrow central aisle for their passage back and forth in the hold.

He thought, with some degree of relief, *generally their quarters were clean. No rats that he could see.* He and Johann had heard stories of the deplorable conditions aboard many of the emigrant ships.

*****

Days and days of endless discomfort and boredom followed. The brothers found they only had a few feet of head room in their berths prohibiting them from sitting upright. Even at that, they felt fortunate to each have a berth to themselves. Family members shared the narrow berths with two or even three people occupying a single birth.

One particular morning as Johann tried to peer through the dank darkness of the steerage deck, he countered their circumstances with, "Did you ever think that your entire private living space could consist of a six by two foot wooden box?"

To which Jacob replied, "Nein, and what's more, I feel my box closing in on me more and more each day." Jacob's voice remained low so as not to disturb those closely packed around them.

"Ach, I notice that you disappear for long periods of time when we go up for our meals on the main deck. Yesterday I searched for you and could not locate you. Where is your secret hiding place?"

"Now if I told you that, it would no longer be secret, would it? Besides, I notice you spending time with the Becker family. Has their young daughter, Katarina, captured your attention?" Jacob came back with a teasing tone in his voice.

"But you change the subject, Bruder, to detract me from my question. I worry that something could happen to you on one of your tours around the deck."

Jacob saw that he could not avoid his brother's probing concern. "I tell you this, little Bruder. I have located a secluded place near the bulkhead where I retreat to write in my journal. Because we lived in landlocked Germany far from the sea, I am curious to see how sailing ships move forward. I jot down my observations and calculations of the wind, sails, and the ship's movement. I need this respite to myself or I will lose my mind in the daily grind and grit of this life at sea."

"Then may it go well with you, Jacob. For to you, thinking and dreaming is like breathing to the rest of us. But be mindful of your surroundings. You are the only family I have on this journey of ours to Texas."

With that, the brothers picked up their empty cans and bowls. They mounted the ladder steps up to the main deck where they would stand in line for their daily provisions of oatmeal and water laced with vinegar. The vinegar was added to avoid contamination.

Most of the time, they found the women and young girls in line ahead of them. Since the privies on the main deck afforded so little privacy, the females of the ship preferred to use them at night or just before dawn. After that, they remained aloft to wait in line for their food and water.

Today the seas seemed more choppy than usual. Each time the ship lurched, the passengers struggled to maintain their footing and not lose their place in line. An air of urgency and apprehension permeated the mood of the passengers in line—more jostling and pushing than usual.

Katarina Becker, just two ahead of Jacob and Johann in line, noticed them and called out, "There was a red dawn this morning. My Mutter said, 'When the sky is as wounded as this one, there is sure to be a storm sowing and sorrow reaping.' "

Johann responded by pointing to the east, "Ja, I see off to the east the swelling waves rising and falling with increasing force. Your Mutter may be right."

A rush of passengers came to get provisions and then hurry to the fireplace on the main deck before it shut down. Jacob, in particular, made haste to cook their oatmeal.

Noticing his brother hurrying to eat, Johann queried, "You seem to gulp down your food. Are you alarmed because of the possibility of a storm, Bruder?"

"Ja, only because I want time to stay on deck and watch what the Captain and crew do to the sails to prepare for a storm." Then looking up towards the sky where the usual sea birds flew about the ship, Jacob added, "Also, I am curious to know about those sea birds. Where in this vast expanse do they go during a storm? I intend to go to my usual place and discover these facts for myself."

"But Jacob, promise me you will not get so absorbed in your observations than you do not heed the ship's warning whistle to go below deck in case that storm blows close," Johann's urging came just within earshot of Jacob's departing back.

Waving a hand as he left, Jacob called, "Ja, ja, I take notice." Then stopping only long enough to point with his other hand, Jacob called back again, "Perhaps you should make some observations for yourself. Do you not see Fraulein Becker at the fireplace frantically trying to help feed her brothers and sisters?"

With that admonition, Johann turned to see that indeed the Becker family could use some assistance in getting their hungry brood of six children fed and settled.

*****

"Du, Bruder! Wake up!" Johann shook his brother's shoulders, "Are you to sleep all the way to Texas? Get up! Captain Springer just sent word for us to gather on deck. He has good news for us!"

Jacob jumped up. "What? Where are we?" Then looking around, he realized they were at sea. "Ach, now I am not dreaming! We are still at sea. But we *are* safely through the storm, ja?

"Bruder, find your bearings. We need to go to main deck."

*****

Captain Springer wanted the emigrants to bring their musical instruments to the main deck that night and have a dance to celebrate their safe passage through the storm.

They lost not one soul during the storm. There were the usual cuts and bruises but nothing life-threatening. In addition, the Captain had other good news: according to his calculations, the storm had blown them closer to their destination. Galveston should be within sight in the next three days. Weather permitting; they should arrive October 22, 1846—slightly less than two months after they had left Antwerp on August 25, 1846. His face shining with pleasure, the Captain announced they were ahead of schedule.

A warm and gentle breeze graced the evening. *The Element* furrowed through the water as if she knew her destination was near. Meanwhile her inhabitants danced lightheartedly on her decks to the polkas and waltzes coming from Johann's harmonica and the accordion played by jovial, chubby Emil Becker.

Jacob stood to the side observing with pleasure the joyful dancing and listening happily to the rhythmic German tunes. What a contrast from the night two nights earlier.

Strolling over to where Johann merrily played his harmonica, he whispered in his brother's ear, "This music-making man is losing the girl to that dance-making man."

Johann grinned, and then leaned over to whisper something to Emil Becker. Quickly, the older man changed the lively polka beat to a waltz and the lilting strains of "The Blue Danube."

Putting his harmonica in his vest pocket, Johann walked straight over to where Katarina Becker danced in the arms of one of the other single, young men. Johann tapped him on the shoulder. Smoothly, Katarina slid into Johann's embrace and they glided over the makeshift dance floor. Jacob watched the two of them a few more moments, then slipped off unobserved to the aft part of the ship.

Standing by the same bulwark where he nearly lost his life, Jacob looked out over the calm sea. He allowed his mind to wander back to the stunning moment right before the storm worsened—the moment he knew without a doubt what Gott wanted him to do with his life in Texas. He would construct an air ship! A vessel that could fly above and over the storms the way he witnessed the sea birds doing at the beginning of the storm. A vessel that could be at home in the air or on the sea. A vessel that would eliminate the struggles of long sea voyages such as theirs.

Jacob sensed Gott's hand in allowing the great storm to overtake them. As he had prayed and had thanked Gott for His deliverance even before the fact, his faith was honored. *The Element* rode safely through the strong gales and exploding lightning—a horrific storm which caused Captain Springer to say they were lucky to survive.

Gratefulness for Gott's goodness swept over Jacob. In an impossible moment, Gott was with him, guiding him in knowing what to do—step by step.

Jacob wept with gratitude.

Reaching into his vest pocket for a handkerchief, he felt his hand brush against his journal. Smiling through his tears, he brought it out of his pocket along with the handkerchief. This journal, with all his notes and observations, made it safely through the storm. Water-logged though it was, the information remained legible to him.

Now, he must use these remaining days at sea to draw and label details of how birds used their wings in flight. Moreover, this remarkable ship proved her true sea-worthiness amid the powerful and thrashing waves beating against her. Likewise, Jacob sensed his own life and newly found ideas about human flight must endure equally difficult storms. He vowed to ride out the trials as they came just as *The Element* rode out the storm.

*****

True to Captain Springer's word, the crow's nest sighted Galveston just a little before the sun appeared on the horizon on the third day. The emigrants up and dressed, waited on deck eager for their first glimpse of Texas. In the pre-dawn light, the passengers saw what appeared to be a group of dull, drab warehouses lining the waterfront and the shoreline.

"I wish the sun would hurry and rise so that we could get a better view of Galveston," said Gretchen, a little girl Otto's age, "I want to see the rest of it."

"I'm afraid what you are seeing *is* the rest of it," cautioned Captain Springer.

"But we read Galveston is the largest city in Texas," stated Gretchen's mother, Irene.

"Well, that may be true—but Texas herself is only ten years old. She is just in her infant stages—much like your children here. She is depending on people like you to nourish her and help her grow." added the Captain.

Soon the Captain gave the order to the First Mate who shouted, "Furl the sails." Then presently, "Drop anchor."

As the ship steadied in place, the emigrants saw what seemed to be seven or so flat barges coming out of the harbor rowing toward *The Element*. Galveston's harbor was not deep enough to dock ships as large as *The Element.*

Jacob and Johann stood side by side ready for the moment when their feet would, at last, touch the soil of Texas—their new homeland. They stood much the way they stood in the harbor at Antwerp awaiting their departure—their hair blowing in the wind—their minds already on the journey ahead of them.

Chapter Six
The Landing

The day dawned as drab and colorless as the warehouses and wharf structures passing by their barges. Heavy fog, suspended low in the sky, purported a mysterious forecast of things to come.

Despite the lackluster sights, Jacob sensed his spirits rising just knowing how close they were to land. He turned around to see the same excited feelings flowing freely from the emigrants on the other six barges approaching the Texas harbor.

"Wunderbar, we see Texas at last!" shouted Johann as he hugged Katarina and Jacob at the same time.

Jacob smiled and observed that Johann had maneuvered well to get the two of them and the eight members of the Becker family on this ten-person barge. Nein, he does not let Katarina get far from his sight if he can help it.

Just a few more swishes of the oars and their barge hit the pier. At last they put their feet on solid Texas ground. Now they were no longer emigrants, leaving their old country, but immigrants entering into their new country.

They all strained to see what the people looked like on shore. Almost at the same time, everyone noticed a very tall, gangly-looking fellow coming down along the pier toward them. They had read that many Texans wore buckskins. In addition to his buckskins, this man wore a big, wide grin. As he extended an arm to help pull the ladies ashore, he greeted them loudly with, "Howdy—howdy, welcome to Texas!"

His cheery greeting and lively manner was in stark contrast to the grayness of the Galveston wharf.

"Howdy, my name is Josiah Gibbons, but folks around here call me Stick—Stick Gibbons," then smiling that grin again that seemed to broaden his whole face, "Guess you can tell by looking at me why I got that moniker."

Stick began lifting each of the ladies up on the pier as if they were dainty parcels of silk ribbons. Shaking the ladies' hands with his right hand and holding his large-brimmed felt hat to his chest with the other, he kept repeating the same phrase to each of the ladies. "I'm just so proud to make yer acquaintance."

It occurred to Jacob the English they studied in preparation for the journey to Texas was much more formal than the speech Josiah . . . er . . . Stick was speaking. It seemed Texans had a language all their own.

As Stick let go of Katarina's hand, he noticed her wobbly stance, "Watch it, there, missy. Hold on! Let yer land legs take over. You been out there on that sea fer so long that you grew you some water legs. Still seems like you got 'em, don't it? Don't you worry none now, missy, yer land legs will come back d'rectly."

While Katarina blushed at the mere thought of someone speaking of the appendages under her garment, squeals from little Otto overshadowed her embarrassment. "My legs are floating! Vater, Mutter, what is wrong with my legs?"

Amid the laughter over Otto's reaction and reassurances he would soon have his "land legs," most of the immigrants began kneeling—not from their water legs—but from sheer gratitude for the end of their long hazardous journey.

Emil Becker, a Lutheran minister back in Germany, began a prayer of thanksgiving with, "Our Vater above, we give Thee thanks for our safe passage across the mighty Atlantic Ocean to this mighty Texas, our new homeland. Give us strength now and purpose to do Thy will. Watch over us and guide us with Thy providence. Amen"

"Amen." followed Jacob.

"Amen". . . "Amen" . . . "Amen" . . . echoed other voices in unison.

Finding their land legs for sure, many in the group seem to burst into dancing and rejoicing on the wooden planks of the Galveston dock. Some—too weak from the rigors of their ocean travel to dance—managed to shout, "Danke Gott, Danke Gott! We made it to Texas!"

"Hold yer horses a minute!" shouted Stick Gibbons, "Happy as y'all are to be here, my job is to take y'all to someone who will be just as happy to know y'all have arrived safely."

Next, Stick Gibbons informed them Herr Klaener, the Adelsverein's representative to Galveston, had sent him to greet them and bring them to join Herr Klaener at a lodging place provided for them by the Adelsverein.

No sooner had Stick finished his last sentence than behind him appeared several men rolling wheelbarrows. After loading them with as many trunks and boxes as possible, Stick led their way from the pier to the wide sandy street alongside the wharf. Stick and the other men escorted and helped the immigrants onto three waiting carts, each drawn by a pair of yoked oxen. Obviously, there was not room for all the immigrants and all their belongings to fit in three carts.

Stick solved this problem by offering, "Reckon we will begin with whole families. All y'all single chaps stay back and haul all the rest of yer trunks and boxes to the street here. We will have to make about three trips, I reckon, to get all y'all folks over to yer boarding place. It ain't but a hog's holler away."

Hoping "a hog's holler" was not very far away, the twenty-seven or so single men left at the pier proceeded to get the rest of trunks and boxes hauled up to the street.

Waiting their turn to be transported gave the two Brodbeck brothers a chance to observe the people around them. Surprisingly, this Texas wharf street seemed to have quite a few people walking around. Sandy streets and wooden docks replaced the cobblestone quays of Antwerp they left months ago. The people were mostly dressed in simple homespun clothing. A few of them wore "buckskins"—clothes like Stick wore. The brothers had read about how the settlers made these buckskins from tanning the hides of the deer and buffalo they killed on the Texas plains.

"Ach, Bruder, it is very hot here in Texas," Johann said as he took his handkerchief from his vest pocket to wipe his brow.

"Ja, and it is already past the middle of October," Jacob could feel sweat rolling down his own shirt collar inside his dark woolen suit.

Imagine, here even in October, the weather was uncomfortably warm and humid. He remembered thankfully that along with their woolens, his Mutter had also sewn and packed lighter clothing made from cotton. Letters from earlier German immigrants warned them of the need for cooler clothing here in Texas.

Waiting also meant thinking. When each of the brothers finally settled themselves to sit on their trunks until the carts arrived for them, their thoughts traveled along very different lines.

Johann's thinking focused on the possible separation of Katarina and himself. For two months now, he counted on seeing her every single day. They shared their thoughts and aspirations of what Texas would be like and what each of them hoped to find in this new free land.

At this particular moment—Johann thought—what would happen now? Katarina was only sixteen years old. What if her father's land grant was far from his? Would he be able to continue seeing her and maybe begin to court her? Did she feel that way about him?

Jacob thought not of what he saw on the ground. Ideas of air ships flowed through his mind—air ships flying in among these low hanging gray clouds and landing here at Galveston harbor.

How would such a vessel appear? Would it have wings, and if so, would they be moveable like a bird's wings? What would be its power source? Birds and ships navigated the currents of the air and the sea to carry them. But then they were at the mercy of the same currents when storms overtook them. Was there a power source which could use the mediums of the air and sea, and control them, also?

The sound of oxen's hooves clogging through the sandy street broke the brothers' reflections. It appeared they needed only three carts to haul the single men's belongings. So the waiting was temporarily over.

As Stick rode along with them, he told them the Adelsverein had rented them a vacant warehouse for their overnight stay. Jacob noted, unlike the stone buildings in Germany, the buildings here were made of wood. Stick went on to surmise that while this vacant building may not be as comfortable as a hotel might have been, he bet most of the Germans would be more than grateful to spend their first night on Texas soil rather than rocking back and forth on the Atlantic Ocean. The German men nodded their agreement most vigorously.

As their oxen-pulled carts arrived at their appointed place, a robust and energetic, short man wearing much the same dark woolen clothing as they, greeted them.

"Willkommen! Wie geht es Ihnen?" Herr Klaener welcomed them in their native German tongue, but very quickly changed to English.

"Ja, you must begin to speak in English everyday—there are few Texans who speak or understand German."

With that admonishment, he called for all the settlers (being careful to call them settlers and not emigrants or immigrants) to gather in a circle in the middle of the floor of the warehouse.

"What I have to tell you is not good news," Herr Klaener paused letting his words settle in their minds and giving them time to acclimate before proceeding. Jacob's gaze found Johann as Johann's eyes sought Katarina's. They braced themselves for what was coming next . . .

> *"And he said, 'My presence shall go with thee, and I will give thee rest.' "*
> *Exodus 33:14*

Chapter 7
An Unwanted Turn

As soon as Herr Klaener felt the settlers had prepared themselves for the information he was to give them, he went on,

"Apparently, Prince Solms of Braunfels, who was elected by the Adelsverein to handle their moneys and the procurement of the Texas land grants, did not have good management skills. He has been replaced by Baron Von Meusebach. But before the Baron could arrive in Texas with more money and make needed adjustments, many thousands of German immigrants before you had no place to go and the Adelsverein took them by barges to a place on the beach south of Galveston called Indian Point." He paused to let the settlers absorb what he was saying.

"They have been stranded there awaiting supplies and transportation to the land grants. In addition, the land grants are located about 250 miles inland northwest of Galveston. To get to the land grants means traveling on rugged dirt paths and trails through mostly virgin wilderness. Also there is the threat of Indian attacks along the way, so settlers would need some protection as well."

"How soon can we expect the Baron to send the help we need?" Jacob inquired of the stout little man.

"Ja, Herr Meusebach has experienced additional difficulty in finding enough oxen and carts to make the trip from his headquarters in New Braunfels to Indian Point. Most all of the available oxen and carts are needed to haul supplies in the war effort of the United States against Mexico."

"What war effort? We thought the Texans won their independence from Mexico," countered Doctor William Hermes, a physician in the group of settlers.

"Ja, maybe you did not know of this war. Mexico threatened to go to war against the United States of America if the United States admitted Texas into the union of states. Last year Texas was annexed as the 36th state in the union. Mexico followed through on her threat and declared war on the United States in April of this year. But except for supplies being harder to come by, hopefully the war has nothing to do with us.

"And speaking of supplies, that is what you must be about doing right now. You will spend tonight here in Galveston and then we will take you and your supplies on barges down the coastline to Indian Point. From there, it is our hope that soon Baron von Meusenbach will arrive with more supplies and news of your land grants."

While going about getting their supplies, a new concern troubled Jacob. He was not comfortable buying any kind of gun. He did not even know how to use one. The German merchant who sold them their supplies encouraged the men to each buy a shotgun.

"Ja, you can use a shotgun for hunting and to protect yourself from Indians. Since you do not have any experience with a gun, a shotgun works best for you because it does not require such careful aim."

Jacob and Johann reluctantly bought their shotguns along with their other needed supplies.

The settlers got an early start the next day. Buoyed by a good night's rest and a home-cooked breakfast, most of the settlers' spirits were higher this day even though they were not looking forward to having to sojourn longer at Indian Point.

The Becker family and the Brodbeck brothers managed to get on the same barge as before. During the passage south, the talk seemed to center around news they heard while shopping for supplies in Galveston—news about the tent city of Indian Point.

Most of the children had fallen asleep en route because of the early morning call.

Noting this, Dr. William Hermes, who was on their barge, called to their attention, "Ja, some are calling Indian Point the 'City of Misery.' This unfortunate title is probably because the place has been plagued with diseases such as dysentery, and maybe even cholera, due to the conditions caused by thousands of immigrants having to live in tents and any makeshift dwelling they could find.

He paused and looked around to see if they were listening. They were. "Polluted drinking water and inadequate sanitation was bad enough, but now since there have been so many rains this past spring and summer, hordes of mosquitoes are bringing a disease called meningitis to the settlers as well. These poor souls have no means of leaving and have been stuck there like festering sores waiting for help to arrive.

Shaking his head in deep concern, he went on, "My hands will be full caring for these people when we arrive. I can only hope we find another doctor there who is still alive and healthy to help me. We must all pray Herr Meusenback arrives soon with supplies and ways to get all of our people inland."

"Ja, and pray, too, our stay at Indian Point is short and we do not become ill while we are there," interjected Emil Becker, who undoubtedly was thinking about his wife and six children.

"The ones with contagious diseases have more than likely been quarantined away from the healthy families. I will find out more as soon as we arrive and inform you of any quarantined areas," warned Dr. Hermes.

A hush fell upon them now as they all seemed lost in their own thoughts. The lapping of the choppy, brown waves upon their barges and the swish of the oars propelling them forward seemed to be repeating sounds of possible impending trouble and heartache.

Slush, slap, whoosh . . . no turning back now . . . slush, slap, whoosh . . . going forward . . . coming closer with each sound of the oars.

To keep his mind off whatever might come next in their journey, Jacob took this quiet time to sit back and think about how birds fly. He very quietly removed his bird drawings and notes. As his eyes scanned his drawings, they kept coming back to the birds' wings—the wings were curved across the top of the wing and flatter at the bottom of the wing. He examined them more closely. Their wings appeared to have the curving thickness at the foremost of the wing as you looked down upon the wing and tapered off toward the back of the wing. He wondered if that curve had anything to do with how birds could fly.

He longed for the time when, being settled, he could experiment with various materials in order to construct wings in the likeness of birds' wings. Also, he yearned to find his scientific books in his trunks. He wanted to read about flight theories for he knew that the magic and dream of flying occupied man's thoughts long before consuming his own imagination. He seemed to remember reading about the studies of a Swiss mathematician named Daniel Bernoulli. Yes . . . he was sure that he had read his discoveries about air pressure . . .

An oarsman's voice broke into Jacob's mind images.

"Not far now and we should begin to see the tents of 'Tent City.' "

A bend in the coastline appeared. What lay beyond this jutted-out sand dune with its small scrubby bushes cropping up—hiding what was next in view?

> *"And behold, I am with thee, and will keep thee in all places whither thou goest . . ."*
> *Genesis 28:15*

Chapter 8
City of Misery

Rounding the tip of the next dune, the settlers saw what looked like a deserted beach . . . until a lone boy darted from behind the scrub bushes. He zigzagged back and forth on the beach—intent on chasing or catching something zigzagging ahead of him.

One of the oarsmen supplied by the Adelsverein, cautioned, "Shh . . . be quiet! That young boy is chasing down his dinner—which appears to be a crab. You will learn to eat shellfish such as crab while you are here. Once you learn how to retrieve their meat, you will find them quite tasty."

Suddenly, the young boy pounced on the creature with all four limbs of his body as if he were a crab himself. As soon as it appeared the catch had been safely made, the oarsman hollered, "Wie gehts! Good catch!"

The boy turned with a startled look.

"Do you bring food?" were the first words from the boy's lips.

And so the settlers' early welcome warned them of things to come as they came upon the city of misery. Hours later, Jacob and Johann finished nailing down the last pegs that secured the sailcloth that would provide their shelter for their stay here at Indian Point. The Beckers' makeshift tent was about thirty yards from theirs.

In order to hopefully avoid any further contamination of existing diseases, Dr. Hermes advised them to make their campsite some distance from the settlers already camped there. They had chosen a site just on the other side of a dune where a pool of water collected. This would make it easier to retrieve water to boil for washing purposes rather than trudging back and forth to the beach for it. Their main drinking water was housed in large cisterns in the center of the tent community.

The next night, Dr Hermes called a meeting of the newly arrived group. As they sat around their campfire, Dr. Hermes shared his early observations with them.

"I am a doctor so it is my life's choice to do whatever I can to heal unhealthy bodies. But I tell you this: each of you cannot take the chances I take by being around these poor souls with their contagious diseases. You must keep yourself healthy and strong to face the demanding road journey ahead of you when Baron von Meusebach arrives with oxen and carts. It is my duty to tell you whatever comfort or help you might think you can give the diseased ones will not keep them from dying. Indeed, it will make matters worse because if your own camp becomes infected, there will be more people for Dr. Reuss and I to treat.

"We are fortunate Dr. Reuss is here. He and I have declared quarantine around the area where we have the sickbay. That will be off limits to all of you."

Johann glanced at Katarina to see the impact of the doctor's words on her face. Ashen and stricken, Katarina turned to avoid anyone seeing her reaction. But Johann had seen it. He moved closer to Katarina to whisper in her ear...

"Katarina, have you been to see your friend, Ann Elizabeth, since we arrived?"

"Ja, she and I promised each other when she left in the shipload of Germans before us that when I made it to

Texas, we would do our best to contact one another. I slipped over to their camp early yesterday morning to see if she might still be in Indian Point. And she was! But she is barely alive. She hardly recognized me. Johann, she is dying with cholera!"

"Katarina, you must tell Dr. Hermes that you have been exposed!"

"What good would that do? It would just worry Vater and Mutter and they have enough to worry them." Then clutching Johann's arm and drawing close to his face, "And Johann, you must promise me you will not tell anyone what I have told you!"

"Only if you promise me that you will not go back to see Ann Elizabeth again."

"I cannot promise you that . . . indeed, if you are my friend, you will help me slip away at night to take extra gruel and blankets to her family. They need more food and blankets—especially for Ann Elizabeth."

"Katarina, listen to yourself! Did you not hear Dr. Hermes say we need to stay strong ourselves for the long journey ahead of us? Besides, does your family of eight have extra blankets and gruel to spare?"

"Nein, but Ann Elizabeth can have some of my share. Oh, Johann, do you not understand? She would do the same for me. We have known each other all of our lives. She is dying, Johann! I cannot live with myself if I do not try to make her last days on earth more bearable."

With these last choked out words, Katarina hung her head and covered her face with her shawl to hide the soft sobs coming from deep within her soul.

Johann felt completely helpless. All he seemed to know to do was comfort her with his arm around her shoulder.

*****

Later, as the two brothers settled in for the evening in their barren makeshift shelter, Johann recounted the bleak situation to Jacob.

"Johann, it is your duty to tell Katarina's Vater what is happening. She is only sixteen years old and does not have the maturity to make the decision she is making. She is not only jeopardizing herself, she is putting the rest of this group of settlers at peril as well!"

"But she is so determined! She would never forgive me if I did that! Besides, she trusts me! How can I betray her faith in me?"

"Johann, you are thinking with your heart and not your head!" Then, grabbing Johann by the shoulders, Jacob gently shook his brother until Johann looked at him—he wanted him to see the sternness in his eyes. "Johann, you must be the man you are—you must put personal feelings aside to think of the better good of all."

Johann slumped over with his head between his hands. "Ja, I will talk to Katarina again tomorrow and convince her to see the wider scope of the consequences of her actions."

"Nein, Bruder, there is no time to do that. Katarina may already be infected and be a carrier. She may need to be placed in quarantine herself. This is a serious situation that requires immediate action. Go now to their tent and tell her Vater!"

"In front of Katarina? She will never forgive me."

"Katarina's scorn is a small price to pay for her life and the lives of those around you. Here, let us go together. I will tell Katarina that I was the one who insisted on telling her Vater."

"Nein, it is not your place. It is mine. But I welcome your support. Let us go now to face what we must."

The two brothers made haste and crawled out on the dark beach to make their way to the Becker's tent.

Chapter 9
Dark Skies

When Jacob and Johann asked for permission to enter the Beckers' tent, they were stunned to be greeted by Dr. Hermes with a cautionary tone, "Please wait outside for the moment. I will be out soon to talk to you."

Both brothers sat back in the sand—each silent not wanting to put voice to their fears. It seemed longer, but their wait was over in five minutes. Only Dr. Hermes came out of the Beckers' tent motioning to them to follow him farther away, apparently not wanting to be within earshot of the inhabitants inside.

He went immediately to the point, "I know you two brothers are close to the Becker family. So I tell you this for your own protection. And I must tell you what I have to share with you is only what I fear and not what I know. God willing, may my fears be wrong. It appears the oldest Becker child, Katarina, started having stomach cramps and occasional diarrhea in the last few hours. She does not have a fever and seems to be normal in every other way. But Herr Becker just found out earlier today that Katarina was seen coming out of a quarantined tent yesterday. As soon as he confronted Katarina about it, she told him it was true . . . that she had been to see her childhood friend, Ann Elizabeth Holtz. Herr Becker became alarmed when just a few hours later, Katarina's symptoms began. He came and found me as quickly as he could. It is too soon to tell, but because her friend, Ann Elizabeth, has cholera, I fear Katarina has become infected with it as well."

Johann quickly implored, "When will you know one way or the other?"

"If Katarina just has a disagreeable stomach, she will more than likely be better in twenty-four hours . . . but if it is cholera, her symptoms will worsen. Then we must fight to keep her from becoming dehydrated by trying to force as many liquids as we can down her. But it has been the experience of Dr. Reuss that it is very difficult to get his patients to drink or eat anything. Most die within forty-eight hours. To be on the safe side, until we know if Katarina has cholera and be placed under quarantine, I have asked the Beckers to move their tent and belongings farther down the beach from any of your group. I am going to insist that neither of you go near their tent. Did either of you come in contact with Katarina in the last twenty-four hours?"

"Ja, I spoke with Katarina right after the group meeting we had tonight," Johann answered.

"Did you drink or eat anything together?"

"Nein, we only talked."

"I hate to have to ask this personal question, Johann, but you understand that I must." Dr. Hermes struggled, "Did you kiss her?"

"Oh, nein!" came Johann's hurried reply. Then pausing a moment in slight hesitation, he volunteered, "But I did put my arm around her shoulders."

Briefly pausing, also, Dr. Hermes said, "Perhaps you will be fine. We are not sure how the disease is passed from one person to the next only that it seems to do so very quickly. I will check by your tent tomorrow when I come back to check on Katarina. In the meantime, I need your word as a gentleman that you will not go near the Becker tent." Then reaching out to shake hands with Johann, the doctor asked him, "Can I depend on that?"

Johann placed his hand in the doctor's hand, "Ja, Dr. Hermes. But will you promise me if there is anything I can get for the Beckers—food, blankets . . . anything at all, you will let me know?"

"You have my word that I will do that for you," agreed the doctor.

Walking back to their own tent, Jacob put his arm around his brother's shoulders, "Johann, it is in Gott's hands now. There is nothing you can do now except pray."

Johann said nothing. With his head hung low, he was forcing back great gulps of sobs pushing up from inside his chest.

Once inside their tent, the emotions trapped inside of him erupted with great heaves of stifled breaths.

"Ach, Bruder . . . let it out. Do not be ashamed. The depth of your despair only demonstrates the depth of your apparent love for Katarina. We must never be ashamed of our ability to love deeply. Besides, we are far enough away from others for your tears to flow . . . no one can see you."

Johann could not even answer so choked was he trying to get his breath. But given his older brother's understanding and encouragement to vent his emotions, he began to let it come up. Haltingly, his breathing began to return to normal and as it did so, the trapped tears flowed freely down his face. Without shame then, he allowed the tears to come.

Indeed, Jacob found himself softly weeping as well. As he tried to comfort his Bruder, he realized how much the extreme events of the past several months had taken their toll on both of them emotionally. The tears that came now flowed from frozen nerves at long last unleashed.

Finally, Johann found his voice, "Do you think there is any chance that Katarina does not have the dreaded cholera?"

Jacob paused before answering. One part of him wanted to give his Bruder hope, but another part warned him to prepare Johann for the worst. Not knowing which of the two urgings to follow, Jacob turned instead to seek out the still, knowing voice inside of him that never let him down.

"I think, Bruder, instead of trying to answer that question, it is time to kneel and ask for the Lord's help and His will."

As the two brothers knelt and entreated the Lord's presence, a soft rain began to fall outside. The subtle drops on their tent roof seem to whisper God's abiding presence in their tent.

Jacob's low voice intoned, "Our heavenly Vater, we lift our precious one, Katarina, and her family up to Thee. We implore Thee to strengthen her body to withstand whatever comes upon it. We beseech Thee to give her comfort, guard her soul, and if it be Thy will, to heal her of any disease. Give Johann the fortitude to face whatever may come. And as always, dear Lord, Thy will be done. In Thy Son's Holy and Precious Name we pray. Amen."

Feeling completely spent, Johann fell quickly asleep. Jacob left him sleeping while he looked around for a cover to place over his head before he slipped outside in the rain. He intended to remove the lid on a large crock pot they had bought as part of their supplies. He wanted to catch some of this rainwater to have for fresh drinking water.

Having done that, he looked up to the darkened sky. With rain still falling, the clouds were moving swiftly by, occasionally revealing tiny sparkles of stars as they passed. The sky was quickly changing in a dramatic way. Jacob took comfort in seeing the stars peep through the pervading, fast-moving clouds.

Was it God's still voice inside him saying . . . *"No matter what darkness betides, look for it to pass. Look for the light under the veil. Keep moving toward the light."*

Just then, a nearby night raven which moments before stood silently and patiently very still, gave a "quock" as it snatched an unsuspecting fish swimming in the dune pool near their tent. As another streak of lightning lit up the sky, Jacob watched the bird, with its captured prey, glide smoothly away with only a few slow and steady wing beats.

What invisible force caused its thrust up into the heavens? It seemed so effortless. How could man duplicate the force behind that thrust? What power did he have at his disposal?

A resounding boom of thunder and then, pouring rain fractured Jacob's speculations forcing him to take cover in the confines of their tent.

Once settled in his makeshift bed, Jacob's mind kept going back to the vision of the night raven soaring away with his passenger albeit his prey. As his body relaxed, he drifted off to sleep. He began dreaming of a huge man-made apparatus lifting up and away with its human passengers on their way to distant lands and destinations—its passengers not afraid of crossing oceans or flying over tall mountains.

> *"Even in darkness light dawns for the upright, for the gracious and compassionate and righteous man." Psalm 112:4*

Chapter 10
Journey On

Despite everything Dr. Hermes and Katarina's family could do, Katarina died in her mother's arms some forty-eight hours later. Because of the quarantine, no one but her family had been allowed inside the Beckers' tent.

The frustration Johann felt at not getting to say good-bye to her was almost unbearable. He did not yet know that among Katarina's last requests to her family was for Johann to receive her Bible and a letter to him she had dictated to her mother.

Jacob knew Johann would need time to grieve this devastating loss, but there was no time. A message had come that Herr Meusebach was finally on his way to Indian Point. They were to be ready to pack up and travel within days.

Finding the materials to construct a casket for Katarina forced Johann and Jacob to concentrate on the matters at hand. Because the only timber around them at Indian Point were small scrub brushes growing from the dunes, most families who lost loved ones were forced to bury them wrapped only in sheets.

A meeting of the able-bodied men closest to the Becker family brought no useful ideas. But then, Phyllis, Dr. Hermes' wife, brought word that Mina Becker, Katarina's mother, had a request. It seems they had built Katarina a hope chest which held family heirlooms for her to have in the event of her future marriage. Since Katarina was petite in stature, she could be placed in her hope chest along with a few of her cherished things. Would the men dig a grave on the highest dune they could find? Would they bury Katarina there facing the ocean?

In the predawn stillness of the next day, the mourners climbed the highest dune to gather around the freshly dug grave. A cross made from two pieces of weathered driftwood marked the head of the grave. Scavenging the night before, Johann and little Otto had found the driftwood. Little Otto located some of Katarina's yellow hair ribbons to lace the crossbars together. Now the little boy held a bunch of beach evening primroses; their yellow blooms popping up on most of the dunes around the coastline. He quickly unlatched himself from his mother's arms and darted over to lay the bouquet of flowers beside the makeshift cross.

"These are for you, Reenie. They are yellow . . . your favorite color."

The Reverend Becker officiated at the graveside of his own daughter. The message, sweet and simple, contained a poem that Katarina had written before leaving Germany. Reverend Becker struggled to read the poem with its haunting and heavenly prophetic message:

Wisdom of the Wildflowers
by Katarina Becker

Matthew 6:28 "Consider the lilies of the field, how they grow; they toil not, neither do they spin."

Consider the lilies of the field;
Joyous in infinite variety,
Springing from rock, crevice or nettle,
Or nestled in many-hued harmony.

They toil not, nor spin, worry or fret.
Tilting vibrant faces to the sun,
Growing abundantly, without restraint,
Resplendent in jubilant abandon!

Gracing and adorning stream or pasture,
In crag or cranny, hillside to roadside,
Blooming in marsh, loam, or wilderness,
What heavenly wisdom do they provide?

Wildflowers, O Wildflowers,

Tho' fragile you burst through cracked stones!
You erupt from hardened rivets of ground!
You spring from crystalline drifts of snow!
Vigorous, yet dainty doth ye abound!

Tell the secrets of your seclusion;
The deep-pinioned dwelling from which you sprung,
Cradled in the bowels of the earth,
Darkened and pressed down by earth's top rung.

Tell of the silence, the aloneness!
Did you spin and strain to push away free?
Free from your temporal constriction,
Free of waiting and longing?

Or

Wildflowers, Wise Wildflowers,

While sequestered, lying still and dormant,
Did you calmly trust your inward design,
Quiescent, serene and confident
Until by God's grace you blossom again?

With the morning sun at their backs and the salty sea mists spraying their faces, the mourners stood huddled together in their grief. Stepping up behind the crude cross with its yellow ribbons fluttering in the breeze, Johann pulled his harmonica from his vest pocket. Haltingly, he began playing a familiar old German hymn, "Be Still, My Soul."

When it seemed Johann might break down, Jacob joined the main verse, his rich baritone voice singing the words in their native German tongue. Soon other voices blended in giving Johann the support he needed to continue.

Stille, mein Wille! Dein Jesus hilft siegen;
Be still, my soul: the Lord is on thy side;
Trage gehuldig das Leiden, die Not;
Bear patiently the cross of grief or pain.
Gott ist's, der alles zum Besten will fügen,
Leave to thy God to order and provide;
Der dir getreu bleibt in Schmerzen und Tod.
In every change, He faithful will remain.
Stille, mein Wille! Dein Jesus wird machen
Be still, my soul: thy best, thy heavenly Friend
Glüchlichen Ausgang bedenklicher Sachen.
Through thorny ways lead to a joyful end.

Singing this beloved German hymn eased their sense of hopelessness. The hymn, based on Psalm 46:10, "Be still, and know that I am God," ironically was written by another Katarina. Katarina Schlegel wrote the hymn in 1752.

As the mourners sang, they clasped hands; each connected in their memories not only of their dear departed one, but from their departed homeland.

When Johann finished playing the last refrain, Reverend Becker captured these feelings in the words of his benediction:

"Our Heavenly Vater, our loved one is in Your Hands now. We give Thee thanks for the blessing of her life to us. Now, Vater, as we turn our backs from whence we have come, bind us together in our faith and give us the stamina to turn our faces to the West where our new destiny lies. In Thy Son's Precious Name we pray, Amen."

After the gathered group paid their last respects to the grieving family and starting disseminating, Mina Becker walked over to Johann. In her hands she held Katarina's Bible with the letter to Johann folded inside its pages.

"Johann, Katarina wanted you to have her Bible. In it you will find a letter to you she dictated to me to write. In the pages of her Bible, she marked many of her own favorite Bible verses and—she said—she marked many of the ones the two of you shared together as well. I hope when our days are not so busy that you take time to find comfort in these, my son, and may Gott bless you now and always."

They embraced as she handed the Bible to Johann.

*****

Sooner than any expected, Herr Meusebach arrived late that evening. Seeing many fresh graves and many sickly folks, Meusebach urged the settlers to speed their packing. He called a meeting of the able-bodied men that night to discuss arrangements. If possible, they would leave in two days, giving him and his men one day to rest before hitting the trail again.

Jacob, eager to talk to Herr Meusebach about a possible teaching position in Fredericksburg, watched to find the opportunity to catch him alone. His chance came early . . . early the next morning before the sun came up. Jacob, always an early riser, found Meusebach strolling up the beach, a coffee mug in his hand.

"Herr Meusebach, might I have a word with you?" Jacob ran to catch him.

"Ja, if you might want to walk with me." Meusebach's tone seemed encouraging and friendly as he went on to explain, "I find walking early in the morning before others arise gives me time to ponder life's questions and needs as well as pray for guidance from our heavenly Vater. Who are you that you get up so early from the rest of the settlers?"

"Ja, I, too, enjoy the solitude of the early morning for the same reasons as you. My name is Jacob Brodbeck. I taught for the King at Württemberg University. I would like to inquire about a teaching position in the town of Fredericksburg you have founded here in Texas. I need a job until the Adelsverein's land grants become available to us."

"Ja, I see . . . 'The early bird gets the worm.' "

"Your pardon?"

Meusebach laughed, "It is just one of the folksy adages I have heard Texans use. Perhaps I should say, 'The early bird gets the job'?"

Jacob, too, smiled and nodded his understanding. Strange, this man amidst death and dying and with so much responsibility on his shoulders could find amusement in small happenings around him. Perhaps this quality of humor helped him be the good leader he had become.

"Herr Brodbeck," Meusebach extended his hand in greeting, "it is a pleasure to meet you and to be informed of your skills and good qualities. At the present time, we have a one-room school in operation in Fredericksburg and we do presently have a school master. However, we may have need for you in the future."

Then he paused trying to size up Jacob in the pre-dawn light, "You seem to be in good health. As you know, I am advising the families with sick ones to travel to New Braunfels where there are more adequate medical provisions instead of journeying on to Fredericksburg. Are you married with a family and ill ones in your care?"

"Nein, I am with my younger Bruder, Johann. We are both unmarried men."

"What profession or skills does your Bruder, Johann, have and is he as healthy as you seem to be?" inquired Meusebach.

"He has very good skills as a stone mason and as healthy as I" replied Jacob and adding, "I, also, am a furniture maker and a land surveyor."

Meusebach smiled at the young man's exuberance. "I tell you this, Herr Brodbeck, while it would indeed be to our fellow German settlers' advantage to have two able-bodied and intelligent young men as yourselves come to help settle Fredericksburg, I would not be fair to you as a gentleman if I did not remind you of what I said at the group meeting last night. Because there are so many sick people in New Braunfels and in Fredericksburg, it would be well for the persons not yet infected to go on to Seguin or San Antonio where the diseases are not so rampant. Having such skills as the two of you have, you will find good jobs."

Meusebach sensed hesitancy in Jacob's response. "Ach, I know it is hard to separate from your fellow countrymen. This I will tell you. You and your Bruder let me know what you decide. If you decide to go on to Seguin or San Antonio, I will give you my word I will send for you when we have a need for another schoolmaster in Fredericksburg."

"Ja,das ist gut. My Bruder and I want to settle in a German community. We thought as soon as we had become settled in a new home, we would be able to bring our family over, also.

Then Jacob continued, "The days on board ship were long and frightful. At times we sailed into severe storms, which caused great discomfort for the crew and the passengers. In the many weeks we were at sea, my thoughts wandered in many directions.

"One thought struck me with a deep conviction—that Gott had made all this possible for me. With my inventive and creative ability, I should be able to develop a much safer way of travel for man. I watched the sea gulls as they glided over the water with such ease and how their wings would control their angle of flight. I thought to myself; *Why not let me build an air ship, so it can use the atmosphere instead of battling these terrible ocean waves?* I also studied the wind effects on the sails of the ship as it slowly moved over the water; without a strong current, we were motionless. This caused us to be at sea months instead of weeks."

Meusebach took pause and then said, "Herr Brodbeck, you have a big dream, and may Gott give you the health and strength to develop this dream of yours."

At that point Meusebach noticed the sun's rays peeping over the horizon. He reached inside his vest pocket and pulled out a pen and paper. "Here, I will write down your name—Jacob Brodbeck, Schoolmaster," then pausing to look over at Jacob, "and Inventor. Now I am writing down how you may contact me when you get settled."

Giving Jacob the piece of paper, Meusebach held out his hand for a handshake, "It is time to get busy. There is much organizing to be done for our trip tomorrow."

Jacob shook hands with Meusebach, "Danke schön. I will talk to you again before we leave tomorrow to let you know of our decision of where to go."

As Jacob watched Meusebach's darkened form walk back to the tents away from the beach, he stood a moment to take in the beauty of the approaching sunrise. Droplets of dew caught by the sun's rays seemed to Jacob like so many crystals sprinkled on the spreading vines creeping all around the dunes of the beach— crystals escaping and falling from the sparkling stars of the nights before—nights of terrible sadness.

But that was it! Had he not sensed Gott's message to him that rainy night after they had prayed Katarina might live?

"Look for the light! Look under the veil for the light!"

Here in this crystalline moment under the veil of the passing sad nights, these luminous dewdrops moved Jacob to perceive the ebb tide of events. He sensed the need to seize this moment. He must go and find Johann. Together they would journey on . . . on through the darkness of their loss and grief, on through Texas trails, perhaps fraught with peril, on until they discovered the light of a new dawn!

Chapter 11
The Trail West Begins

Jacob found Johann outside the tent packing up their cooking utensils. Upon seeing Jacob walk up, Johann motioned toward the campfire, "There is one more cup of coffee there, mein Bruder, if you want another cup."

"Ja, I will take that cup of coffee if I might interrupt your packing to share some news with you," replied Jacob.

"Ja, gut. Bitte, here is my cup . . . just a little more to heat it up."

As the two brothers began discussing Jacob's conversation with Herr Meusebach, it soon became clear to them his advice held merit. Further, they agreed San Antonio rather than Seguin would be the better choice because it was a more established town.

Just as they decided Jacob would go find Meusebach to let him know of their decision, Meusebach found them.

"Herr Brodbeck," Meusebach called out to them as he approached their tent. "I have come with news for you and your Bruder." Seeing Johann beside Jacob, he went on, "Wie gehts, you must be Johann Brodbeck." Meusebach extended his hand in introduction.

"Ja, it is a pleasure to meet you, Baron Meusebach," answered Johann accepting the older man's handshake.

"Nein, in Texas, I do not use the title, Baron. It is too formal for Texan culture," Meusebach said with a smile, "I came to find the two of you this morning after hearing from one of our scouts something that might interest you. There is a group of unmarried German men in

Victoria who have located a few Mexicans with oxen carts. These Mexicans are willing to take German settlers to San Antonio. I have sent word back with my scout that our group of settlers should be in Victoria in about a week. From Victoria, a group of you can break away from our group, cross over to the town of Goliad, where the San Antonio River will lead you into the town of San Antonio. We will, of course, come to the Guadalupe River in Victoria and follow it until we come to New Braunfels and then from there, onto Fredericksburg."

"Ja, then, that settles it. My Bruder and I had decided that San Antonio would be the best place for us to find jobs, so there we shall go," answered Jacob.

After Meusebach walked away, Jacob touched his brother on the shoulder, "Johann, I noticed you have not opened Katarina's Bible or letter, yet. I can do the packing. May I suggest that you take the Bible, walk down the beach until you find a quiet place to sit, and then read your letter?"

"Danke schön, that is thoughtful of you, mein Bruder. But my hurt is too raw right now. The shock is so great. My heart could not endure the bittersweet pain of her letter just now. Surely, I would not hold up to what lay ahead of us if I give in to further grief now. Nein, it is better for me to keep my mind busy. One day soon, there will come the right time when my heart is stronger for me to sit down with my dear sweet Katarina's last words to me."

Jacob stood quietly for a few moments letting Johann gain control of his shaky emotions. After a few still moments he said, "Perhaps, Johann, her words would fortify you instead of weaken you. Have you not considered Katarina knew you well enough that she perceived just the right kind of words to help you gain the strength and comfort you need?"

Johann sat down to ponder what Jacob advised. Jacob pretended to get busy dousing the campfire and putting the tin cups away. In just a few moments, Johann looked up at him.

"Ja, I can agree with you Katarina's words will be comforting to me. But in due time. All I can stand to feel right now is numbness. The numbness is its own comfort and protection for me. During this time, let me take the actions that I must to get us on the road to San Antonio. Then one day when the dust settles along the trail, there will come the time to be with Katarina's thoughts and words."

"Very well, mein Bruder, you know yourself the best. I shall not mention it again until you talk about it to me. Now, pack up your gear. Let us go and discover the 'land of the free and the brave'—this glorious Republic of Texas!"

*****

This glorious republic of Texas seemed to spread out in endless miles and miles of flat grassy prairie. Jacob wondered if all of Texas was this monotonous. Trudging along behind the plodding oxen and listening to the wagon creak as their big wheels slowly turned, made for a long, boring day. Of course, in a way he was glad the oxen were slow because he was not sure he could walk any faster. None of the settlers were accustomed to walking on such a long and continuous journey. Most of the women and children rode in the wagons along with all their provisions while the able-bodied men walked along side.

At least the miserable tent city of Indian Point faded out of sight. Now and then, low marshy ponds appeared like glassy respites amidst the grassy terrain. Jacob took note when they drew close to one such pond. Long-legged birds stood in the shallow waters, their beaks dabbing up and down oftentimes filled with fish. He watched keenly as they took flight, unfolding their wings and rising sharply in the sky. He wanted to stop, sit down and capture their movements on paper. But that was not possible.

He continued treading along; shotgun slung over his shoulder, and allowed his mind to imagine how to design an air ship for mankind. He remembered studying the anatomy of a bird's body. Most of the bones of birds were hollow which made them lighter. Reeds and bamboo stalks were hollow, but they would not be strong enough to support the weight of man. Birds' bones were fused together which made them strong. The bone structure of their wings was then covered with different layers of feathers. These different layers flapped to help propel the bird into the air. How could man duplicate bird wings?

Instead of feathers to cover the wing structure, how about sailcloth like the kind used on their sailing ship? Sail cloth was strong and able to catch the wind. But what kind of wood could be used to replicate birds' bones and how would the wood be fused together? Oh, he would be so glad when he would have the chance to sit down to study solutions for his questions.

Just then a change of motion in the sound of the constant churning of the wagon wheels interrupted his mind dance.

Was the wagon train coming to a halt? As Jacob looked around for the cause, his eyes noted a different kind of bird on the horizon. Dark vultures circling in the sky some distance ahead forecast a warning of some kind of life being damaged or already gone. Perhaps that explained the wagon train coming to a stop.

Jacob turned around and shouted to Johann who was taking his turn driving their wagon.

"Johann, I run ahead to see the reason for the vultures in the sky."

"Are you sure you want to do that, Jacob? The scouts on horseback ahead of us are trained to take care of any trouble and will alert us soon enough."

"Ja, I will be careful. I am curious to find out why the wagon train has stopped. I will come back soon with information."

Jacob trotted as fast as he could alongside the trail of the wagons until he came to the head wagon. It had completely stopped as Meusebach stood ahead twenty paces or so talking with his men. Not wanting to intrude on their conversation, Jacob remained back a little distance waiting to see if any information were forthcoming.

At that juncture, two Texas scouts on horseback came trotting up from ahead. One of them jumped down and hollered to Meusebach loud enough for Jacob to hear, "No sign of any other wounded or dead people as far as we can tell . . . just this one dead man along the trail and his very loyal dog. That poor hound's a whining and a whimpering, and a licking his master's face doing his best to revive him. We couldn't find any cause of death . . . no bullet wounds, no arrows in him."

Reaching into his pocket, the scout pulled out some wadded-up paper. "We did find these papers on the dead man. You might want to look at them, sir."

Taking the papers from the scout's hand, Meusebach quickly scanned their contents. "It appears you have found a scout of the United States Army. He was on his way to Goliad with what looks like a coded message for the command post there. The second paper asks if he is wounded or killed and found by Texans, that his message is taken on to Goliad for him. He also makes a plea for his dog, Happy, to have a good home. He writes that Happy is a good hunting dog and very loyal."

An idea popped into Jacob's head. He quickly pushed himself forward, excusing himself as he did. "Herr Meusebach, might my Bruder and I take the message with us to Goliad to the Command Post there? We would also be glad to take in the poor man's dog. As you know, my Bruder has also suffered a loss. Perhaps he and the dog would be good companions for one another. Besides, we are not good hunters. Maybe Happy can teach us how to find our supper."

Meusebach looked around at the other men standing about them. "If no one has any objections . . . that is fine with me." None of the men had anything to say, so Meusebach handed the papers to Jacob. Then looking to the scout who had brought him the papers, he said, "Ben, take Herr Brodbeck to where the dog is guarding his master.

Take a few volunteers with you to help you bury the gentleman as well."

Ben, a worn-out looking man who wore the garb of most Texans, adjusted his wide-brimmed hat, got on his horse and looked down at Jacob, "Here, hop up on the horse behind me and ride with me. It's just a few hundred yards ahead of us."

Then he barked a few orders to the other scouts who quickly ran for shovels to come along and help dig the grave.

By the time they rode up to where the body lay, Happy was lying down right beside his master. The soulful look in his eyes touched Jacob's heart. The dog didn't

whine or whimper or even move when they got down and came over to where he lay.

Ben crooned to the dog as he petted him on his head, "Hey, there, Happy. Bet you're all tuckered out and hungry to boot." At that, Happy wagged his tail faintly seeming to show his sadness but friendliness as well.

"How long do you think this man has been dead?" Jacob asked of the scout.

"It's hard to say . . . maybe a day or so. The weather's cool . . . that might keep the body from smelling right away." Then looking up at the buzzards circling overhead, he said, "It doesn't take long for those buzzards to find dead meat, though."

Having said that, Ben looked back down at the body, "Wonder what happened to him? We looked for his horse, but found nothing. From the looks of that worn down grass behind him, I'd say he even dragged himself up to the trail here."

Then the Texan reached down to turn the body over, apparently looking again for further evidence of his death. Just as he did so, Happy let out a slow, low growl that warned the Texan he would not allow any further tampering with his master.

Jacob remembered the hard biscuit and dried meat in his knapsack. Reaching for the food, he called out to Ben, "Wait a minute. I have some food here for the dog. Let me try to make friends with him."

"Good enough. He's all yours. I'll get a rope from my saddle so that you can tie him up if need be." Ben stepped over to his horse for the rope.

Happy responded immediately to the food Jacob offered him. "There, boy . . . good dog. Are you hungry? I wish I had some water for you." Jacob squatted down and kept his distance while the dog ate the offered food. Then to Jacob's surprise, when the dog finished, he whimpered and started crawling over to where Jacob knelt. Jacob gingerly patted him on his head, talking soothingly to him.

"There now, Happy. You certainly are a friendly dog. No rope for you." Jacob carefully put his arms underneath the dog until he could lift him up to cradle him in his arms. “Are you too weak to fight me, Happy? Do not worry, boy, there are better times ahead for all of us.”

Jacob decided to walk back to their wagon carrying Happy. He was surprised to feel how light the dog was. Happy, for his part, made little or no objections . . . finally laying his head submissively in the crook of Jacob’s arm.

The wagon train had begun moving again so that Jacob came up to their wagon sooner than he expected. Johann’s face, when he spotted Jacob walking up to the wagon with the limp dog is his arms, registered both curiosity and consternation. What did his Bruder have in mind, now?

Chapter 12
An Unexpected Sojourn

At first Johann objected to the addition of Happy to their wagon train claiming he was another mouth to feed. However, Jacob's reasoning that Happy could help them find game for food made sense. The sealer of the deal was Happy himself. The dog seemed to sense the kindred, sad and aching spirit in Johann. Until his strength was renewed, Happy seemed content to ride on the wagon seat alongside Johann with his chin resting near the bend of Johann's knee. The comfort that the warmth of their bodies gave to each of them came to soothe both their spirits.

For himself, Jacob volunteered to skip his time driving the wagon—glad to allow Johann and Happy the time needed to help mend each other's wounds. In less time than either man expected, the food, water, and loving care restored Happy to the jolly, energetic dog that apparently earned him the name of Happy in the first place. In a matter

of days, he was taking detours off the trail to track rabbits, squirrels, and other game for the men to kill. His distinctive wailing howl when he was on the scent of quarry alerted Johann or Jacob to grab their shotguns and run for the hunt.

Uncannily, Happy sensed when it was time for more game and limited his excursions in the wild to those occasions. Otherwise, he ran happily alongside their wagon never scurrying off the trail on wild goose chases. He had obviously been well trained by his former owner.

One afternoon the wagon train came upon a small winding creek. To their relief they saw for the first time on their journey . . . trees. The grassy bank sheltered by tall, spreading oak trees looked to be a perfect camping site. Even though it was early in the day to set up camp, Meusebach decided not to pass up the opportunity—they would make up the time by leaving an hour or so earlier in the morning.

Everyone seemed to need the couple of hours respite from the grinding and churning days on the trail. Johann decided to settle on the bank to try a little fishing. Happy jauntily scampered up and down the creek banks chasing turtles and frogs into the water.

Jacob decided he would slip away to have a talk with Frau Becker about Johann and to see how the whole family was doing. He felt concerned that every time he mentioned going to visit the Beckers at night when they camped, Johann made excuses not to do so. It had been nearly a week since they left Indian Point and according to the scouts, Victoria was only about a day's journey away. In Victoria, things would get hectic as he and Johann split off from the group to go to Goliad. They might not get another chance to visit with the Beckers in a quiet and unhurried setting.

An hour or so later, Jacob returned after his talk with Frau Becker. He located Johann fishing along the bank.

"Johann, I have just come from visiting the Beckers. I implore you while you have the chance to go and pay your respects to them before we arrive in Victoria tomorrow. And Frau Becker has something she has found of Katarina's that she strongly feels is meant for you to see."

Johann hung his head in abjection. He didn't move. At first, Jacob thought Johann hadn't heard him and started to speak again. About that time, Happy trotted over to where Johann was sitting on the bank. Gently he nudged his brown nose up under the still hand that rested on Johann's knees. Looking up at Johann with his liquid, brown eyes, Happy whimpered softly.

Jacob stood still watching this quiet moment of affection and sympathy pass between animal and man.

As Johann responded to Happy by patting his head and rubbing his long, floppy ears, he began speaking to him almost as if he were an old and understanding friend,

"I know, boy, what you are telling me. It is time for me to adjust to what has happened to me just the way you have—face up to what I must do—make the most of the skills I have and the opportunities Gott has given me."

Happy moved a little

closer to Johann—then reaching up with his head, gave Johann a few licks on his cheek. "I hear what you are saying, boy, and I am on my way."

Jacob smiled as he watched man and dog head down the trail towards the Beckers' wagon.

Arriving at their wagon, Johann learned from Reverend Becker that Mina Becker had gone to watch the sunset from a rise of land just beyond the winding creek. Johann could just see the back of her head as she sat at the top of the ridge. Johann chatted awhile with Reverend Becker, paid his respects to him and the rest of the family, and then he and Happy left to join Frau Becker.

As Johann came to the base of the small hill, Happy ran over to investigate a newly dug hole in the ground. Johann decided to let him explore and continued up the hill. Just as he approached the top of the slight ridge, he came upon a scene so exquisite in radiance and beauty that it startled him to stillness.

A fiery array of brilliant crimson and scarlet-tinged stratus clouds streaked across the low horizon. Burnished gold and coppery orange streams of sunlight burned brilliantly through and behind the painted clouds. Beyond the setting sun, blue violets and deep indigos blended together until they gave way into the sweet amen of a deep blue sky. A grove of small trees nearby, glistening in their autumn foliage, stood silhouetted against this glorious display.

Instinctively, Johann knelt down. Keenly aware of all his senses for the first time in weeks, he was stunned at how vibrant a Texas autumn sunset could be. The intensity of the rich hues on the horizon brought wonder again to his heart.

He sensed the cool and misty autumn breeze refreshing his skin and perhaps sinking down to moisten his dry soul. As he listened to the ripple of the falling leaves and looked upon the changing colors of the sky, he felt the wind's embrace and inhaled the aroma of a changing season. Johann became acutely aware that he could no longer numb his senses as he had been doing.

"Johann, is that you?"

Mina Becker's voice jerked Johann's attention to his immediate surroundings. He noticed Frau Becker standing, and now walking over toward him looking at him with a quizzical expression.

"Are you all right? You have such a strange look on your face."

Johann hopped up and smiling his usual smile, said, "Ja, I am fine. The beauty of the sunset overwhelmed me." As he spoke, he spread his arms out as if to frame the event. Then leaning down to embrace Frau Becker, he inquired, "Wie gehts, how are you, Frau Becker?"

Mina Becker returned his gesture, smiled and answered, "I, too, am fine—and I, too, feel wonder at this splendor before our eyes. Finally, we see the beauty of the Texas of which we have read. Here, walk over and sit down on my quilt with me and we shall have us a visit as we watch the sun sink out of sight."

Johann obligingly did so. After a few moments of gazing at the horizon, Mina Becker spoke, "Jacob tells me you have not yet read Katarina's letter to you."

Johann continued gazing into the sunset for a few moments more and then said, "Ja, just now upon seeing and indeed, feeling this amazing autumn sunset, I realized I could no longer keep my feelings deadened. Can you understand that I wanted to bury my feelings the way we had to bury Katarina?" Then turning and seeing Mina Becker's tear-brimming eyes, Johann paused a moment longer to steady his voice. He was struggling to stay in control of the raw emotions welling up within him.

He looked away into the sunset as if to detach himself from his feelings. Then he spoke with some hesitancy. "I just could not bear to read her letter to me. I could not allow myself to get that close to her. I did not think I had the strength to continue on with our journey if I gave in to the crushing agony I felt. I even feared I might fold up and die from the sheer pain of it."

Choking back the mounting knot coming up in his throat, Johann continued in a hoarse rush of words, "I did not want to let Jacob down. He counts on me and needs me to be with him on this journey." Then swallowing hard, he tried to explain, "You know how he can be at times—with his head in the clouds daydreaming about his inventions. He forgets time and sometimes he even forgets where he is."

Thinking of this image of Jacob brought chuckles from both of them—somewhat relieving the pent-up sadness they both felt.

Mina Becker reached across and placed her hand on top of Johann's. "My son, your Bruder worries over you and you worry over your Bruder. That is how it should be.

"Before I go on, I have some good news to tell you. Word just came to our wagon that Ann Elizabeth has survived the worst part of the cholera. She is still very weak, but alive. Katarina may have helped save her life by sharing her gruel and clean water with her."

"Ach, what blessed news." Johann paused before saying more. "Ja, praise Gott that Katarina's sacrifice was not in vain. Ja, praise Gott!"

"Ah, so be it. Amen." Frau Becker paused. She wanted to say more, but seeing the light of day fading, she felt a sense of urgency to proceed. "I am glad Jacob finally persuaded you to come and talk to me. I can tell you with almost certainty what Katarina dictated to me in that letter for you will comfort and fortify you, Johann."

Then reaching inside her skirt pocket, she pulled out a small hand-sized book. Handing it to him, she went on, "Somehow this little journal of Katarina's became displaced after the ship journey. It popped up in my trunk the other day. At first, I was not sure if anyone should read her private thoughts. Emil and I discussed it, prayed about it, and then remembered the many times that Katarina herself would read us passages from her journal. She loved to record all that happened each day; and sometimes, she composed poems of the day's events which she often read to us.

"So after a while, we felt at peace to read at least portions of it." Handing it to Johann, she added, "My son, you have just enough daylight time left to read some of the pages I have earmarked for you. It will do you good—you will see. And, ja, let those tears go that are clogging up your system. Perhaps reading these journal pages will encourage you to read Katarina's letter to you, also. I will leave you alone now with your Gott and this wonderful sunset He has provided for you. You can bring the journal and this quilt by our wagon on your way back."

As Mina Becker got up to leave, Happy came trotting up the hill towards Johann. Johann called to him and the loyal dog obeyed his new master, wagging his tail as he came. Soon Happy settled his head on his master's lap, waiting for the strokes of affection Johann was sure to give him. Happy looked at Johann with love and empathy showing in his eyes. He knew without knowing Johann was terribly sad.

With his trusted pet's warmth near him and the sky's colors illuminating him, Johann began reading the words of the one dear to him.

The very first passage Frau Becker marked for him to read began thus . . .

Sunset at Sea

Beautiful palaces in the western sky,
God's crowning glory greets shimmering sea,
Daylight, twilight, and then starlight nigh,
Partake this wonder on bended knee.

These words, these thoughts from Katarina, this day beside this sunset. It was almost too much to take in. Suddenly, the imprisoned gush of grief broke loose from Johann's inner being so forcibly that he shook from its impact. Great heaves and gulps of sorrow overcame him to the point that Happy started whimpering and licking his master's tear-drenched face.

As dog comforted man, nature's plan for pain began its healing process. Instead of the torment Johann dreaded, he began to feel release— and finally, relief. In the next moments, he knew he wanted to read Katarina's letter. Indeed, he knew he must read her letter even before he read any more of her journal. Reaching inside his left vest pocket, where he carried it next to his heart, he grabbed Katarina's small Bible and quickly opened it to find her letter tucked inside its pages.

Trying to focus his vision through his watery eyes, Johann wiped the tears away with his sleeve. As if to signal him to begin, Happy laid his head down on Johann's knee. Taking in a few deep breaths, he finally began to read Katarina's last thoughts to him written in Mina Becker's careful script.

November 5, 1846

My Dearest Johann,

May Gott give me the time and fortitude to allow me these words and thoughts for you. When I think of you, I think of gratefulness and cheerfulness. The gratefulness is mine to give you. The cheerfulness is yours to give me.

I give you my gratefulness for your happy nature and your unyielding faith. When we were imprisoned below deck during that terrible storm at sea, you led us in singing "A Mighty Fortress is Our Gott". What a gift! You turned our fear into faith. When we were near to shore, you gave us your happy harmonica playing for dancing and celebrating.

Please remember me by giving me the gift of sharing your cheerfulness and faith to all those around you. If you miss me and feel sad, remember to be still and find that deep silent place inside you where Gott resides. He will comfort you.

My father once gave me the writings of New York born missionary and writer, Arthur Tappan Pierson. He wrote that there is a part of the sea known as "the cushion of the sea." It lies beneath the surface that is agitated by storms and churned by the wind. It is so deep that it is a part of the sea that is never stirred. Indeed, it may have remained completely undisturbed for hundreds, if not thousands of years.

Rev. Pierson went on to write that the peace of Gott is an eternal calm like "the cushion of the sea." It lies so deeply within the human heart that no external difficulty or disturbance can reach it. And anyone who enters the presence of Gott becomes a partaker of that undisturbed and undisturbable calm.

Go there, Johann, during sunrises or sunsets. Go there to find your peace and come away with encouragement, cheerfulness and faith to share with others.

My love and gratefulness to you always,
Katarina

> *"From the rising of the sun unto the going down of the same the LORD's name is to be praised."*
> *Psalm 113:3*

Chapter 13
On Birds' Wings

Jacob became concerned about Johann as the sun sank out of sight. He expected him to be back from the Beckers' wagon before dark. He was just about to grab his shotgun to go look for him when he heard Happy's familiar baying sound—that meant he was hot on the trail of game. Jacob smiled and grabbed his shotgun anyway knowing Johann was not far behind the hunting dog. He would lend another hand at getting some game.

He followed the sounds of the wailing dog and came upon Johann and the very excited hunting dog just after the kill. Tonight's supper would be roasted prairie chicken. As the two men gathered the several prairie chickens and started back to camp, Jacob queried Johann.

"Did you get to see Frau Becker, Johann?"

"Ja, after we watched the glorious sunset together for a while, she let me see some passages in Katarina's journal she had discovered just a few days ago. Then she left me alone to read them. Unbelievingly, the first passage Frau Becker marked for me to read was a poem about sunsets that Katarina had composed while out at sea.

Johann's voice quivered a little as he went on, "Jacob, as I read her poem, I felt Katarina sitting there beside me while I watched the last rays of the sun disappear in the sky. No longer was I afraid to face my grief because I felt her presence comforting me. Truly, at that point, I hurried to read her letter to me. I quickly retrieved it from my breast pocket. And ja, you were right, mein Bruder—her words and thoughts helped me, even inspired me," and then pausing, Johann added, "Her words renewed my faith Gott is still with us."

Sensing Johann's need to pause and take a breath, Jacob quietly encouraged him, "I am so glad, mein Bruder."

No more needed to be said at this point as the two brothers approached their campsite. Maybe later, other words might be helpful. Now, their hunger took over and drove them to work quickly to pluck the hens and get them roasted for their supper.

The next morning, Johann told Jacob over coffee, "Jacob, I forgot to tell you last night. Frau Becker invited me to ride with them today so that I might read more of Katarina's journal. Would you drive the wagon today?"

"Ja, of course."

During the morning's ride, Mina Becker decided to remove pages from the journal she sensed Katarina would want Johann to have. Johann tucked them away in Katarina's Bible to read them over and over again later.

As the wagon train rolled and creaked along, there appeared sad remains of the German settlers who had traveled this trail before them. Pots, pans, and other discarded items lined either side of the trail. Dotted here and there, the make-shift graves told the story of the immigrants' unsuccessful march to New Braunfels, a march later to be known as "The Death March to Comal County."

Even now, their own wagon train halted many times as sick ones in one wagon or another succumbed to dysentery, cholera, or malnutrition that had been a part of their life at Indian Point. Using whatever means was available given the short length of time and scarcity of materials, their families buried them alongside the trail.

At first all the settlers would get out, try to take part and comfort the grieving ones. But after the eighth or ninth stop, it was just too much. Soon, just the close family members would bury their own and the wagon train would continue plodding on—trying to get to Victoria where hopefully, medicines and fresh supplies awaited them. Meusebach had said there they would find a doctor who would help them.

Just before sunset after what seemed like the longest and most grueling day thus far, the wagon train slowly wound itself around into the main square of Victoria. To the German settlers, it was comforting to see houses and buildings again. Not since their brief overnight stay in Galveston did they have reminders that civilization actually existed here in Texas.

Meusebach lost no time in locating the doctor reported to be treating and helping German settlers as they passed through Victoria on their way to New Braunfels.

Dr. Felix Webb had his practice in his home. He began treating the settlers by first trying to group them in order of priority of the severest ill. At once, Jacob and a few of the other single and healthy young men volunteered in helping Dr. Webb get the groups organized. Johann, meanwhile, chose to stay back with the Becker wagon. Emil and Mina Becker were weak from so little food and really needed help with getting food and supplies for their five remaining children.

Jacob and the other single men followed Dr. Webb around the porch and yard of his house as he surveyed all the settlers and their ills. As he quickly as he could, the doctor assessed each patient's degree of illness. He pinned strips of paper on each patient with the numbers 1, 2, or 3. Dr. Webb instructed them to take all the patients with a number one pinned on them to the waiting room just off the doctor's office. There, he would see each of them first because they needed immediate attention. He asked for the healthy men and women of the group to make this first group as comfortable as possible—giving them water or providing pillows and blankets for them if they needed to lie down on the floor. Group Two settled in the drawing room while Group Three remained on the porch.

Some of the men went on into town to gather as much food as they could to feed the waiting patients. Jacob ended up seeing to the people in Group Three on the porch.

For everyone, the day drug into a long and exhausting one. Jacob gave a sigh of relief when Dr. Webb finally sent many of them back to the wagon train to spend the night.

As Jacob wearily headed down the dusty road to where the wagon train had camped for the night, he was joined by Johann coming from the Beckers' wagon nearby.

"Mein Bruder, you have a haggard countenance. It was a hard day for you, ja?" questioned Johann.

"Ja, so many sick and discouraged ones. I can only pray this stay in Victoria will strengthen and give hope to our people for the next leg of their journey."

"Speaking of legs . . . it appears we will be moving ours very quickly. When I went into to the General Store with Reverend Becker today to get our supplies, I was introduced to the other single men waiting for us here in

Victoria to go on to Goliad. They have waited over a week for us to get here from Indian Point. The Mexican guides they hired last week to take us on to San Antonio are restless to start the trip. They want to leave early in the morning for Goliad. I told them we would be ready to go. We will meet them back at the town square."

"Did you already buy more provisions for us then?"

"Ja, I have. They are packed in the wagon. It is time for you to get a good night's rest. I have said our good-byes to the Beckers. "

"Ach, and so be it. How did the single men you met seem to you?"

"They are all German settlers as well. They have been stranded in Victoria since last April waiting for oxen and carts to be freed up from the war to take them on to San Antonio. Finally, when they were able to hire the Mexicans with their carts and oxen, they had word from Meusebach to stay and wait for us. So you can see why they are anxious to be on their way. But other than that, they seem like kind and honorable countrymen."

The morning came soon enough and found the small band of wagons leaving the main wagon train in Victoria and heading on southwest to Goliad. Johann took his turn walking letting Jacob drive their wagon. Happy trotted spryly along beside him.

Jacob was left alone again with his thoughts as he guided the bumping, joggling, plodding motion of the wagon.

He gazed out over the shimmering sea of grassy plains. The buffeting from side to side of the wagon, reminded him once again of the slish-sloshing, back and forth movement of their ship at sea.

His thoughts returned to the smooth gliding motion of the birds overhead and to his ideas of an air ship.

How effortlessly the birds rode the air waves. Why not man? What joy and freedom to sail and soar over the impediments below. But again, he dreamed. Instead of dreaming, he wanted to literally put wings to his dreams with some kind of action. He wanted to draw, to plan, to experiment. He wanted to be done with this dreaming—to make his first concrete steps in the pursuit of his ideas.

But here he was—trapped by the confines of his existence—shackled to the requirements of survival. Surely it was Gott who placed this dream in his head during that storm at sea. Why had He given him this dream with no providence for its fulfillment?

"Jacob! Jacob! Why have you stalled? What is the matter?" Johann's urgent voice jolted Jacob back to the here and now. He looked at the reins in his hands. They hung limp—just like the thoughts in his head.

"Ach, Dummkopf!" Jacob muttered to himself and then went on to ask aloud, "Did I fall too far behind . . . where are the rest of the wagons?"

"Nein, they have stopped just ahead, but not to wait for us. Another couple of wagons are just ahead of us. We have stopped to find out who they are and where they are going. Hold up . . . I will drive us up the trail until we get to where they are stopped."

Jacob expected Johann to rib him about daydreaming again, but instead he seemed more interested in the strangers in the wagons ahead.

Several hours later, the two wagon groups were camped together at a nearby creek. Ironically, the new group of wagons held a German notable and his traveling companions. They, too, were being driven by Mexican guides on their way to Goliad. Because there is safety in numbers, the two wagon groups decided to travel the rest of the journey together.

Sitting around campfire late that afternoon, Jacob and Johann were introduced to Dr. Ferdinand von Roemer. Dr. Roemer, like many Germans in Texas, was quick to drop the "von" from his name. A naturalist and geologist, Dr. Roemer had been sent to Texas by the Berlin Academy of Sciences to help survey the land of Texas where the Adelserein had its jurisdiction. Jacob was immediately excited to be in the presence of another scientist, especially one who might be able to shed light on the study of birds.

It was not long before the two men were so engrossed in their talk of birds they were completely oblivious to the rest of the travelers. Indeed, Dr. Roemer soon took Jacob with him to his wagon to rummage through his collection of drawings that he had sketched on birds during his travels in Texas.

One particular drawing of an eagle in flight fascinated Jacob. Upon seeing Jacob's keen interest, it was not long before Dr. Roemer was digging out his books on birds. He began leafing through their pages, looking for the book that detailed the anatomy of birds' wings and bones and also explained the process of bird flight. Though Jacob had a few of his own books about birds, none were as detailed and graphic as these of Dr. Roemer's.

Finding the particular book he wanted, Dr. Roemer asked, "Herr Brodbeck, I know you are a teacher by profession, but your avid interest in birds is more than your profession would demand."

Then Jacob shared with Dr. Roemer his dreams and plans to build an air ship. When Dr. Roemer heard of Jacob's ideas of manned flight, he became excited and very spirited. For Jacob, Dr. Roemer's encouragement and enthusiasm were beams of light dispensing the darkness, doubt, and dreariness of the last days gone by.

Before the wagon group arrived in Goliad, Dr. Roemer invited Jacob and Johann to stay with him in his guest house while they were in town. In this way, Jacob could avail himself of Roemer's materials and take the time to sketch and copy drawings he needed for his flight research.

During this time, Johann agreed—as they had promised they would—to take the coded message from Happy's dead master to the military command post there in Goliad.

Later that evening, as Jacob lay his head on his rolled-up blanket under the starry night sky, he felt the reassurance of Gott's hand guiding him in his plans for manned flight. Just when Jacob needed a boost of confidence, along came Dr. Roemer.

Ja, Gott ist sehr gut.

Chapter 14
Comes a Message

Four months passed quickly after the Brodbeck brothers arrived in San Antonio on near the end of November in 1846. Four months without one crisis. Four months of regular jobs and a firm roof over their heads.

Time possessed its own wings in this idyllic old Spanish town. Brightly colored flowers blooming from lush green-leafed plants offered their sweet nectar to swift-darting hummingbirds adorned with brilliant plumage and butterflies with exotic wings. The sparkling San Antonio River, winding through the town, boasted various shade trees including willow trees whose leaves whispered during the slightest breeze.

In the more affluent sections of town, houses with low and flat roofs made of adobe bricks or stone, often had enclosed garden patios. Pink-flowering vines cascaded down along the walls offering a cool respite from the dust and heat during the hot summer months.

Thus nature invited the native inhabitants to slow their pace of living in order to enjoy the beauty around them. Finding a two-room adobe hut to rent from an elderly German couple, the brothers continued the custom many brought from Mexico of taking daily naps over the noon time hour or "siestas" as they called them. Happy was happy to snooze as well lying on the concrete floor with his tail wrapped around his body.

During one of these afternoon siestas in late March, Jacob sat with a coffee mug in hand reading San Antonio's first newspaper, *The Western Texian*. Neither brother had a mind to nap in the middle of the day, but both tried to observe the locals' custom by stopping their work schedule in order to remain quiet for the hour.

Johann swung through the open door and smiled as he ambled over to where Jacob sat. He casually slipped a letter in between the pages of the newspaper in Jacob's hands. Then he went over to pour himself a cup of coffee as Jacob turned the letter slowly, over and over again. As Johann pretended to get busy in the cooking area of the room giving Jacob a few moments of privacy, he nonetheless slyly observed Jacob continuing to ponder the significance of the letter.

All the while inside Jacob's head, thoughts and memories swirled about in scattered abandon. He sat there needing to let his mind settle before opening and digesting the contents of this letter.

He reflected . . . some of life's distinctive moments seem to repeat themselves. Was it only two years ago Johann sauntered into the kitchen in their old home place in Germany and placed in between the pages of the *Stuttgart Zeitung* he was reading, a brochure expounding the virtues and exciting opportunities found in the grand and glorious Republic of Texas? That one life moment, maybe even as this one, changed the entire course of their lives.

These last few months in San Antonio had brought some order into their lives. Johann found work in his field of stone masonry. This brought some needed joy into his life again because he used his hands to create things of use and permanence. Jacob's own work in building furniture kept him busy by day and helped pay for their room and board. By candle light at night, he worked on his drawings and did research that kept his dreams of an airship alive. Both of them finally enjoyed some routine and with routine came a stability that brought peace. But here in his hands lie what could be a different piece of his future. A piece of life that might usurp the serenity they found currently in their lives.

"Du, Bruder! Are you only to gaze at the letter in your hands or will you decide to read it sometime during this century?"

Johann's impatient voice brought an abrupt halt to Jacob's reflections. Happy looked up from his slumber as he sensed a change in the atmosphere.

Chuckling at his brother's overstatement, Jacob explained, "I experienced . . . er . . . what is the French word for it? Ach, ja! 'Déjà vu!' Then an impulse to reminisce overtook me. Was it only last May at this time we started planning for our July voyage to Texas? So much has happened in that year. It is as if we have lived several lifetimes since then."

Knowing what Jacob meant, Johann acknowledged with a grin, "I know! The minute I came into the room with that letter for you and saw you intently reading the newspaper, I could not resist my own impulse to reproduce that far away moment in time. But now, for heaven's sake, read that letter from Meusebach before our beards grow even longer."

Jacob carefully took the letter from its sealed enclosure and looked at the neatly scripted message inside.

"Ja, Herr Meusebach writes to me in German. I will read it aloud. It is good to hear the message he sends in our native tongue."

Both men had already surmised this message from Meusebach offered news he needed Jacob to teach school in Fredericksburg. So the only surprise was how soon they needed him. Meusebach's supply wagon would be in San Antonio a week from today. If Jacob wanted the teaching position, he was to meet the supply wagon at the livery stable located in the Military Plaza across from the Alamo.

Instead of talking over the matter immediately, both men found themselves going about the usual routine of the afternoon and evening. After his workday, Johann fixed a simple meal of cabbage stew along with some cheese and bread from the market. Both men sat quietly eating their meal. Then as usual after supper, Jacob got out his drawings and books to study by the candle light.

Johann, as he often did many nights, took out Katarina's Bible to read. Happy readjusted himself to lie down near Johann's feet. Johann reached down to pat the friendly dog on his head.

Not only did Johann reread her earmarked pages over and over, but now he began to study the Bible from cover to cover. He was currently in Deuteronomy. He could not help but parallel the lives of the Israelites as they traveled to their promised land to that of their journey across the great Atlantic. They, like the Israelites, hoped to find their promised land here in Texas. And like the Israelites, even though they were here, it seemed they had to travel in circles before they could finally reach the actual land promised to them by the Adelsverein and what was then the Republic of Texas.

Thinking thus, Johann finally interrupted their evening's silence with the question: "Jacob, do you think

Herr Meusebach has at last procured the land promised us by the Adelsverein?"

Jacob looked up from his intense focus on his drawings, then decided to put them away for the evening. As he did so, he answered Johann's question, framing his words carefully . . . "Ja, before you came in with Meusebach's letter, an editorial about our land grants caught my attention. It seems the Fischer Land Grant sold to the Adelsverein turned out to be right in the middle of Comanche territory. That's why Meusebach chose Fredericksburg to colonize before heading on northwest about fifty or so miles to Mason County where the land tracts are. He knew the Comanches to be one of the fiercest of the Indian tribes in Texas. The article also stated Meusebach was soon to attempt a meeting with the Comanche Chief to work out some sort of peace plan. Accomplishing this, Meusebach hoped the German settlers who were willing and healthy could claim their tracts of land and settle down."

"That could be you and me. Did the article say how long this might take?" ventured Johann.

Jacob shook his head, "Nein, the article appeared more speculative than factual. I only wish it could be soon. We have been gone from Germany for a year now. Our Mutter is getting older. If we do not settle on our own land soon, I fear she will be too old and feeble to make that trip across the ocean."

There was a silence then as both men pondered their situation. Finally Johann spoke first, "I am thinking, mein Bruder, until we know more about when our land will be available to us, it would be best for me to remain in San

Antonio. Here, I have good employment and a roof over my head. Teaching is more your profession than building furniture, so of course, you must go. Additionally, you will be right where Meusebach is and he can instruct you about where the best land opportunities are."

"Ja, I thought you might be thinking that way. You are right, of course." Then looking levelly into his brother's eyes, Jacob continued, "It will be as difficult separating from each other as it was leaving our family in Germany."

"Nein, mein Bruder, for there is no ocean between us. Besides, I will have Happy here to keep me company until we meet again."

Then with a twinkle in his eye, and walking over to slap his older brother on the back, he teased, "Besides, you can fly your air ship over the hills between here and Fredricksburg and be here in no time!"

Jacob chuckled at the image this brought into his mind. He decided to play along with his brother's light-hearted spirit by adding, "Ja, and just imagine the shock on the Comanches' faces when they look up to see a white man inside a machine flying like a bird."

Johann laughed and conjectured, "Maybe Meusebach could bargain with the Comanche Chief using your flying machine as a defense weapon!"

Suddenly, Jacob turned serious, "The air ship may be in my head now, Johann, but one day, I promise you, we will not talk facetiously, but factually about a new form of transportation for mankind. Ja, I know it, not only in my mind do I envision it," then pointing to his heart, he said softly, “but here in my heart, where Gott placed this dream, I just know it.”

> *"Trust in the LORD with all thine heart; and lean not unto thine own understanding. In all thy ways acknowledge him, and he shall direct thy paths." Proverbs 3:5-6*

Chapter 15
Fredericksburg, Texas

March 1847 . . .

Riding in the rumbling supply wagon down the wide dirt main street, Jacob noticed very few log cabins in this frontier town—probably because it took considerable man hours to build just one.

Still he admired the accomplishments of the German people since starting this settlement in May, 1846. Now nearly a year later, despite the blustering and biting early March winds, their gardens stood cultivated and ready for spring planting.

Arriving sick and weak with disease, the settlers used whatever materials they had at hand to erect simple shelters. Setting poles close together in the ground, they put clay and moss in the narrow crevices to keep out the cold. They covered the sides of the structures with ox hides and used thin cross poles for the roofs over which they placed more ox hide. They cut the tall and abundant grasses growing all around them to layer on top of the ox hide roofs for further insulation.

Jacob could not help thinking, how had so few German immigrants accomplished so much in just one year? Not only had they come sickly and weak, they came heart-broken and sad from so much loss. They came to an untamed wilderness commanded by the marauding Comanche Indians.

Ah, but perhaps this boundless Texas exacted from its vanquishers more than muscle and sinew, more than courage and daring. Nein, this republic's founding cry of

"Remember the Alamo" yielded itself to hungry hearts and huge hopes.

And Jacob Brodbeck was one such man—his heart hungry to educate its future citizens—his hopes huge that given the time and experimentation, his air ship could become a reality.

But first there was this little matter of survival. For starters, how does a man find food and shelter, help build a town, help educate its youth, fight off savage Indians, and still find time to plan experiments, secure the equipment, materials, and locate a secret place to fly an air ship?

For might not these good Fredericksburg citizens riding in their horse-drawn buggies think him daft if they witnessed him attempt to fly like a bird in a manmade contraption?

One man could not do all this. But one man's Gott could. Had Gott brought him safely across a vast ocean only to abandon him now? Nein, in Jacob's heart, he heard Gott's still small voice saying, "Lean on Me and I will direct your path."

Jacob's path began as the wagon master pulled up to a small boarding house. Just until he could locate lodging of his own, he knew Meusebach had contracted for him to stay in the Nimitz boarding house run by Captain Charles Nimitz and his wife, Sofie.

After settling the oxen, Earnest Klein, the wagon master, turned to Jacob with a smile, "Herr Brodbeck, I will be leaving you in very good hands. Captain Nimitz will ply you with schnapps while Sofie Nimitz fills you with wonderful German food. Welcome to Fredericksburg, Texas. Aufvedersein!"

"Danke shön und Aufvedersein!" Jacob extended his hand to clasp Herr Klein's.

Captain and Frau Nimitz greeted Jacob in the drawing room of their boarding house. Just recently built with only four rooms, but with a huge central fireplace in the drawing room, the Nimitz boarding house was already garnering a reputation for its fine German food and clean beds.

After introductions, the hosts gave Jacob the first night to unpack and become settled. Over breakfast the next morning, Frau Nimitz said to Jacob, "Herr Brodbeck, I took the liberty of inviting our schoolmaster, John Leyendecker, to dinner this evening. No doubt, you have two have many questions for each other. It is much more pleasant to meet and then dine together whilst exchanging information, ja?"

"Ja, Frau Nimitz, das ist richtig. Danke schön. It is so kind and thoughtful of you. I shall look forward to it. What time do we dine?" asked Jacob.

"We eat at seven, but my husband welcomes the men boarders to gather with him around the fireplace at about six for schnapps and news of the day. He and Herr Leyendecker anxiously await conversation with our new schoolmaster," Frau Nimitz's invitation came with a smile of encouragement.

"Ja, then I shall not disappoint them." Jacob assured Frau Nimitz.

When Jacob met the schoolmaster, John Leyendecker that evening, he liked him immediately. Evident in his speech and manner, was the devotion shown to his wife and children and likewise to the students he taught.

The men's conversation around the fireplace mostly centered on the upcoming meeting between Herr Meusebach and the Comanche Indian chief. Could a treaty be signed and if so, would both parties abide by its rules?

Frau Nimitz soon rescued the men from their continuing talk of Indian skirmishes. She ushered them into the dining room for a sumptuous meal of sausage, red cabbage, fried potatoes, and fresh green beans. The group sat around the large dining table speaking comfortably in German. They spoke of their home towns in Germany and any news from letters received from the Vaterland.

It had been some time since Jacob ate such good German food and he felt completely at ease speaking in his native tongue and not struggling to speak English. Indeed, as the meal and the warmth of the schnapps relaxed him, he found himself fighting feelings of homesickness. Leaning his face down, he placed his hands over his mouth to cover a fake cough.

Jacob's gesture did not fool Sofie Nimitz. Her observant eyes caught the tenderness nearing tears in Jacob's eyes.

Standing up, she took Captain Nimitz's hand and said, "Captain, we are thoughtless to detain our guests when they have so much to discuss."

"Ja, that is true, mein Schatz. Let us wish our guests a restful night's sleep and bid them a gut nacht," bowing politely Captain Nimitz seemed adept at sensing his wife's lead.

As they said their good nights, Jacob thought to himself, Gott placed these two people in the right profession. How congenial and hospitable they are.

Back again beside the roaring fireplace, Jacob sat listening closely to Herr Leyendecker's description about the Vereins Kirsche (Community Church) where Jacob would be teaching.

"Ja," Herr Leyendecker went on to explain, "as the name suggests, it was built for the purpose of a church for all denominations, but it also serves as our school, a central meeting place for the townspeople . . . and a look-out tower to warn us of any Indian raids. It was the very first structure built in Fredericksburg. You will see it tomorrow. You will know it because in contrast to all our tentative dwellings, it is a tall octagonal building in the very center of the town."

"Ja, it is much more than what I expected for a school building . . . much, much more," Jacob admitted.

"Ach, do not get your hopes up. It still has a sand floor and only simple backless benches for seating the students. In addition, there is a scarcity of books and supplies."

Smiling, Jacob said, "Before I left Germany, the King gave me a set of books just in case I had the opportunity to teach in Texas."

"Ja, das ist sehr gut."

Then with great care and interest, Herr Leyendecker gave Jacob detailed reports on all of his students.

"Our class size fluctuates as the seasons change. During planting and harvesting times, the older eighth grade boys are needed in the fields. We currently have 18 students."

Jacob listened with gratitude for the information Herr Leyendecker shared with him on each of the students. When he had finished, Jacob said, "Danke schön, Herr

Leyendecker, for your insight and guidance. With your detailed records, you have made it much easier for me than I thought it would be."

Herr Leyendecker handed the records to Jacob and they shook hands. Then he bid Jacob a "gut nacht" and made his way home.

Much later as Jacob lay in the quiet stillness of his room on his sublimely comfortable bed, he mused over Herr Leyendecker's discourse of his classroom—the classroom Jacob would soon inherit. Was he prepared for the challenges of a frontier classroom and would there be enough time afterwards to work on his "air ship?"

Chapter 16
Vereins Kirche

Like an anxious mother repeating her supper call to her children playing outside, the church bell atop the cupola in the Vereins Kirche rang out its summons for the parishioners to gather for Sunday morning services.

Seated in one of the front pews, Jacob counted as the bell pealed ten times. When the last of the flock seated themselves, Jacob felt relief that, as usual, he came early. He intended to exemplify punctuality as the new schoolmaster of their school.

Jacob felt the deep unity among the parishioners as they stood singing the opening hymn. Lutheran, Catholic, and Methodist alike stood shoulder to shoulder joyfully singing in thankful worship to their Gott.

The Reverend announced his message for the day, "Today I base my sermon on scripture taken from 1 Samuel 7:12, 'Thus far has the Lord helped us.'

He paused and gave the congregation time to absorb the Lord's Word.

With only the sounds of the birds twittering in the trees outside and the warmth of the spring sunshine streaming through the windows, the congregation settled to listen to the Reverend's words.

"Part of my sermon today I take from the writings of the great English theologian, Charles Spurgeon, and later we shall sing a wonderful old English hymn as well. We must honor our English brethren. For if not for those early Christian pilgrims who sought religious freedom in America and who later pushed westward and on to Texas, we might not be standing here today.

"The words 'thus far' are like a hand pointing to the past . . . 'Thus far has the Lord helped us.' Whether through poverty, wealth, sickness, or health, whether at home or abroad, on land or sea, and whether in honor, dishonor, difficulties, joy, trials, triumphs, prayers, or temptation . . . 'Thus far has the Lord helped us'

"We always enjoy looking down a long road lined with beautiful trees. The trees are a delightful sight and seem to form a temple of plants, with strong wooden pillars and arches of leaves. In the same way you look down a beautiful road like this, why not look back on the road of the years of your life? Look at the large green limbs of Gott's mercy overhead and the strong pillars of His loving-kindness and faithfulness that have brought you thus far. Indeed, through much tribulation, but also, with much joy has our Gott brought us thus far to our town of Fredericksburg, Texas.

"Do you see any birds singing in the branches?" The Reverend pointed to the windows and paused . . . and as if on cue, the birds sang their happy choruses.

"If you listen and look closely, surely you see many, for they are singing of Gott's mercy received 'thus far.'

"Ah, but these words also point forward. Someone who comes to a certain point and writes the words 'thus far' realizes he has not yet come to the end of the road and that he still has some distance to travel. There are still more trials, joys, temptations, battles, defeats, victories, prayers, answers, toils, and strength yet to come.

"So dear believer, 'be strong' and take heart. And with thanksgiving and confidence lift your voice in praise, for:

The Lord who 'thus far has helped you'
Will help you all your journey through."

At this point, Jacob thought with gratitude, I feel as though the Reverend is speaking to directly to me. Thus far, Gott has brought me here to Fredericksburg. Surely He goes before me to help me build my air ship as well.

He looked around at the rapt faces nearest to him; he saw they mirrored his own thoughts—that the Reverend spoke directly to them. As he turned his attention back to the sermon, Jacob smiled thinking, the Reverend is a good messenger of Gott's Word.

Reverend Basse continued, "As some of us might remember from our Vaterland, the Shepherds of the Alps have a beautiful custom of ending the day by singing an evening farewell to one another. The air is so pure that the songs can be heard for very long distances. As the sun begins to set, they gather their flocks and begin to lead them down the mountain paths while they sing, 'Thus far has the Lord helped us. Let us praise His name!'

"Finally, as is their enchanting custom, they sing to one another the courteous and friendly farewell . . . 'Gut Nacht . . . Gut Nacht!' The words then begin to echo from mountainside to mountainside, reverberating sweetly and softly until the music fades into the distance.

"Now as we await Herr Meusebach's safe return from the tribal meeting with the Comanches in the hills north of us, let us also call out to one another until the darkness he faces becomes alive with the sound of many voices, encouraging Gott's weary travelers."

With the Reverend's last words, the organ's strong chords called the worshipers to stand as they sang loudly and joyfully, the old English hymn . . .

O God, our Help in ages past,
Our Hope for years to come,
Our Shelter from the stormy blast,
And our eternal Home!

Later just after the benediction, the Reverend motioned to Jacob to come forward to be introduced to the congregation.

"My brethren, please give a hearty welcome to our new schoolmaster, Herr Brodbeck."

As the worshipers applauded, the Reverend motioned for the families to come forward to meet Jacob and shake his hand.

"Willkommen . . . Wie gehts" . . . So many smiles and well wishes.

As each family came by to meet Jacob, he tried to keep their names and faces together. Then among all the new people he was meeting, he heard a strangely familiar voice.

"Jacob Brodbeck . . . is that you?"

Gently pushing through the other greeters, Mina Becker came with Reverend Becker and the rest of their brood not far behind.

Smiling broadly, Jacob answered, "Ja, do you know any other Jacob Brodbeck? But when did you arrive? I did not see you come in the church."

In the midst of hugs and greetings, Reverend Becker explained, "Ja, one of our wagon wheels came off on our way to church this morning and we had to walk the rest of the way. We were to have been introduced also but we just now arrived. Herr Meusebach encouraged us to come and settle in Fredericksburg. He asked me to assist Rev. Basse here at the Vereins Kirche until a Lutheran church is built. We have only just arrived two days ago. We heard that you are the schoolmaster now. It is so good to see you again."

Mina Becker hurriedly wanted to know, "How is Johann? Is he still in San Antonio?"

Jacob replied, "Ja, he is still there and I hope he is well. The mail is slow, so I have not heard from him in a few weeks."

At the mention of Johann, Mina Becker's eyes started to brim with tears. "You know, I cannot think of Johann without thinking of Katarina."

Reverend Becker knew they needed a quick diversion. “Say, Jacob, are you ready to teach our youngsters, especially little Otto here who is now in the second grade?”

Feeling hands wrap around his, Jacob looked down at little Otto impishly grinning up at him.

And so Herr Brodbeck prepared his classroom for those students new to him, but also for those very familiar and dear to him.

Chapter 17
Departures

1849 . . . Two years later . . .

Squeals of glee and enchantment erupted from the schoolchildren as they witnessed an unbelievable event. Small winged contraptions soared above them in all directions. Winding the little coils inside each machine as fast as he could, Schoolmaster Brodbeck then propelled each of them into the air. They sailed a hundred yards or so until the coil spring unwound forcing them to glide to the ground.

The children darted here and there retrieving each one to bring back to their schoolmaster shouting as they came, "Fly it again, Herr Brodbeck . . . fly it again!"

But one young man, grasping a small airship in his hands, ran back with a different request, "Herr Brodbeck, how do you make the 'air ships' stay up in the air? Their wings do not flap like birds' wings do."

Schoolmaster Brodbeck looked into the lad's earnest eyes, "Ja, but Little Otto, notice how the wings of the air ship are shaped. I tried to construct them like birds' wings. Here, touch the front part of each wing . . . see the thickness there and then notice with your fingers how it thins out toward the back part of the wing. And see how the top of the wing is curved while it is flat underneath. The unwinding of the little spring coil inside the air ship causes thrust, or a forward motion. Lift is created by air moving over the wings as the air ship moves forward. The combination of the low pressure above the wing and the downward thrust of air under the wing causes the lift of the air ship into the air. As long as there is the thrust caused by the spring coil unwinding, there is lift and the air ship stays up. When the coil unwinds, the air ship glides back down to earth. Does that make sense to you, Little Otto?"

"Ja, in some ways I understand and in other ways, it is still a big mystery to me. But Sir, please . . . you promised not to call me Little Otto anymore. I am nine years old now and I am even tall for my age."

Schoolmaster Brodbeck smiled, "Ja, I make a mistake. Any young man who can understand even part of the mystery of flight is certainly not little anymore. What about this? At recess tomorrow I will demonstrate how to rewind the coils inside the air ship and then, you may be the first student to fly one. Would that excuse me from my mistake?"

"Ja, ja . . . danke shörn, Herr Brodbeck, das ist sehr gut! Tonight I will not sleep one wink, I will be so excited!"

*****

In that same fall of 1849, Jacob filed for his citizenship certificate. Having arrived in Gillespie County in 1847, he had to wait five years from that date to receive his United States Citizen Certificate. He looked forward to becoming a citizen of his adopted homeland.

At the end of the year, Jacob felt he could no longer manage on his small teacher salary. He had heard of available work as a furniture maker in the new settlement of Castell. Built along the north back of the Llano River, the community was arranged with thatched-covered log cabins in a single row. As new settlers arrived, they needed furniture. Would that provide him with a better living than teaching did?

Then he heard the new Protestant minister, Reverend Dangers, was also a teacher. Perhaps he would take over as the teacher at the Vereins Kirche?

It was a time of indecision.

Finally, he decided he would ask the Reverend about teaching for him and the Reverend agreed.

That forced Jacob to take a chance and move to Castell.

It turned out to be a fortuitous move. For in Castell, he crossed paths with people who later had a deep impact on his life.

Right after he moved to Castell, he met Dr. Ferdinand Von Herff, a doctor and a surgeon. They found a common denominator in each other—their scientific minds. As they became fast friends, Jacob was able to share his ideas of manned flight with someone who understood. Dr. Herff not only understood, but believed in Jacob and encouraged him to pursue his dream.

A native German, Dr. Herff was a brilliant surgeon who was interested in all sorts of intellectual pursuits. He kept abreast of medical advancement both in Germany and in Texas.

One evening as the two visited, Dr. Herff advised Jacob, "Ja, it was good you moved away from Fredericksburg at this particular time. The dreaded cholera disease from which you and your brother escaped at Indian Point has spread to Fredericksburg. It is believed it might be spreading because of so many settlers traveling through

Fredericksburg on their way to the Gold Rush in California."

"Ja, das ist richtig." Jacob paused and with a grin said, "In addition, my dear friend, Castell has introduced me to you!"

Dr. Herff nodded his head, smiling in agreement.

*****

While Jacob lived in Castell, he helped teach the school-aged children because no school had yet been established in the new town. It was then he became acquainted with the Behrens family—a family who would affect his personal life in years to come.

They had three children—ages six to fourteen. Jacob helped with the instruction of all three, but Christine, even at six years of age, captured his attention with her bright mind and lively personality.

Jacob enjoyed his time in Castell, but could not see himself putting down roots there. He missed the advantages offered in the more settled town of Fredericksburg. He had heard of a furniture-making job becoming available to him in Fredericksburg. Also, Dr. Herff had left Castell and had gone back to Germany to be married. Jacob was not sure when he would return.

Nein, it seemed best to accept this new job back in Fredericksburg. He needed to get settled in a place where he could concentrate on his flight experiments.

Chapter 18
God-Fearing Gumption

Three years later, Fredericksburg, Texas . . .

Jacob sat in the parlor of the Nimitz boarding house enjoying a rare stein of beer. The Nimitz Boarding House was the last stage stop for passengers to bathe, eat a good meal, and rest before the long run to El Paso.

Johann's letter, arriving moments before on the weekly stage from San Antonio, held Jacob's avid attention. Jacob read:

> Dear Bruder,
>
> I greet you in good health and hope yours is the same.
>
> I send good news to you. As I wrote you last, your good friend, Dr. Ferdinand Herff has moved back to Texas. I decided to share your small "air ship" drawings with him. By the way, Dr. Herff has become a very influential doctor and man of renown here in San Antonio.
>
> I allowed him to read your letter about your students. He was delighted in your description of the joy experienced by your students upon seeing your small air ships fly for the first time.
>
> I sensed his excitement about your invention; whereupon, I invited him to come witness the flights in person.
>
> Thus far, he thinks the small air ship might be a clever idea for toys and amusement. He insists that I accompany him at his expense so that we may all see each other again. I am by no means certain that he

intends to offer you some financial backing for your small air ship project much less manned flight; but you might prepare a defense in that regard.

We make plans to leave by stagecoach on Saturday, October 25. Barring no unforeseen incidences en route, you may expect us two days later, Monday, October 27. We can stay only two nights as both our work schedules demand our prompt return. Our dear neighbors, the Martinez family, have agreed to care for Happy while I am gone.

There is one other item of important news about Dr. Herff. Being an excellent surgeon and ever a forward-looking man, he is now the first doctor in Texas to successfully use ether in his surgeries. The inhalation of ether fumes provides the patient an almost complete and safe state of unconsciousness, thereby alleviating the pain of the surgery. Most outstanding!

We shall soon see each other to share all these matters in person.

I remain your admiring and loving Bruder,

Johann.

Jacob let out a deep sigh of contentment and took another swig of beer. All too soon, the hustle and bustle of travelers coming in and out of the boarding house interrupted his reverie. No more time for dawdling . . . he must walk back to his cabin to make preparations for his guests before they arrived in two days.

*****

Johann, leaning back on the stagecoach's upholstered seat, felt at ease bumping along on their journey from San Antonio to Fredericksburg. After all, former Texas Ranger, "Bigfoot" Wallace, their stagecoach driver or "Charlie" as drivers were sometimes affectionately called, sat above them in the "Box" driving the six-horse team. Bigfoot Wallace earned his reputation as a sharpshooter and skilled tracker fighting border bandits when he served under Texas Ranger Jack Hays.

Surely, he and his partner, Lefty Logan, who rode shotgun beside him, offered the best of protection from the increasing numbers of stagecoach robberies brought about by the gold rush of '49. Stagecoach lines now joined the east to the west going from the shipping port of Galveston to San Antonio, on to Fredericksburg, then to El Paso on their way to San Diego, California. These stagecoaches carried not only passengers, but important mail, and now of late, gold and silver bullion, and other valuables heading both east and west.

"Johann, you seem most comfortable and relaxed. Did you say this is your first ride in a stagecoach?" inquired Dr. Herff, who sat across from Johann.

"Jawohl, I prefer the stagecoach to my usual ox-drawn cart mode of transportation." Continuing this jovial manner, Johann went on, "Dr. Herff, I want to thank you again for providing this trip in order for both of us to witness Jacob's model air ships in flight."

"Nein, it is my pleasure. I look forward to the meeting of the three of us together. It seems longer than three years ago when I first met Jacob in Castell. Moreover, I need a small reprieve from my medical practice in San Antonio. In any case, the stagecoach, though more expensive than the ox cart you mention, is much faster. It allows both of us to save money in the end. You can get back to your stonemasonry sooner and I to my medical practice."

"You are most gracious, Doctor. Speaking of speed, I can only hope my letter advising Jacob of our visit arrives sooner than we do".

"Worry yourself not, my man. We will find him how we find him . . . expecting us or not. It might be an interesting surprise for all of us."

Dr. Herff looked through the curtains off the side window of the coach, vaguely aware of the post oaks and scrubby cedar trees dotting the landscape. He leaned back as well, looking forward to a little vacation time. He mused over finding his absent-minded inventor friend involved and entangled in wires and contraptions of his latest project. What fun they would have exchanging their latest scientific thoughts.

An abrupt interruption was about to intervene on Dr. Herff's thought processes.

One lone rider approached the stage from up the trail ahead of them. He stopped about fifty yards in front of the stage and held his hands up for the stage to halt.

"Gee . . . yahhhh!" Bigfoot shouted to the team of horses as he reigned them in to slow them down.

"Wad de ya think he wants?" ventured Lefty to Bigfoot.

"Don't know. Seems ordnary enuff . . . no bandana on his face. Don't see no six gun hangin' from his hip." Bigfoot surmised.

“Hey, you yonder,” yelled Bigfoot, “Do ya need somethin’? Better make it pronto! Don’t yer know it’s a federal offense to stop the United States Postal Service?”

Quicker than a rattlesnake’s strike, another rider appeared from behind a cedar clump and rode up along the right side of the coach. As he came close enough, he leaned over from his saddle and in one swift motion, grasped the top rail of the stagecoach with his left hand, released the reins, slipped off his horse and with his right hand grabbed for the door handle.

Seeing the second rider appear, Bigfoot yelled, "Robbery!" He cracked his whip over the lead horse. “Heaah! Horatio! Fly like the wind.” Hollering at his fastest steed, Bigfoot counted on him to propel the team with him.

“Lefty, throw a load at that hombre ahead." Bigfoot urged.

Lefty took aim at the rider ahead of them and managed to hit him knocking him from his horse.

“Wahoo! I bagged him!” But Lefty’s glee was cut short as the stagecoach hit a bolder on the trail throwing the stage in a lurch to the left almost launching him into space, but he caught the hand-rail in the nick of time.

The same lurch that nearly unseated Lefty, slammed the second rider hard against the side of the coach. As the coach righted itself, the rider found himself swinging awkwardly on the stagecoach door out into space. However, when the swinging door came back around to the opening of the coach, he was able to grab onto door frame. Like a lizard, he slid into the coach and slipped into the seat beside the good doctor and across from the startled Johann.

The bandit pulled a pistol from his waist band and pointed it at Johann's face, "I want the money you swindled from me back in San Antone. Hand it over."

Before Johann could protest mistaken identity, another jarring jolt threw the bandit from the seat to the floor.

A loud bang!

His pistol discharged in a billow of white smoke. The bullet struck Johann in the left side of his chest.

As the pistol recoiled from the surprised bandit's hand, Dr. Herff reacted purely from a gut level and twisted the pistol from the bandit's grip.

In the next second, Lefty thrust himself through the right side door. He pounced on the bandit and pinned him down on the floor.

"I've got 'em, Doc! You tend to yer buddy there." Lefty shouted.

Handing the pistol to Lefty, Dr. Herff grabbed his medical bag and crossed over to the seat where Johann slumped forward. Blood oozed out between Johann's fingers where he grasped his chest.

Dr. Herff pulled out bandages to put pressure on the wound in order to slow the bleeding. He screamed to Lefty, "We need to stop!"

"No can do, Doc. Might be others. It ain't far to Fredericksburg. They won't chase us into town. Just keep him alive 'til we get there."

*****

Meanwhile . . . back in Fredericksburg, a few folks gathered outside the Nimitz Boarding House anticipating the arrival of mail and passengers on the stagecoach.

Jacob, waiting for his dear brother and their distinguished guest, stood amongst the eager early birds.

Their wait ended abruptly. The hurdling stagecoach rounded the San Antonio Trail onto Main Street with Big Foot pulling in the reins and bellowing from the driver's box, "Clear the way! There's been a hold-up! We got a wounded man on board."

The crowd parted and made a path.

The next moments blurred in Jacob's head as the ensuing events unraveled. He knew Dr. Herff and Lefty carried Johann inside the hotel as Big Foot and Sheriff Martin took the bandit, known in these parts as Rattlesnake Dick, to the jail. Everything else remained peripheral.

With the town's only doctor away on a call to deliver a baby, they took Johann to Jacob's cabin as quickly as possible before Johann lost more blood.

When they got to the cabin, the reality of the situation struck Jacob square in the face as he found himself at the most difficult impasse of his life.

Dr. Herff asked Jacob to assist him in the removal of the bullet from Johann's chest. But that was not all Dr. Herff needed Jacob to do. In assisting the doctor, Jacob would be required to administer the ether the doctor had pioneered in Texas. Along with the ether, Jacob needed to keep track of Johann's pulse as well.

When Jacob registered reluctance, Dr. Herff hit him with the alternatives.

"Jacob, number one—I operate without the ether but you will have to hold your brother still while I dig and probe for that bullet. No amount of whisky will help him endure that pain and remain still. Number two—if we do not remove that bullet soon, he may bleed to death. Number three—I'm asking you to assist me because I know you have a steady hand. We are losing time. What is it to be, Jacob?"

"Ja, of course . . . I do as you say, Dr. Herff," Jacob's decision came with a gush of air rushing from his lungs—pent up air due to shallow breathing.

Dr. Herff laid his hand on Jacob's shoulder and advised, "Take a few deep breaths. Then round up some blankets for our patient. His temperature will drop when we start administering the ether."

Chapter 19
Steady Hands

"**H**old it steady, Jacob, just over his mouth and nose so that he inhales the fumes."

Jacob tried to keep from shaking as he applied the inhaler to Johann's face. The blown glass globe attached to the inhaler held sponges saturated with ether. Drawing atmospheric air over the ether-soaked sponges through the glass mouthpiece into the patient's lungs rendered the patient unconscious.

"Now, Jacob, this is what I want you to do. Keep your attention on Johann's breathing. Let me know immediately if it becomes shallow and irregular. That means his heart might be failing or his respiratory centers are becoming paralyzed. Then we must discontinue the ether until deeper and more regular respiration is established. Do you understand?"

"Ja, Doctor, I watch very closely." Jacob's eyes focused on Johann's face as he began inhaling the ether fumes. At first his face became very flushed. He moaned a little and then Jacob, with his free arm, held him as tight as he could to keep him still. Johann's facial muscles began twitching and seemed to register a conglomerate of reactions from outright glee and whimsy to awe and bewilderment. Moments passed before Jacob noticed a calming effect pass over Johann's face. Then an almost blank, faraway expression replaced the earlier exhilaration.

His breathing became even and steady. Jacob looked up to see Dr. Herff nod to him and say . . .

"He is ready . . . keep your eyes on him and not me."

Jacob kept his eyes centered on Johann's breathing. In and out . . . in and out . . . was his breathing slowing down? Jacob was not sure. Still he forced himself not to look at Dr. Herff, but continued listening and watching Johann's face and his breathing.

Soon Jacob noticed his own breathing slowing down to match the rhythm of his brother's. He became conscious of wanting to hold his breath to keep it from interfering with the sounds of Johann's. In what seemed an eternity and a fleeting second all in one, he soon heard Dr. Herff say, "I have the bullet! It did not go deep. It lodged at an angle making it easy for me to locate. Now keep steady, Jacob, as I stitch him up."

Jacob continued watching Johann's even and slow breathing . . . amazed he did not register any pain. But now his face seemed to be more flushed than it was earlier. Jacob, with his free hand, wiped and smoothed wisps of hair from Johann's forehead. Noticing how hot he felt to the touch, he glanced to see if Dr. Herff had finished.

Completing the last stitch, Dr. Herff looked up to see the apprehension on Jacob's face.

"Is he fading, Jacob?"

"I cannot tell for sure, Doctor, but he feels very hot."

The doctor wiped his hands and then felt Johann's forehead.

"He is feverish . . . . which is to be expected. Fever is the body's way of fighting off disease. He has lost a lot of blood. The next twenty-four hours are crucial. We have to keep him warm and get some broth down him. Then watch, wait and pray for the Good Lord to take over where we left off." Then looking directly into Jacob's eyes, he said, "It is in His hands now, Jacob."

After helping Dr. Herff remove Johann from the hard kitchen table to Johann's bed, Jacob set about getting broth prepared and making coffee while Dr. Herff kept close vigil at Johann's side checking his pulse and watching his breathing. Johann rolled slightly back and forth in a fitful sleep.

Just as Jacob handed a tin of hot coffee to Dr. Herff, they heard a loud banging at the door.

"Is the Doctor still there? Open up, we need a doctor fast!"

Not recognizing the voice, Jacob quickly shot a glance at Dr. Herff to check his reaction. When he looked puzzled, Jacob lost no time in locating his shotgun. He moved to the small window to get a peek. The sun setting on the other side of the house cast long dark shadows obscuring the visitor's face.

"Identify yourself, sir!" Jacob shouted back.

"My name's Lefty. I rode shotgun on the stage into town. If the doctor is there, he knows me."

Dr. Herff nodded recognition to Jacob and shouted back, "What can I do for you, Lefty?"

"Bigfoot's been shot. It looks bad, Doc. Do you think you can spare the time to look at him? He's back at the boarding house. The town doctor is still away."

“Just wait a moment and I will be with you.” Dr. Herff then whispered to Jacob, “You stand guard there by Johann. This could be a ruse.”

Crossing the room to get his revolver, the doctor avoided the window as he stepped to one side of the door.

He abruptly opened the door with revolver aimed.

“Don’t shoot, Doc. I’m by myself.”

Stepping out and glancing from right to left, the Doctor made sure the man spoke the truth.

“Come in then. Where is Bigfoot shot?”

As Lefty Logan entered the cabin, he pointed to his own left shoulder and explained hurriedly, “Right through the shoulder. The bullet went right through . . . tearing up his shoulder pretty bad, Doc.”

“When did it happen and has he lost much blood?”questioned the doctor.

“ 'Bout half hour ago. Rattlesnake Dick got sprung from jail by his gang and in their escape, one of their shots found Big Foot’s shoulder. They all got away, but we may have wounded one of them . . . . so yer right to be careful. If they find out where ya took Mr. Brodbeck, they may show up here to get yer services."

Dr. Herff began packing his medical bag and then asked Lefty, “Would you mind staying here with Jacob? He needs to take care of his brother and you could stand guard for him.”

Before Lefty could answer, Jacob spoke up, “What about you, Doctor? It is your services they want. What if they are bedded down just outside of town and apprehend you? Rattlesnake Dick would recognize you from the stage. Lefty should go with you to protect you.”

"I will be fine. It is just a short distance to town. Surely they rode miles out from town before stopping." offered the Doctor.

"I think the Doc's right about that. You take my horse, Doc, and I'll be glad to stay here and guard the place," countered Lefty.

Darkness fell as the Doctor rode away. Jacob lit just one lone candle and offered Lefty a cup of coffee. He checked the broth on the stove and went over to sit by Johann. Feverish and moaning slightly, Johann restlessly threw off the blankets around him. Jacob covered him again and sat down next to him. Glad that Lefty seemed content sitting by the fireplace drinking his coffee, Jacob allowed himself to take in a deep breath for the first time since the operation. As he slowly let out his breath, he uttered an urgent prayer.

"My Gott . . . my heavenly Vater . . . take not my Bruder this day. Give him back to me. I ask for no other thing in this world than he may survive and be healthy again."

Then he hung his head and wept . . . . not ashamed that Lefty who sat a few feet away might hear him weeping.

> *"In whose hand is the soul of every living thing, and the breath of all mankind."*
> *Job 12:10*

Chapter 20
Shared Plans

As Jacob wiped the tears from his eyes, he glanced quickly toward Lefty. Lefty, having finished his coffee seemed solely absorbed in keeping guard by the window. The late October wind rattled the window pane causing Jacob to notice the chill in the air. Instinctively, he rose to fetch more logs for the fireplace.

"The fire is burning low," he explained to Lefty as he crossed the room to the door.

"Naw, you stay here. I'll get the logs," insisted Lefty.

"Nein, sir, it would do my body good to stretch a little. The wood stack is just at the corner. I will be careful."

Lefty nodded and then stood in the doorway. As Jacob went outside, he noticed tonight's sky was vividly clear with clusters upon clusters of shimmering stars. He wondered . . . how could anything be wrong on a night like this?

As fast as he could, Jacob piled the logs into his arms. His thoughts did not linger on the starry night as he hurried back into the cabin. After getting the logs in place, he let Lefty poke the fire as he went back to see about Johann.

He was worried about Johann's temperature rising. He placed his hand on his brow, surprised that it felt cool and dry. Had his temperature broken? He felt his face and hands. He seemed cooler everywhere. Surely this was a good sign. He seemed calmer as well. Still asleep, he was breathing evenly.

Jacob knew in his heart he had been right when he stared up into that starry night sky and said aloud, "How could anything be wrong on a night like this?" Now, Gott had delivered his beloved Bruder back to him. He knew it in his heart.

Hours later, shortly before dawn, Dr. Herff came riding up. He almost fell from his horse, his entire body worn and haggard.

Jacob and Lefty rushed to make coffee and breakfast as the doctor went immediately to check on Johann. Pleased with his patient's progress, he at last sat down to drink his coffee and eat the sausage and eggs Jacob offered him.

"Jacob, I believe your Bruder is out of the woods. Now, what he needs most is complete bed rest," then with a bit of tease in his voice he went on to say, "You are a good nurse."

"Nein, Sir, you are a good doctor," Jacob responded.

Not able to hold back, Lefty wanted to hear about Bigfoot's condition and the whereabouts of Rattlesnake Dick and his gang. He pummeled the good doctor with question after question. Listening to Dr. Herff's short replies and oftentimes only nods and grunts, Jacob knew the doctor needed rest and sleep even more than coffee and food much less more of Lefty's inquisition.

Once they knew Dr. Herff arrived in time to stop the bleeding from Big Foot's shoulder wound and the local doctor came back in town to take care of Big Foot, Jacob interrupted Lefty's next volley of questions.

"Dr. Herff, your bed is just over here in the corner. Draw this curtain for privacy and to shut out some light. Surely you need to rest after such an eventful day and night. I am aware of what to do for Johann and if his condition changes, I will awaken you."

"Ja, I almost fell asleep here in the chair several times. Danke shörn, I appreciate that."

"Aw, shucks, Doc, I'm plumb sorry fer hammering you with all these questions. I shouda realized how tard you were. I can get my answers about Rattlesnake Dick and his gang from Big Foot himself now that I know he's all right. I'll be saying my good-byes now and be off fer town. I'm still riding shotgun on the stage and it's bound to leave Fredericksburg as soon as a replacement is found for Big Foot because the line is now runnin' late.

"Jumpin' toad frogs! Come to think of it . . . I just might be that replacement!"

Lefty raced to retrieve his hat from the hook by the door, put it on his head, and tipped it in a farewell fashion to the two men.

*****

During the next two days, Johann slept around the clock giving Jacob and Dr. Herff time for endless talk about Jacob's air ship.

"Jacob, I came prepared to offer you backing for your toy air ships and now, I must admit your ideas and plans for a manned air ship intrigue me. But you are correct in thinking this kind of venture would take more money than one man might be prepared to gamble. Ja, I like the idea of selling shares for your air ship. With many working together, you can achieve your goals much sooner than just with a few of us. I will be glad to back you in the amount I had originally planned for the toy air ships and that should get you started and also, help you get the shares printed."

Jacob took a moment to control his mounting exuberance; he felt as if he could jump high enough to fly himself without any wings. He wanted to laugh, dance, and give a Texas "Yee Haw" all at once, but felt the doctor might consider it unscientific to display such emotions. Also, he did not want to wake Johann. So instead, he immediately reached across the table to shake Dr. Herff's hand vigorously.

"Dr. Herff, Dr Herff . . . you make me a very happy and grateful man. I thank you with all my being not only for this opportunity that you give me, but for saving my Bruder's life."

"Jawhol! What are friends for . . . especially we Germans must work together here in Texas. And speaking of working together, I think Johann will probably heal just fine, but it may take a while. He should remain here with you instead of going back to San Antonio anytime soon. I think you should try to talk him into living here with you now. They may not hold his job for him in San Antonio anyway. He needs you and you need him . . . you can work together to achieve this dream of yours."

"I agree with you, Doctor. But the first thing on his mind when he wakes up will be concern for his dog, Happy. The two are inseparable. I believe you know our kind neighbors, the Martinez family? They are keeping

Happy until Johann returns for him and we don't know when that might be. Would it be possible for you to go by their house to explain what has happened?"

"Ja, of course, I know them to be good people. Besides, down the street from where the Martinez's live, there is a young woman who is about to have a baby. I need to go see about her as soon as I get back. I will be sure to stop by and talk to the Martinez's about Happy while I am in the neighborhood."

"Ach, danke schön! That would mean so much to Johann."

" For myself, I must leave early in the morning because my practice cannot wait on me much longer. So today, do you not think we should immediately proceed with designing a share of stock for your air ship?"

And that night in a Texas one-room log cabin illuminated only by homemade candles, two men sat admiring a draft of a share of stock in Jacob Brodbeck's future air ship.

Quarter Share No. 36

$ 1. 25. *San Antonio*, *T*,, *June* 27th 1865.

Six months after the sale of a U. S. patent right for an airship, invented by me, I promise to pay to Dr. Herff ONE DOLLAR and TWENTY EIVE CENTS, together with his share of One Fourth of the amount receivcd by such sale, expenses deducted, or two months after the term for which a U. S. patent will be granted to me, together with a yearly payment of his share of One Fourth of the profits accrued by the saie of such airships, as the case may be, value rcccived.

J Brodbeck

Chapter 21
Christine

The first public schoolhouse in Fredericksburg opened in 1856. The Behrens, whom Jacob met when he lived in Castell, decided their youngest daughter, Christine should attend this new school. Now eleven, Christine was the lively and bright six-year old who made an impression on Jacob when he taught her in Castell.

As the Behrens still lived in Castell, they sent Christine to live in Fredericksburg with her Uncle Hermann and Aunt Rita who lived just a few blocks from the school.

The school had just one room. In the center of the room, a pot-bellied stove radiated as much heat as it could muster. A blackboard to one side had assignments carefully scripted for the older students to follow. As soon as the day started, they began reading their text books, then writing on their stone slates.

August Siemering, the Schoolmaster at the new school, taught oral lessons to the younger ones while the older ones worked independently.

After the first several months of school, Schoolmaster Siermering had concerns about one of his students. He had heard of Jacob Brodbeck's reputation as an excellent teacher. Perhaps Herr Brodbeck could come by the school after work and advise him on what approach to take with this student.

When asked, Jacob was happy to comply. The Schoolmaster only mentioned that the student was an eleven-year-old girl named Christine. As Jacob listened to the Schoolmaster, he did not connect this Christine to the six-year old he had taught at Castell.

"Christine . . . ahhh, Christine. How do I explain Christine?" the Schoolmaster lamented. Pausing to put his thoughts in order, he went on, "Christine has the mind of a twenty-year-old trapped in the body of an eleven-year-old girl. The sad part is that she has no intellectual equal in school.

"From her fifth grade class on, there are no students until seventh grade. Among the girls in that class only two are anywhere near Christine's intellectual level—Abigail and Hildegarde. Both hard-working girls, but shy and lady-like. No match for Christine.

"In eighth grade there are two boys—Alfonz and Gus. Both struggle to maintain their grades—perhaps because they miss quite a bit of school due to seasonal chores.

"Alfonz can be obstinate if he thinks anyone makes light of his intelligence. Therein lies the quagmire. Because I feel Christine's mind needs challenging, I sometimes allow her to participate in the older students' oral lessons. Being an avid reader, she outshines all the older ones, and moreover; she does it without any modesty or decorum—almost flaunting her supremacy—especially to the older boys.

"Most of the older students manage to tolerate her behavior, but not Alfonz. I often see him seething beneath his skin and glaring in Christine's direction. Even taking Christine aside and talking to her about her demeanor has not helped. She seems oblivious to her behavior and fearless where Alfonz is concerned.

“One idea I had was to suggest to Mrs. Behrens, Christine’s mother, that she might be tutored at home. Would you have the time or the interest to tutor her?”

Jacob’s attention stopped at the name of Mrs. Behrens. Ach, so this was the Christine who was giving the teacher such angst! But well, he was not surprised.

“Ja, I happen to know that family. I taught little Christine at Castell.” Jacob paused to formulate his thoughts. “And ja, any extra time I have, I work on my experiments.” Thinking further, he said, “Before you speak to Mrs. Behrens again, might I observe Christine at school one day? Perhaps this would help us make a better recommendation.”

“Ach, wunderbar! What a good idea. Ja, when would you like to come?”

“I have some time tomorrow morning. Would that be satisfactory?”

They agreed on the time and talked about how to plan the visit.

*****

Jacob entered the classroom just after school had begun. As prearranged, Schoolmaster Siemering only nodded when Jacob took a seat at the side of the classroom, then looked toward the desk where Christine was seated. When Jacob looked in that direction, the Schoolmaster indicated that was Christine.

A neatly dressed and dark-haired girl with her pigtails tied up in a bun on the top of her head, Christine sat working very hard at her desk. So engrossed in her studies, she did not notice Jacob when he entered the classroom.

Her book open, she was reading the material, and then with exacting diligence, writing the answers on her stone slate.

True to form, Christine finished her fifth grade numbers, writing and spelling assignments in short order. While she waited for her work to be checked, she glanced up and noticed Jacob. Jacob thought he saw a look of recognition on her face. The Schoolmaster noticed it as well. He went over to Christine and whispered in her ear.

Christine smiled and looked back at Jacob. Not wanting to disturb the other students still working on their assignments, the Schoolmaster said in low tones, "Christine, I believe you know Herr Brodbeck. As a former teacher, he agreed to come in and help with my classes today. Would it be all right for him to check your work?"

"Yes, Schoolmaster." Then looking up at Jacob, she said, "I remember you, Herr Brodbeck."

"I am glad you do and I remember you, too. You were a very good student. Let me see if that is still so."

Her work showed accuracy and it was written in a well-formed penmanship. She glanced up at Jacob with a smile of satisfaction, as he nodded his approval of her work. Then without further ado, she excused herself and went to where the first and second grade children were doing their assignments. She quietly began helping them, obviously well-trained to do so by her teacher.

As Christine helped the younger students, the Schoolmaster began checking the older students' written work as each one was finishing. Jacob noticed the older students reading quietly in their history books while waiting for their work to be checked. He also noted that often two students shared a book. Like the students he had taught here in Fredericksburg, they were adept at working this out with each other without the teacher directing them on how to manage it. Ja, these frontier children were expected to make the most of their time and the scarcity of materials.

Jacob remained quiet as he watched Christine work with the younger ones. At this point, Christine impressed him with how much help she offered. Would that not be missed if she were gone?

Shortly, the Schoolmaster announced it was time for the older students' oral history lessons. Christine quietly went about arranging the younger students on benches behind the older students. The younger students were expected to sit quietly and listen to the instruction even though they understood little of it. The belief was that they might absorb some of it and then be more adapted to the content once their time came around.

The Schoolmaster nodded in Christine's direction and she nodded in acceptance. She remained with the younger ones, but Jacob surmised the Schoolmaster's nod signaled permission for her to participate orally in the History lesson to follow.

As Christine's hand popped up over and over during the question and answer phase, the Schoolmaster ignored her as long as there were older students raising their hands.

Then he asked a higher level of knowledge question: "The battle of the Alamo in San Antonio eleven years ago this month culminated what economical and social issues of the Texans?"

Now only one hand remained raised.

Christine rose to answer when the Schoolmaster called her name. In a clear and confident voice, she explained, "The Texans faced many of the same conditions that forced our German fathers to leave Germany. The Texans had to follow laws given to them by a ruler who did not live among them, but lived in Mexico. Their economic needs went unmet by not being understood by the Mexican government mainly due to distance and a language barrier; therefore, they did not have adequate representation of government. Many of the Texans were not Catholic by faith and yet were being forced by the Mexican government to practice that religion. In addition, there was a cultural clash between the two entities. Parallel to that in Germany . . ." but before Christine could finish her statement, the Schoolmaster interrupted.

"Christine, you aptly answered the question. You are now into next week's lesson."

Jacob heard the snickers around the room—mostly from the eighth grade boys when the teacher reprimanded Christine. Jacob watched Christine's composure wondering if she would show any embarrassment or discomfort.

Instead she smiled gleefully in Alfonz's direction and with a swish of her skirt sat down with all the aplomb of the Queen of Sheba.

Alfonz, on the other hand, held down his resentment with some effort and only glared in Christine's direction.

So now Jacob knew the perplexity of the situation. With Christine's gifted mind would it be in Christine's educational advantage to be tutored at home? Would her social skills be acquired more readily in the classroom? She was such a big help with the younger students. Would it be beneficial to remove her from that?

He wondered—how does an eleven-year old girl leave such an indelible impact on all those around her?

Jacob was about to discover all that and more besides.

*****

That Saturday, Jacob made a trip to Castell. He wanted to discuss Christine's schooling with her parents. Christine would be home for the weekend from her aunt's house.

Sophia Behrens came to the door when Jacob arrived. He removed his hat and greeted her. She curtsied and said, "Guten tag, Herr Brodbeck. How very nice to see you again. My husband sends his regrets. He had to be away for the day."

She invited him in the small cabin where the children stood lined up to greet him. "I wanted you to see how the children have grown since you last saw them. You remember Henry, the oldest, nineteen, then Henrietta, fourteen, and of course, Christine, eleven.

Each one smiled, bowed or curtsied, and said politely, "Guten Tag, Herr Brodbeck." All, that is, except Christine. When introduced, she tipped her dark head to one side and peered up at him. Her face bore no apparent smile. Instead one corner of her mouth turned ever so slightly upward in a lopsided closed grin that all the more emphasized her large brown eyes staring directly up into his. He found himself intrigued with the apparent intelligence those eyes expressed.

Mrs. Behrens, noticing her youngest daughter's bad manners, said quickly, "Christine, greet your former teacher, Herr Brodbeck!"

Only then did Christine offer a slight curtsy, but never cast her eyes down with bashfulness as her sister did. Instead, holding her head to one side, she raised her hand to her forehead to brush away a wisp of dark hair that had escaped from the bound braids atop her head, but not taking her eyes away from looking at Jacob.

Jacob decided to keep his greeting short to her, "Guten Tag, Miss Christine."

Still she said nothing, but instead, nodded her greeting to him.

Her mother gave Christine a stern look, turned and said, "Henry, please escort your sisters to the kitchen. Aunt Patricia and Aunt Rita are waiting for your help with the canning."

They bid their ado's and walked away. Christine, with feigned nonchalance, turned back to look at Jacob. For just a second he found himself watching her look back at him. Then he turned his attention to Mrs. Behrens.

Once they were seated, Mrs. Behrens offered the best explanation she could for her daughter. "Since an infant, Christine has never done what was normal for other children . . . except when it appealed to her to do so." Chuckling a little to herself, "I am never quite sure what she will say or do next. Ja, she has the independent spirit of Texas in her."

Jacob smiled and said, "I, also, am unconventional. So ja, I understand Christine's nature."

As they talked, Jacob began to form opinions about what was best for Christine. After seeing her at home, he was more convinced that Christine needed the discipline of the classroom and the social skills it offered. He sensed her mother was frustrated trying to manage the strong-willed Christine. That frustration would just increase with Christine not in school and being home all the time. Nein, even though there were concerns, Christine fared better in the school environment.

After explaining his reasons, he concluded with "Ach, Mrs.Behrens, in my judgment Christine is better served in the public school. If you like, I will speak to the Schoolmaster. I have some materials I could loan him for Christine and I might be able to offer a few ideas about teaching a bright, but independent, student like Christine."

Sophia Behrens trusted Jacob's opinion. She expressed her gratitude for any suggestions he might offer the Schoolmaster.

Chapter 22
A Wedding Dance

Two years later . . . Castell, Texas.

"**M**utter, why can we not go to the Grossmann wedding dance if we are going to their wedding?" Christine relentlessly questioned her mother.

Sophia Behrens took in an extra deep breath before trying to deal with her very obstinate youngest daughter. She missed her husband's steady hand with their children but the most of all with Christine.

Not yet a year ago, while on his way to Fredericksburg, Henry Behrens was shot by rebel Indians. He suffered a sudden death from the poisoned arrows. The grief of his quick passing still lingered for Sophia. She was unsure of how it still affected Christine.

Going to where Christine sat on the side of her Mother's double bed, Sophia put her arms around her daughter's shoulders before she tried another approach with her.

"My dear, do you not want to honor your Vater's memory? I know it must be hard at your age to understand the propriety of not attending celebrations until the proper mourning period is past, but we do it not only to honor your Vater but also to not cause our friends and neighbors to feel uncomfortable as they celebrate around us."

"Das ist nicht rechtig! Does wearing black and avoiding dances mean I love my Vater more? My grief for my Vater is my own! Is it determined, or even diminished, or lengthened by propriety? I think not! My grief is mine to disclose or not."

Christine stood up, pressed the quilt smooth on the bed where she sat and with a flick of her dark curls and her chin up, she strode out of the room leaving her Mutter shaking her head in bewilderment. Christine's strong will and independent spirit were so much harder to manage without her husband's influence.

*****

At another cabin . . . Fredericksburg, Texas.

Johann winced as he helped Jacob lay another log on top of the others as they constructed another room to Jacob's cabin.

"Does the wound in your chest still bother you, my Bruder?" asked Jacob.

"Nein, I am fine. It just reminds me it is there from time to time. Besides, the sooner we get this room finished, the better we will feel. Then you can spread your air ship plans and parts out like you desire without worrying about my comfort. Which reminds me, speaking of comfort, have you decided yet whether you are going to the Grossmann wedding?"

"How is the Grossmann wedding related to my comfort?"

Johann chuckled beneath his breath as he answered, "Since when do you feel comfortable at weddings and dances?"

"Since I know Wilhem Grossmann. He is a good neighbor . . . he does not judge me to be crazy for building my air ship like the other neighbors do."

"Did you ever think, Jacob that is because he also comes from Stuttgart like us? He is familiar with your status as an inventor for the King, and so he does not doubt your sanity. Perhaps if you would allow Wilhem to tell others of your inventions, then they, too, would have fewer doubts."

"Nein, Johann, it is not the responsibility of Wilhem Grossmann to promote my saneness. Let people think as they will. Besides, maybe I will be bothered less by their curiosity and time-consuming questions if they think I am a little daft." Jacob pointed to his head with one finger smiling to himself as he chinked up spaces between the logs.

"I assume that means a "yes" of sorts. You will be attending the Grossmann wedding and dance?"

"If you will remind me, Bruder, when the day comes what time I am to be clean and in my Sunday-going clothes, I shall be ready."

"Ja, I will. Did you know we had a letter from the Martinez's about Happy?

"Nein. How is Happy doing?"

"They say he is *happy* chasing around with their other dogs and playing with the neighborhood children as well. They have taken him hunting in the nearby wooded hills. He treed a raccoon. Though it was so hard for me to give him up, I know he has a better home with the Martinez's. At our cabin, he would be alone most every day while we worked. Ja, it was the right thing to do for Happy."

Jacob said, "Ja, sometimes the right thing to do is the hardest thing to do. And the right thing for me to do is to go to the wedding of Wilhem Grossmann."

At the Wilhem Grossmann place just one mile north of Jacob's cabin, the Kauffmann wagon pulled up in front of their cabin. On board were Mr. and Mrs. Kauffmann and their daughter, Jane, the intended wife of Wilhem. An impending problem with the wedding ceremony had transpired. Their selected organist had taken ill and the Kauffmanns wondered if Wilhem would ask his friend, Jacob Brodbeck, to play the music for the wedding.

So on a bright Saturday morning, Jacob sat at the organ playing the wedding processional for his friend, Wilhem and his bride, Jane. The wedding was taking place at the Veriens Kirche as many weddings did.

*****

On one of the back benches sat Sophia Behrens, dressed in a high-necked, button down the front, long black dress. Beside her sat her three children, all in dark colors except for Christine.

Christine wore a green gingham dress with white lace tatting around the neck, sleeves and bodice. The skirt flared full from the waist as full as she could get her Mutter to spare the extra material to make it full. Christine knew the green color of the dress complemented her clear brown eyes and dark hair.

When Christine noticed it was Herr Brodbeck playing the organ, her crimson cheeks turned even more scarlet with excitement. She had wondered and dared to hope Herr Brodbeck would be present today. This was even better than her young heart imagined . . . to hear him play the organ. She enjoyed the way in which he touched the keys and the melody flowed almost effortlessly. Yes, indeed, it had been worth the compromise she made with her Mutter. Christine would be allowed to wear her best dress instead of the dowdy navy jumper her Mutter had in mind if she would give up on the idea of attending the wedding dance.

Christine lost track of the ceremony while she kept an intent awareness of Herr Brodbeck's every move. She was glad they sat in the back so that she could observe him without notice. The last time she saw him flashed across her mind . . .

After he visited with her mother about her schooling, he came the next Monday morning to the classroom. He carried with him a box full of materials. Her Mutter had told her he was to help the Schoolmaster with her instruction. She assumed that meant he was going to tutor her. How exciting! She thought Herr Brodbeck the most handsome and amazing man.

When the Schoolmaster and Herr Brodbeck came over to her desk, she could not believe what she heard the Schoolmaster say, "Christine, Herr Brodbeck has come to loan us some books and reference materials. These will make your studies more interesting. Won't you thank him for his thoughtfulness?"

Instead of gratitude, her voice rang with deep disappointment, "Is Herr Brodbeck not to stay and tutor me?" When she saw each man look at the other with questioning expressions, she went on to say with a twinge of defiance in her voice, “I prefer to have Herr Brodbeck tutor me. He knows what I need to learn.”

“Ach, Miss Christine, we cannot impose on Herr Brodbeck. He has already taken the time to help you. Now show your manners. Say thank you to him.

Instead, she put her head down on her desk and in between sobs, she said, “I will not!”

Though Herr Brodbeck tried to reason with her, she would not listen. Soon, he said no more and quietly left the classroom.

She had not seen him again. Now here he was. Oh, she wanted the chance to apologize to him and show him how much she had grown up.

While the pastor proceeded with the wedding service, she watched as he slipped over to the front bench. He sat beside a younger gentleman, quite handsome actually. Herr Brodbeck seemed to know him. She had never seen him before.

When the ceremony ended and Jacob played the recessional, Christine wanted to linger in the building in the hopes of an opportunity to approach Jacob without others around. But her Mutter kept ushering her outside with all the other wedding guests to greet the new married couple.

Once outside, she looked back to see if Herr Brodbeck followed the crowd outside. She could not see him. Was he still inside?

“Come along, Christine, and help us with the food in the wagon,” her Mutter took her hand, apparently making sure they all stayed together.

All the friends and neighbors brought covered dishes to share for the huge meal planned on the grounds. Later in the afternoon, the dance would begin with the wedding couple leading off with the Grand March. Of course, at that time, Christine knew the Behrens family would quietly leave. Now she began to wonder if she made the right bargain with her Mutter about the dress.

*****

Bringing tables and benches from all over town and providing a hard surface for the dancing fell to the men of the community. Jacob and Johann lent their hands to helping with this chore.

The Becker family had extended an invitation for Johann and Jacob to eat with them. It seemed they could not get enough of seeing Johann now that he lived in Fredericksburg again. As they talked, Jacob remembered the wedding gift he and Johann had designed for the bride and groom.

"Johann, I will go get the clock we made." Johann nodded his consent.

As Jacob walked back from their wagon with the clock in his arms, he spotted the Behrens family nearby taking food from their wagon. He had not seen the family since his visit to their home in Castell. Word had come to him that Henry Behrens had died.

As soon as he placed the clock with the other gifts, he must go and pay his respects. Suddenly, the last time he saw young Christine Behrens flashed across his mind. He could only hope she had outgrown her apparent schoolgirl crush on him or at least transferred it to someone else. Just as he leaned down to place the clock on the table with the rest of the gifts, he felt a slight tap on his shoulder.

"Hello, Herr Brodbeck. It is so nice to see you again."

When Jacob stood up, he was not exactly sure who this comely young lady in the green gingham dress was. She certainly knew him. She continued smiling and looking directly into his eyes as if she were enjoying the fact he had no idea of who she was.

"You will be glad to know, Herr Brodbeck, the book you left for me to read, *Pilgrim's Progress*, I have read twice over." Christine continued talking about the book to Jacob, but he heard not a word she said. Could this be the same child who bewildered him and the Schoolmaster that day in the classroom nearly two years ago?

She was absolutely stunning and so full of confidence. He felt like a schoolboy . . . stammering to find the right words to say.

Chapter 23
Romance Hearkens

Finally, Jacob found his voice, "Christine Behrens! My, I did not recognize you. You have grown into a young lady since . . ." Jacob again paused searching for the right words, "since the last time I saw you."

"Oh, I do hope I have changed since that day, Herr Brodbeck. I fear you must have thought my emotional outburst quite unseemly and I do apologize if I embarrassed you."

To Jacob, Christine's confession along with the flush on her cheeks seemed to accentuate her youthful winsomeness. He felt a rush of heat rising from the collar of his shirt up to his face. Absentmindedly, he loosened his tie and shirt collar.

"W-W-Why, no, Miss Christine, I was not embarrassed but instead concerned for the anguish you must have felt when what you expected did not happen." Jacob hoped what he said did not hurt Christine's feelings further.

"Herr Brodbeck, you are too kind. But I have not stopped thinking you must be the best teacher ever."

As he tried to think of an appropriate answer, Johann appeared behind him as if he were a heavenly apparition sent to rescue him.

Smiling and tapping Jacob on the shoulder, Johann inquired, "My dear Bruder, who is this lovely young lady who has your exclusive attention?"

Jacob heaved a sigh of relief, and then hoped it was not too apparent how flustered he was as he introduced his younger brother to Christine. He fully expected Johann's youth and charm would certainly divert Christine's attentions away from him.

On the contrary, Johann seemed determined to keep the focus of their conversation on Jacob, going on to tell Christine about the progress on Jacob's air ship.

Christine paused a moment, then demurely looked up at Jacob and boldly asked, "Herr Brodbeck, the Grand March is about to begin. I would be so delighted if you would be my escort and tell me more about your exciting air ship." Christine was taking the chance that once she was out on the dance floor with Herr Brodbeck, her Mutter would not interfere.

Again Christine caught Jacob dumbfounded and practically mute. As he furtively looked around for some course of escape, he detected Christine's mother standing some distance away with her two older children. Now at last his mind cleared. He had been on his way to pay his respects to this grieving family when Christine overwhelmed him.

"Miss Christine, I see your Mutter, Bruder and Schwester over there. It reminds me I have been remiss in paying my respects to you and your family upon the loss of your dear Vater. Allow us to go and do so."

Now there was no argument. Both Johann and Christine bowed their consent and walked with Jacob over to where the Behrens family stood.

It was during the conversation of respect and regards to Mrs. Behrens and her family that Mrs. Behrens said, "Herr Brodbeck, it is providential we should see you today. I wanted to you to know the materials for Christine's instruction you loaned the Schoolmaster and your suggestions for her studies helped each of them. Schoolmaster Siemering sends home good reports on her progress. Danke schön.

"Ach, I am pleased to hear Schoolmaster Siermering and Miss Christine have worked *together* to achieve her academic progress. Das ist sehr gut!"

Jacob's emphasis on the word, together, did not escape Christine's attention. Not wanting the conversation to linger on her schooling, Christine inquired, "Herr Brodbeck, do you and your Bruder live far from Fredericksburg?"

"Ja, our cabin is only a good stretch of a walk from town . . . but today we brought the wagon so we could bring the wedding gift with us."

Before Christine could continue, Mrs. Behrens caught her by the hand, offered their regards, and took their leave from the picnic grounds and from the dance.

Christine, for once, did not object. She waved good-by all the while thinking . . . *auf wiedersehen. I know we will meet again.*

*****

On their ride back to their cabin, Johann brought up the meeting with the Behrens family. Attempting to hide any tease in his voice, he ventured a query, "Why have you not mentioned your association with the Behrens family? They seem like such a nice and interesting family . . . especially the youngest daughter, Christine."

"Why, yes, they are. But I have not seen them for nearly two years now and the thought of mentioning them did not come up until seeing them again today."

Johann could tell Jacob deliberately kept the tone of his answer neutral and unaffected. But he decided to persist anyway.

"Did you not think Christine a lovely young girl?"

"Ja, lovely and very *young*," replied Jacob with just a hint of consternation.

Johann went on, "Regardless of her age, she seemed very taken with you, Jacob. Surely you noticed."

"Ja, I noticed," replied Jacob curtly.

"Then why should you ignore her interest in you? Any available woman in these parts is rare . . . much less an obviously intelligent and pretty one such as she," exhorted Johann.

"Then why do you not take an interest in her yourself, my dear Bruder?" Jacob retorted.

"Because for one thing . . . it is obvious she has eyes for you . . ." then looking away in the distance with his voice softening, "And for the other, my own heart has no room in it for another love."

Changing his tone as well, Jacob tenderly asked, "Oh, my Bruder, do you still yearn for your Katarina after all this time?"

"Nein, because of her dear letter, her poetry, and her Bible, the yearning in my heart has turned into a beloved chapter in my life forever enfolded in time. And I desire it that way. It was so lovely and delicate, that I dare not lose it nor diminish it in any way by encroaching upon its chambers. Though we never had the chance to marry, Katarina and I are one in heart and mind forever."

Then putting his arm around his brother's shoulder, Jacob admitted, "Ach, Bruder, we have been so busy with all my things . . . that I did not take the time to ask you about what you are feeling."

Quickly Johann responded, "Nein, nein . . . feel no sorrow for me. I am fortunate to have known Katarina even for a short time. And it was your urging that gave me courage to believe such a wonderful girl could have a deep and meaningful connection with me. That is why I now encourage you to look into your own heart to find out if it can connect with another's. It is a beautiful thing, my Bruder. I want you to experience it like I have."

Jacob shook his head, "But my own heart is full as well. How could there be any room left when my dream of providing man with air travel is so encompassing?"

"That may be true to you now. But I sense Miss Christine may have ways of fitting herself into your dreams and into your heart," and then Johann smiled and added, "And perhaps with little protest from you at all."

Jacob reined in their horse as they approached the cabin. He turned to Johann and said, "Johann, I have not time or money for a family. Miss Christine will have a batch of suitors before long who will offer her what she desires. I do not have the makings to be a good husband nor a provider."

Still Johann smiled and said to himself . . . "We shall see . . . we shall see."

> *"The flowers appear on the earth; the time of the singing of birds is come, and the voice of the turtledove is heard in our land."*
> *Song of Solomon 2:12*

Chapter 24
Duly Waiting for the Dew

Several months later . . .

Life began to settle into a routine for the brothers as soon as they finished building the extra room onto the cabin for Johann.

"Now that my *room* is finished, my Bruder, today I look for work to provide my *board*," quipped Johann with the old twinkle in his eye.

Jacob smiled at his brother's attempt at jocularity. "And where shall the search begin?"

"From talk at Nimitz's Boarding House, I learned about the need for laborers at Lange's Mill. Unusual flood waters these past few weeks washed away the saw mill and part of the old grist mill. The building of a dam and reconstruction of the saw mill and grist mill may require just the kind of masonry skills that I possess, do you not agree?"

Jacob nodded his head in consent, "I wholeheartedly agree. Shall I expect you home for supper?"

"Why, yes and no, my Bruder. Ja, I shall probably be home by then, but nein, you do not have to stop your work on your air ship to cook for us."

"You answered my mind instead of my words. Are you sure you should not look for work as a magician instead of a mason?" returned Jacob. "Ach, go find a job! I am eager to get started again."

Johann began working at Lange's Saw Mill that same day while Jacob fervently poured over the plans he and Dr. Herff discussed during his stay with them. From his small model air ship, he would draw up plans for a man-size machine. He hoped to make enough money at odd jobs to build the air ship himself. If he could not, he would make copies of the share they designed to promote funds for its construction.

He used daylight hours for the tedious work of trial and error. By night, lamplight found him pouring over his blueprints correcting errors gleaned from the day's efforts. Somehow amid these labors, he earned meager wages from odd jobs here and there: building furniture, giving music lessons, or surveying land.

The thought of Christine rarely, if ever, crossed Jacob's mind. Left to his own devices, Jacob and his one-track inventor's mind, honed in on how to solve the problem of flight.

Johann's masonry work ended when the sun set. He felt tired and completely ready for bed when he came home at night. At first, he marveled at Jacob's energy and drive for his project. As Johann blew out his candle at night, Jacob sat hunched over his air ship plans by the light of the only coal oil lantern they owned. When Johann arose before dawn to get to the mill, Jacob stood chiseling away at either a piece of furniture or parts on the air ship's frame.

After a few weeks went by, Johann began questioning the wisdom of Jacob's intense involvement in his work. Could any man maintain physical (or for that matter, mental) health continuing in the manner Jacob drove himself? Several times in the evening, he began to voice his misgivings to Jacob. Jacob waved him off with hand motions and vigorously shook his head sideways communicating to Johann without words not to interrupt him.

A precipitous incident forced the issue.

Just an hour or so before dawn on that particular day, an acrid odor wafted in and out of Johann's sleeping subconscious. Even with his eyes closed in a semi-dreamy state, Johann's ever rational mind wondered . . . why does a person's sense of smell arouse him before any of his other senses?

Clink--Clunk--Clatter--Clang--Thump--Clack--Thud--Whomp!

Johann sprung from his bed like a bullfrog from a frying pan. More clanging and banging. It sounded like every pot, pan, jar, and cooking utensil in their pantry was coming off their shelves. And that reeking smell! What was that? It had a familiar odor. . . but he could not identify it. He fumbled for his rifle under the bed all the while hollering, "Jacob, are you hurt? What did you do?"

No answer. More clinking, crashing sounds. With the rifle square in his hands, Johann shouted again, "Jacob! Are you here or are you deaf?"

Jacob for his part, sat transfixed at the table as the last clanging sound subsided and what appeared to sound like soft thuds retreating out the door. Johann's repeated questions finally penetrated Jacob's confusion.

"Ja, I am here." Then . . . "Oh, nein! I feel kerosene oil all over the table. My plans! My plans! Are they ruined?"

By this time, Johann held up a lighted candle to survey the situation.

Jacob sat at the table looking down at an overturned kerosene lantern with the kerosene dripping off the table. He scrambled to retrieve the plans not yet soiled by the oil.

"Wheh!" Johann said in disgust, "No wonder they call it 'skunk oil!' That at least explains the odor."

Seeing no one else in the room, Johann laid the rifle down. He reasoned that before he tried to help Jacob recover the plans, he better not set the candle near the spilled kerosene.

"Let me put the candle on the fireplace mantle and then help you." As he held the candle in that direction, the scene of the pandemonium materialized.

Strewn amongst many of Jacob's metal tools, screws, nails, and other paraphernalia were cooking pots and pans, a sack of meal ripped apart, and several jars of molasses, one of which was broken with molasses oozing out into the whole muddle and mess.

Both men shook their heads in bewilderment. Muttering under his breath, Johann carefully made his way to the mantle.

"Do not bother helping me with the papers . . . I have all the dry ones . . . the rest we will wait and see what the daylight brings."

As Jacob spoke, Johann looked toward the slightly open door which revealed the first faint light of dawn. He wanted light shed on the mystery inside as well.

"Why is the door unbolted, Jacob? What caused all this? Did a thief try to rob us?"

"I remember going outside earlier in the evening to get more materials that I have stored in the shed." Rubbing his forehead in confusion, Jacob continued, "Perhaps I did not bolt the door again once I returned and . . ."

"And then later, because you were utterly and completely exhausted, you fell asleep at the table while working on your plans," Johann finished his brother's sentence for him.

"Ja . . ." Jacob admitted, "It is possible." Looking down at the soiled and crumpled plans, Jacob let out a deep sigh. Hours and hours of tedious and pain-staking work to do all over again.

Sensing his brother's dejection, even from across the room, Johann let some moments lapse.

Then he walked over to his brother, placed his hand on his shoulder and motioned for the two of them to sit at the table.

With a smile on his face, Johann quoted an old German proverb: *"Ordnung lerne, liebe sie; Ordnung spart dir Zeit und Müh."*

Jacob smiled back and repeated the proverb in English:

"Learn good order, love it too,
It saves time and trouble for you."

"Das ist richtig, my Bruder. I remember not so long ago . . . when I lay wounded and recovering from the bullet Rattlesnake Dick shot into my chest . . . that my Bruder devoted the first hour of his day to journaling, meditating, and talking to our Heavenly Vater asking for His guidance in our lives."

"Ja, du hast recht, as you said . . . I have been so busy doing things my own way to even consider Gott's way." The dejection on Jacob's face moments earlier melted into mellowness and composure.

The two men decided first to put the cabin in order. Who or what had been their mysterious invader they could pursue later. Possibly a raccoon? No matter. The *who, what, why, or how* were not nearly as important to ponder as the *when. When* Jacob needed redirection, Gott provided it.

That evening, both men sat reading the scriptures by candle light. Johann seemed drawn to the Psalms while Jacob found himself reading in Proverbs.

As they read quietly, Jacob looked over at his brother and said, "Johann, there's scripture here about the *dew.* Have you ever thought much about the *dew*? The only time you see it is early in the morning . . . and then how it sparkles with the first rays of light. How beautiful but fleeting it is for not every morning brings dew. Our Vater used to say, "When the night is still, the wind calm, you awaken to a dewy morn."

"Ja, I remember that, too. Vater was both a poet and a prophet it seems. But more practically speaking . . . he was saying, the conditions have to be just right for what you need and what you ask for. Remember the Israelites after they left Egypt when they were so hungry in the desert? Just at the needed moment— early in the morning—there on the dew Gott left manna for them to eat."

"Ja, even though they were clamoring as loud as our intruder this morning, Gott chose a quiet, still place to send them what they needed."

Johann only smiled and nodded in agreement.

Later when Johann slept, Jacob crept out into the night. Stars twinkled through some drifts of ribbon-like clouds. The still air was cool about him. Jacob knew in his heart that Gott formed these words in his mind:

"Do not make haste and do not fear. Spiritual dew comes from being quiet and still before Me. Linger with Me until you feel saturated with My presence. Then go to your next duty energized with the freshness of Christ."

As Jacob looked into the heavens, he knew he would awaken to a dewy morn.

> *"The LORD by wisdom hath founded the earth; by understanding hath he established the heavens. By his knowledge the depths are broken up, and the clouds drop down the dew."*
> *Proverbs 3:19-20*

Chapter 25
Desires of the Heart

Early the next morning as Jacob witnessed the dew glistening on the blades of grass; he joyously understood the love and grace of God. He knelt on his knees in the dewy grass to pray and thank Him for this precious sign of His attention to Jacob's needs. Though he felt no immediate guidance, he felt a growing awareness of His Lord's presence and perhaps the need to do as Johann suggested—relax more and become aware of life's joys around him.

Later that evening, he and Johann talked about what relaxation meant.

Johann smiled and said, "Ja, ja . . . I say relax a little and just enjoy the life Gott has given you. By the way, I heard at work today the Founder's Day Picnic committee is looking for a choirmaster to form a youth choir to sing during the picnic. I know how much you enjoy music. Why not volunteer for the position?"

"Ja, but it will take time from my air ship. It is the German way to work hard and be careful with all details."

"But perhaps too much work wearies the mind and leaves no room for inspiration. Let me ask you this. When you watch the birds fly do they seem to work hard to fly or do they seem to fly effortlessly?" inquired Johann.

"Ja, that is a good analogy. So I am to be like a bird and fly with ease?" Jacob countered with a gleam in his eye.

"Nein, but perhaps Gott wants you to stop trying so hard and depend on Him more. Delight in His accomplishments instead of pushing so hard for your own. What do you think?"

"Ja, could be." Placing his hand under his chin, he mused, "Now, I wonder . . . what is Gott's first delight for me?"

*****

Approximately fifty miles north in the community of Castell, Christine felt extra excitement as she finished the last part of her packing. After her weekend stay at home, today her mother would take her back to her Aunt Rita's house in Fredericksburg. Today was different because after seeing Herr Brodbeck on Saturday, she just knew in her heart they would soon meet again.

Mrs. Behrens walked into Christine's room to hear her daughter singing . . .

Du, du liegst mir im Hersen,
Du, du liegst mir im Sinn;
Du, du machst mir viel Schmerzen,
Weisst nicht, wie gut ich dir bin.
Ja, ja, ja, ja,
Weisst nicht, wie gut ich dir bin.

"Christine, sing it in English, my dear. Texas state law now requires English to be taught and spoken in your school."

Christine nodded and sang,

You, you are in my heart, dear,
You, you are in my mind;
You, you make me much heartache,

Don't know how much I love you.
Yes, yes, yes, yes,
Don't know how much I love you.

"But Mutter, it sounds better in German. Besides, I always hear you older folks talk about preserving the German ways . . . what better way than to continue to sing our favorite folk ballads in German?"

"Ja, that is true, too." Then with a twinkle in her eye, she teased, "Perhaps I was just testing you to see how well you could translate the song into English. And you did a very nice job of it, too!" Then as she added folded linens to Christine's packing, she asked, "But tell me, does the "You" in your song happen to be Herr Brodbeck?"

"Oh, Mutter, why does that come to your mind? Besides, I just mentioned it is a popular German folk ballad we all sing!" Christine answered with just a shade too much indignation.

"Perhaps . . . but maybe it comes to mind because I sense your attention is centered on Herr Brodbeck." Then catching Christine's hand, Mrs. Behrens went on, "Let us sit and talk about this secret desire of yours, Christine."

"It will not be a secret if I talk about it!"

"Then I should say 'deep desire' instead. Even though you have not talked directly about your fondness for Herr Brodbeck, your actions have communicated the message to anyone who was watching. Christine, as your Mutter, I more than anyone else know how strong-willed you are. When you have a desire for something, you will use every skill and talent you have to possess it. But a man's heart cannot be possessed solely by your will. What

I am suggesting is . . . depend more on Gott's will in this matter than your own. He sees both hearts and both their lives. If it is to be, allow Gott to bring you together in His own way and His own time. That way it will be a good fit."

Christine's features registered signs of relief instead of the indignation reflected earlier.

"Oh, Mutter, I thought you were about to preach to me about how young I am and how I do not know my own heart or how much older Herr Brodbeck is." Wrapping her arms around her mother's neck, she gushed, "Thank you, Mutter, so much for understanding me."

"Ah, my dear, but do *you* understand *my* intentions? I have discovered that preaching against something to you only makes you more determined to do what it is you want to do. Ja, you are very young and Herr Brodbeck is very much older. But instead of stating the obvious, I want to ask you to do one thing for me in this last night at home before we see each other again. Do you think you can do that?"

Christine, still relieved about receiving no lecture, dutifully nodded her head and said, "Ja, Mutter, whatever you wish."

"Please get your Bible and come sit by me," requested Mrs. Behrens. Christine held back a curious look and quickly retrieved her Bible from one of her valises.

"Bitte, turn to Psalm 37:4."

Christine leafed through the pages until she located the chapter and verse.

"Now . . . ." Mrs. Behrens reached into the right pocket of her apron and pulled out a very delicate lace cross the size of a bookmark. "I have tatted this for you."

Placing the cross in Christine's hand, she went on to say, "Please use it to mark this passage in your Bible. I would like for you spend at least a half hour tonight meditating on it. You may memorize it, if you like. But more importantly, let it penetrate into your innermost being. Then allow this scripture to direct your thoughts and actions toward Herr Brodbeck." Looking straight into Christine's wide brown eyes, she said, "First, would you read it to me?"

Christine looked down at the scripture and read aloud: "Psalm 37:4 'Delight thyself in the Lord and He shall give thee the desires of thine heart.'"

With searching eyes, Christine returned the deep gaze into her mother's eyes hoping to find added meaning.

Softly her mother advised, "I said that I would not preach so I shall not add to what the scripture says. Just promise me you will ponder upon it. Write down what you think Gott's word might be saying to you through this scripture. Will you agree to that?"

Christine smiled a wide smile and agreed, "I agree. Ooooh, as much as I like going to school, I miss you so much while I am gone." She squeezed her mother as hard as she could.

Her mother returned her bear hug all the while thinking that Christine was much too immature and imaginative to conceive of the idea of a heavenly Father guiding her life decisions. But she was her Mutter and she at least could plant this tiny seed. It would be up to Gott to grow the seed into a garden of faith for her Christine.

"My, that was a big hug. I miss you, too, my baby daughter, more than you know. But we will come to the Sunday House at the end of this month. You can stay with us there that weekend. On Sunday, we will all go to church together."

Later that night in her room beside a lit candle, Christine read once again Psalm 37:4. What did it mean to 'delight oneself in the Lord?' What did one do? Go to church? Sing hymns? Read the Bible? Was she to delight herself in the Lord like she would other things in which she found delightful? Like dancing or reading or daydreaming about Herr Brodbeck? Or was that what it meant? Christine did not know, but she wondered . . .

Chapter 26
Delightful

Christine watched as the Schoolmaster placed the morning's assignments on the board. How she wished it was Herr Brodbeck who was writing the assignments for the day. She wondered when they would meet again and almost started daydreaming about how and where their next encounter would be. But always the ardent student, she shook herself free of those thoughts, and immediately became absorbed in her class's assignment.

The only girl in the eighth grade class, Christine knew it was a privilege to be attending school when most girls her age were at home helping with chores. She intended to make the most of it. She scarcely noticed the two boys in her class. She thought they were like tadpoles in a pond . . . too immature and wiggly for her taste.

To her total surprise later in the day, her schoolmaster began talking about Herr Brodbeck.

"Herr Brodbeck will come by the schoolhouse today to talk to those of you in the eighth grade and older who are interested in singing in the choir he is organizing for the Founders' Day Picnic. As you know, the picnic is coming soon in May. Let me see a show of hands from those of you who want to participate."

Christine's hand flew up first and the expression on her face registered not only participation, but eager participation.

The schoolmaster counted hands and then said, "Good! When he arrives, those eight of you will go outside with him where he will talk to you about your practices."

Of course, now there was absolutely no way Christine could focus on her studies. Fortunately, she could pretend to read her reading assignment while her mind raced about pondering other things . . . like how she looked . . . what she was wearing . . . what she would say or what he would say . . .

She did not have to stew very long. Within the half hour, the door opened and in walked Herr Brodbeck. Christine felt her heart jump to her throat. The Schoolmaster introduced each of the choir students to Herr Brodbeck, but when he came to Christine, he said, “And you remember Miss Christine?”

“Ja, how are you, Miss Christine?" Jacob kept his greeting brief.

Feeling a little lightheaded, Christine was barely audible when she answered, "I am well, sir, and you?"

"I, also.” Then to the whole group, he said, “It is a fine April day. Let us go outside. We can sit on the benches under the trees while we discuss our practice times."

Thoughts accelerated in both Jacob's and Christine's heads while their bodies casually carried them outside. Ironically, their thinking ran along parallel lines.

I had forgotten she would be here, Jacob thought. *She seemed different somehow . . . more subdued. I wonder why?*

While Christine wondered, *somehow he seemed different toward me . . . perhaps more interested in me?*

Just as the short meeting ended, the school bell rang indicating the close of the school day. Christine started walking silently back to the classroom, her usual audacious manner gone.

She hung her head pondering why she was so shy and unsure of herself. Perhaps reading and meditating on Psalm 37:4, as she promised her Mutter she would, was having an unusual affect on her. She wanted to find a way to talk to Herr Brodbeck alone, but her mind seemed like mush . . . not allowing her to follow through on her desires. What was wrong with her?

Just as she reached the schoolhouse door, she heard Herr Brodbeck call out to her, "Miss Christine, I have not inquired about your family. Are they well?" Jacob surprised himself by his need to detain Christine. As she turned, and a beautiful smile spread across her face, his desire to talk to her intensified.

"They seemed well the last time I saw them. They will come the last weekend this month. We plan to come to church that Sunday. I enjoyed hearing you play the organ at the Haufmann wedding. Do you play the organ in church on Sundays?"

Jacob walked up to stand beside her and answered, "Nein, I asked for a sabbatical so I could give more time to the development of my air ship."

"But you took time off to be the choirmaster for this event?"

"Ja, at the bequest of my Bruder, Johann. He suggested I was working too hard and relaxing too little. Music relaxes me, you see."

"Ja. Music is good for the soul," Christine added remembering how her Mutter teased her when she found Christine singing a German folk ballad.

"And how would such a young Frauline know what is good for the soul?" Jacob teased.

In all due seriousness, Christine replied, "Texas Fraulines grow up fast by necessity, do you not think, Sir?"

*****

For the next several weeks, Jacob continued to find reasons for Christine to help him after practices. Without him realizing it, they began to get to know each other. Jacob found himself eagerly looking forward to choir practice. He was surprised that he and such a young girl could talk so easily to each other. But then he remembered, two years ago the Schoolmaster said Christine had the mind of a twenty-year old. She was old beyond her years.

He was glad Johann had encouraged him to relax by taking on this activity to offset his work on his air ship. But he worried about the strong affection growing between him and Christine.

One afternoon just after Jacob's last choir practice at the schoolhouse ended, Johann came galloping up on his horse. Hurrying to dismount, he ran toward the open door of the schoolhouse. Just as he approached the door, he heard hearty laughter coming from inside.

He knocked on the door several times, then because he was in a hurry, he went on inside. He saw Jacob and Christine laughing as they sat together at the organ.

"I, too, would enjoy a good laugh . . . ja, what is so funny?" he inquired.

"Ach, du lieber! Johann, what are you doing here this time of day?" Jacob's response showed total surprise at seeing his brother.

An equally surprised response came from Johann, "You mean you have not noticed the dark green clouds brewing outside? A hailstorm is sure to follow. They let us go early at the mill so we might tend to our livestock and protect our gardens. The wind just changed directions to the southwest. You know that means the storm is not far behind. When I rode by here on my way home, I was surprised to find you still here."

"Ja . . . we have been so busy, we did not notice the weather change. Christine, get your things. I will drive you home in my buggy."

"Nein, I will be fine . . . I can walk the block to my Aunt's house. You go on with your Bruder to tend to your livestock."

"Nein, Jacob is right. He should take you home," Johann turned and winked at Jacob so that Christine did not see. "Besides we only have one cow. I can get her in the shed. You go on, Jacob. I will see you at home."

All three raced out as bolts of lightning lit the darkening sky and thunder rumbled all around them.

No sooner had Jacob delivered Christine to her doorstep than a torrent of rain broke loose. In seconds, he said good-by, then dashed through the pouring rain to his buggy.

By the time he reached their cabin, hailstones started pelting the buggy top. He drove the buggy up to the shed. He unhitched the horse to move him inside with Johann's horse and their Guernsey cow. As Jacob looked around for Johann, he saw him covering as many of the garden plants as he could with canvas sheets. But as the hailstones started coming faster and thicker, both men ran as fast as their legs would carry them for the safety of their cabin.

Once inside, Johann built a sturdy fire while Jacob got the coffee ready. After both of them changed into dry clothes, they sat down to drink their hot coffee beside the fire.

Jacob knew what was coming next. And he was right.

"Well, mein Bruder," Johann began, "It seems my little lecture on relaxation has manifested itself in the form of Miss Christine Behrens. How delightful!" Johann's grin spread all across his face.

"Ach, it is nothing. She helps me prepare for the next day's choir practice. Besides young people laugh easily . . . that is all," he protested.

"Jacob, why deny the two of you are attracted to one another? Why not enjoy it?"

"Because she is much too young for me to be feeling that way about her," Jacob conceded. Then with a perplexing wrinkle showing on his brow, he stated, "I must put a stop to it and soon."

"The feelings you are having for her are Gott-designed, mein Bruder, and you can no more put a stop to them than stop that hail from falling outside."

"And my feelings could lead to as much damage as that hail may cause," Jacob moaned in an anguished voice. "What kind of marriage would it be? I am thirty-five years old and she is thirteen. I am easily old enough to be her father. She deserves someone who is intent on providing well for her and spending time with her. I do not deny that I enjoy her company . . . but only at intervals. At other times my whole being is focused on my air ship. What kind of husband would that be for Christine?" Jacob reasoned.

"Apparently the kind of husband Christine wants. She is a very strong-willed young lady. Seems to me she does not think she is too young or that you are too old for her. Am I right?" Johann persisted.

"Ja . . . she calls herself a Texas Frauline who is old for her age," admitted Jacob.

Then Johann leaned forward and spoke in earnest, "Jacob, her age might have mattered in Germany. But she is right. In Texas, girls her age marry all the time. Here on the frontier where far too many die in childbirth, there is a lack of women. So it is more out of necessity that girls marry so young. There is no shame in it. It is just the way it is. Be joyful that Gott has given you this chance at personal happiness."

"Ja, those things are true. But it may be true as well that Christine's young romantic mind keeps her from seeing the reality of the harsh way of life she might be facing. The desire I feel to be with her should not be stronger than my desire for her happiness and well-being, should it?"

Johann would not be put off, "Ja, well, sometimes passion is stronger than good sense. Perhaps that is why it says in 1 Corinthians, 'But if they cannot control themselves, they should marry. For it is better to marry than to burn with passion.' "

"Bruder, you are beginning to quote scripture like a preacher!" Then peering out the window, he noticed, "Ach, the hail has stopped. And look! The grass is no longer green, but covered with white. We should go check to see what damage the storm caused.

*****

Christine sat by her bedroom window looking at the white bumpy earth all around her. Her heart felt as cold as those lumps of ice. Even seeing her cousins running outside with such glee throwing the icy stones at each other gave her no youthful delight. Why could she not be like one of them? Instead she felt miserable because choir practices were now over. After the Founders' Day Picnic, would she ever get to be with Jacob again?

Chapter 27
Strong Desires

Jacob continued his practice of studying the Word early each morning and then, in quiet meditation, seeking the presence of the Lord. Most often his meditations took place outdoors, weather permitting. It was during these moments of solitude and stillness he often experienced thoughts, directions, and guidance from the Lord.

In this manner, he found when he began his workday, things went much smoother. Even the tedious tasks got accomplished with less frustration. And new ideas came upon him daily. He felt fresher and more confident when his days started with these quiet times.

On Sunday, the brothers rode to church in their buggy as was their custom. Jacob had now resumed his position as the organist at the Vereins Kirche.

The fresh April rain made the air crisp and slightly chilly. As they rode along, Jacob sat relaxed while Johann drove. He even wondered if Christine would be in church today. But he knew she spent most weekends with her family at Castell.

During Holy Communion, Jacob softly played the hymn, "Just As I Am." He knew the hymn by memory so his eyes roved over the congregation as members came forward to receive the sacrament.

His eyes stopped as they gazed upon a dark-haired head bowed before the altar. Was that Christine? He continued to watch until her head came up. In one tantalizing moment, their eyes locked. Finally, in what seemed like five minutes to Jacob instead of seconds,

Christine lowered her eyes, a demure smile forming on her lips as she lifted her eyes to catch Jacob involuntarily smiling back at her.

Then he did something he never did . . . he hit a wrong key. It so unnerved him he sat up straight and focused his eyes completely on the music. Had anyone noticed the wrong key? He hoped not.

Someone noticed, however. Johann. He sat nearby taking in the preceding scene. He chuckled to himself as he observed his brother's feigned preoccupation with the organ's keyboard and sheet music.

On this particular Sunday, a boxed lunch was planned. Jacob and Johann brought cheese, bread, dried sausage, and dried plums. Being bachelors, their boxes held only simple food. But usually, their kind neighbors invited them to sit with their families and share in the women's baked confections.

This Sunday, Pastor Dangers and his wife, Paula, asked the two men to join them.

As often as he dared, Jacob glanced around to see where Christine sat. He soon spotted her with her relatives—Uncle Hermann and Aunt Rita.

Christine, fully aware of Jacob's sideway glances, kept herself engaged in the conversations at their table. She seemed to know intuitively she must remain still now and let Jacob make the next move.

Johann leaned over to Jacob and whispered in his ear, "You know you want to say "hello" to her. Go over and do it!" he urged.

"But what would I say?" Jacob whispered back, "Nein, I think it too improper."

"That is sometimes your problem, mein Bruder, you think too much!" Then to Pastor and Mrs. Dangers, Johann said, "Jacob and I have spotted some of our former neighbors and one of his former students. May we be excused to go over and give them our regards?"

Pastor Dangers smiled, "Ja, by all means. But remember Frau Dangers' pound cake, or you know it as Sandkuchen, is coming up for dessert soon. You do not want to miss that!"

"Ja," smiled Johann, "How could we forget? We will soon be back." Johann maneuvered a hesitant Jacob over to the relatives' table.

"Gut Abend! Are all the family members enjoying this day?" asked Johann cordially.

Uncle Hermann stood up to shake hands with the two men. "Wie gehts, a splendid day! It is good to see you. Please join us for dessert. Rita baked kaffeekuchen," then turning to Christine, "And I believe Christine baked a fresh cobbler from dewberries she picked herself."

Christine smiled and nodded her affirmation.

Johann turned to Jacob and said, "Jacob! Dewberry cobbler! That is your favorite." Then without giving Jacob a chance to answer, he went on, "Jacob, you must stay and have some." Then turning back to the table, Johann answered, "I must decline your gracious offer as I accepted an invitation from Frau Dangers to join them for her delicious pound cake. Jacob, I will offer your apologies to Frau Dangers."

Johann scurried back to the Dangers' table leaving Jacob rather awkwardly standing there. Aunt Rita quickly saved the moment by offering, "Herr Brodbeck, please sit down. There is plenty of room there at the end of the table."

After dessert, most of the children drifted off to join in the various games being played. Even Uncle Hermann and Aunt Rita left to play dominoes with another couple.

"Miss Christine, do you want to join in any of the games?" inquired Jacob.

"Nein, but I would enjoy a walk along Town Creek. Would you be so kind as to escort me?"

Jacob knew as a gentleman, he could not refuse her invitation. He hoped no one noticed as they slipped away under the old oak trees down to the creek. He wanted to cause no impropriety.

As they passed down the slope toward the creek and out of view, Jacob relaxed to enjoy the warm spring day and Christine's exuberance. She wanted to pull off her shoes and dangle her feet in the water, but Jacob managed to convince her that the waters were still too cold for that. Instead, they walked along the creek side, both quiet and a little nervous. At last, Jacob asked, "What are your plans when school is out for the summer?"

"Oh, I do not want to think about that. Even though I miss my family, I will miss school more." Then looking up earnestly into Jacob's eyes, she said quietly, "But most of all, I would miss seeing you."

Jacob's first thought was—watch out— you are getting too close. However, some unfamiliar force inside him took over as he gazed deep into Christine's eyes. The same hitherto unknown force took his arms and wrapped them around Christine. She snuggled up next to him and fit like the last missing piece of a jigsaw puzzle.

"Oh, Miss Christine, what am I going to do with you?" he whispered.

Christine hugged him even tighter and said, "You might begin by simply calling me Christine."

> *"How fair and how pleasant art thou, O love, for delights!" Song of Solomon 7:6*

Chapter 28
Wedding Bells

Two weeks later, Sophia Behrens came to the Founders' Day Picnic and to Christine's surprise her Mutter came escorted by Henry Hasse and his two small children. Christine knew Herr Hasse, a close neighbor of theirs, had recently become widowed. At first Christine was a little taken back to see her Mutter with a man other than her Vater.

As she pondered the situation, she began thinking, *It is over a year since Vater's death. How could I deny my Mutter the need to have a man provide for her as well as have the chance for companionship? I could not.*

A little after that, she thought: *I believe this is Providence. With my Mutter's mind attending to her own courtship, perhaps she will be less focused on mine.*

Later when the youth choir finished their last song and the applause finally died down, Christine quickly slipped over to her Mutter and said, "Mutter, please bring Herr Hasse over to meet Herr Brodbeck and his Bruder, Johann."

Mrs. Behrens followed dutifully along between her daughter and Herr Hasse. After the introductions, Christine again took the lead and said to Herr Brodbeck, "I am certain we have plenty of food to share with you and your Bruder. Would you please join us at our table?"

"That would depend on your Mutter as well as my Bruder." Jacob slightly nodded and bowed in Mrs. Behrens's direction to offer his respect.

"Ja, ja, Herr Brodbeck. We would be delighted for you and your Bruder to join us. Herr Hasse has brought his homemade sauerkraut and we have many pies and cakes to share. Bitte, join us."

When Jacob gave Johann a look to ascertain his choice, he nodded and said, "Ja, I am happy for the food and the company."

The sunny and busy day with its speeches, domino games, horseshoes, and other contests turned into a balmy, breezy spring night. Johann joined the dance band on several occasions to play his harmonica. Jacob danced first with Frau Behrens to a Schottishe. They all enjoyed the "Herr Schmidt" dance. They swapped partners now and then to the waltzes and polkas. The first strains of the Lilly Dale Waltz found Jacob and Christine standing side by side. Then, as if it was meant to be, it was natural to glide away together to the waltz's swaying rhythms.

At one point, Jacob looked down at Christine and in the same moment, she looked up at him. A dazzling smile lit up her face. She leaned in a little closer so that only Jacob could hear her when she said, "This is the happiest moment of my entire life, Jacob. I wish it would last forever."

Christine's choice of Jacob's Christian name had not escaped him.

*****

After the picnic, Jacob found he had trouble focusing on the air ship. Even Johann noticed Jacob spent more time doing odd jobs here and there than he had before. And it seemed the odd jobs here and there often brought him by the school house just as Miss Christine was walking home from school for the day. Jacob walked her home, letting his trusty horse trot along behind them.

When working on his air ship in the cabin, Jacob often discovered himself filled with thoughts and visions of Christine instead of thoughts and visions of his air ship.

On one such occasion, Johann looked up from the candlelight where he was reading, and noticed Jacob staring out the window in a dream-like trance.

"Jacob, what are you seeing out that window?" Johann inquired.

"What . . . uh . . . oh . . . nothing. I . . . I was just thinking."

"Thinking about the same blueprint you have been working on for the past two weeks?"

"Ja, I guess I am not making such good progress lately."

"Perhaps, mein Bruder, it is not so easy to work when your heart is in two different places."

"Is it so obvious?"

"Ja, it is. And what is also obvious is that I better start looking for another place to live before long."

As it turned out, Johann did not move. Instead, that winter, Jacob accepted a new teaching position at the Grape Creek School. With a little extra income as well as his part time jobs, Jacob felt he could make a move.

Jacob rode to Castell to the Hasse home where Christine's mother now resided. He wanted her permission to ask for Christine's hand in marriage before asking Christine.

*****

A few months later . . . February 9, 1858

The wedding took place at the Vereins Kirche with Pastor Dangers presiding. Christine wore her Mutter's wedding dress which was handed down from her Mutter before her. Made of muslin, it featured a square neckline bordered with hand-tatted lace. The empire waistline was trimmed in the same lace. The dress draped smoothly down from the bodice to the floor. The hem was banded with six inches of delicate muslin lace which flowed into a train a yard long in the back. It thrilled Christine she was about the same size as both her Mutter and Oma and she could wear this priceless heirloom. Besides, she loved the early nineteenth century dress styles. To her, they were simpler and more elegant than the day's current bouffant skirts and petticoats.

To the bride and groom, the time honored words of the marriage vows seemed brand new and fresh because this day, the words were spoken to and for the two of them.

"Eternal God, our creator and redeemer, as you gladdened the wedding at Cana in Galilee by the presence of your Son, so by His presence bring Your joy to this wedding. Look in favor upon Jacob Frederick Brodbeck and Maria Christine Sophie Behrens and grant that they, rejoicing in all Your gifts, may at length celebrate with Christ the marriage feast which has no end."

And thus Pastor Dangers began the marriage ceremony which ended with the bride and groom joining hands and looking into each other's eyes as they each repeated after the Pastor their vows . . .

"I, Jacob Frederick Brodbeck, in the presence of God and these witnesses, take you, Maria Christine Sophie Behrens, to be my wife, to have and to hold from this day forward, for better, for worse, for richer, for poorer, in sickness and in health, to love and to cherish, until death parts us, and I pledge you my faithfulness."

Neither took their eyes off the other as Christine repeated her vows to Jacob.

When they exchanged their rings, Jacob, in his nervousness dropped Christine's ring, but caught it in his vest. A slight ripple of laughter spread across the congregation.

They each repeated, "Receive this ring as a pledge and token of wedded love and faithfulness."

Pastor Dangers led the bride and groom to the altar where he wrapped his stole around the ring hands of the bride and groom, saying:

"Grant Your blessings, O Lord, to Your servants Jacob and Christine that they be ever mindful of their solemn pledge and, trusting in Your mercy, abound evermore in love all their days; through Jesus Christ, our Lord. Amen."

The bride and groom kneeled, and Pastor Dangers said, "Now that Jacob and Christine have consented together in holy matrimony and have given themselves to each other by their solemn pledges, and have declared the same before God and these witnesses, I pronounce them to be husband and wife, in the name of the Father and of the Son and of the Holy Spirit.

What God has joined together, let man not separate. Amen."

The Pastor then led the couple and the congregation in the Lord's Prayer.

At the end of the prayer, Jacob and Christine stood and turned to face the congregation. Pastor Dangers introduced the bride and groom to the congregation, "May I now present to you, Mr. and Mrs. Jacob Brodbeck."

*****

When the festivities of the day were over, Jacob and Christine suspected that a shivaree would take place soon after they blew out the lantern in the cabin Jacob had found for them near Grape Creek. So they decided to go to bed with their clothes on . . . ready for the revelers when they arrived.

Lying side by side so close, but fully clothed, was strange but still exhilarating for each of them. A few awkward moments passed, and then both of them spoke at once.

Laughing quietly, Jacob whispered, "Ladies first."

Christine whispered back, "Do you think they are out there, yet?"

"Maybe . . . but I think their plan is to wait as long as they can in order to surprise us."

"So we are whispering so they cannot hear us and will think we are asleep," Christine surmised.

"Ja, but chances are, they will not think that," he chuckled.

"Oh, Jacob, why not light the lantern, go outside, and invite them inside since we know they are out there and they know we are in here?"

"Because, mein lieber Schatz, that would spoil the fun of the occasion."

They lay still for what seemed at least thirty minutes to Christine. Just when she was about to fall asleep, the worst clanging, banging, and yelling Christine ever heard exploded outside their window.

By the time Jacob had their lantern lit and scrambled to their front door to open it, they spied their friends and neighbors coming out from behind bushes and trees ringing cow bells, beating on pots and pans and hollering loud enough to wake the dead. They came from all directions holding canned goods, baked goods, one pound bags of coffee, pound bags of salt, pound bags of ground meal, a pound of this and a pound of that. Everyone came laughing, slapping Jacob on the back and hugging Christine.

"My goodness, I will not have to cook for a month!" Christine exclaimed. "Look at all this food. It is so much! Oh, danke shörn, everyone!"

Soon someone broke out their fiddle and the music began along with the dancing. There was not much room in their cabin to dance, so soon the couples filled the porch outside as well.

By the time the last soul left, it was nearly two in the morning.

Christine had been nervous and a little scared of their wedding night. Her Mutter had said very little to her. "Just do as your husband tells you to do. Jacob is a kind man and because he is so much older than you, he will be extra gentle with you."

Christine wanted to ask why it was necessary to be "gentle" with her, but her Mutter evaded any further conversation on the matter.

Just as they cleared the last remains of the party, Jacob leaned down to kiss Christine's forehead and said, "We are both so tired tonight. Let us get a good night's rest. Does that meet with your pleasure?"

"Oh, ja, please." Christine hoped her response did not indicate too much relief. As she looked at her husband, he was already yawning as he took her hand to lead her to their bedroom.

> *"I am my beloved's and his desire is towards me."*
> *Song of Solomon 7:10*

Chapter 29
Wedded Bliss

Christine, kneading dough to make bread for their supper, smiled to herself as she marveled at how unbelievable it was she could love Jacob more now than before they married. But truly she did.

She loved and treasured how Jacob prepared her for their lovemaking. As she formed the dough into two loaves, she began reliving it again in her mind almost like it was a scene from a book but with romantic characters other than the two of them . . .

When they had finished breakfast on the morning after the shivaree, Jacob grabbed his Bible, and led her outside on a walk down to Grape Creek. He motioned her around the bend of the creek where he showed her a large rock protruding out over the water.

She clasped her hands together gleefully as she said delightedly, "Oh, Jacob, a 'sitting rock' for me! You remembered how I love to sit and dangle my feet in the water."

"Ja, I remembered. And when I told Johann how you would miss your 'sitting rock' on the banks of the Llano River, he smiled and said, 'Well, it just so happens than I am a mason and I know about rocks.' He and I managed to get this one from Lange's Mill and we brought it here in the buggy."

Then bowing and gesturing his arms towards the rock, he said in a grandiose tone, "Your throne awaits, my lady."

They sat together on her "sitting rock." When she pulled off her shoes, Jacob did, too. With their feet dangling in the water, Jacob put his arm around her and she laid her head on his shoulder. Then he opened his Bible and read Solomon 7:10 to her. "I am my beloved's and his desire is toward me."

Quietly and gently, Jacob explained to her how God designed a man and a wife to make love and become as one. He explained that they both would learn together as he had not lain with a woman before her. He asked when she would want to begin learning together. And she asked shyly, "Would tonight be too soon for you?"

Jacob smiled and kissed her on her temple and said, "Ja! Ja! Tonight is gut!"

Married nearly a month now, Christine thought she and Jacob were really quick learners with the lovemaking part of their lives. She wondered if everyone did as well as they did. Of course, she knew she could not ask or even tell anyone other than her husband. But, my goodness, it seemed the daily chores were not nearly as tedious when she anticipated making love at night. It was quite a wondrous thing to her and she wanted to sing out loud and tell everyone just how happy she felt.

Instead, after her chores were done and before Jacob came home from his teaching and other side jobs, she scampered down to her "sitting rock." There with feet dangling, she sang her heart out to the fishes in the creek, the frogs and turtles, the occasional rabbit, coon or armadillo, and the many birds flitting through the trees. There, too, she also recorded faithfully the daily events in their lives.

This particular day, Jacob stood on the side of a hill about two miles away from where Christine playfully sang to nature around her. With his survey instruments, he worked on one of his side jobs surveying land for the county.

As he worked, he thought about Christine as well. He knew Christine to be passionate about life in general, but he was surprised, and well . . . delighted that her passion also extended to the bedroom. Perhaps it was her tender years and innocence that caused her to be so unabashedly enthusiastic about making love. Though he looked forward to their nights together, he also missed having more time to work on his air ship. Working hard all day, then attending to a young, vivacious wife at night left Jacob with scant time and energy to create the transportation wonder of the future.

*****

A few days later, Johann rode up on horseback at just around suppertime. He had an envelope tucked away in his pocket and he knew Jacob would want to see the contents of the envelope before they saw each other in church on Sunday.

"Wie gehts, Lovebirds! What is cooking for supper?" He sniffed the appealing aromas in the air.

"Prairie chicken stew and cornbread," announced Christine. "I will set out an extra place."

To Jacob, Johann said, "I see you have had to kill some game at last." Then to Christine, "He always insisted that I was a better shot and coerced me into doing most of the hunting."

After supper, the two men sat out on the porch while Christine cleaned the supper dishes.

"Not that you are not always welcome, but what brings you out to our house in mid-week, mein Bruder?" Jacob questioned.

Johann reached inside his shirt pocket and pulled out the envelope. "It must have been Providence I happened to be at the Nimitz Boarding House the same day and hour our dear friend was passing through. He was only there an hour while fresh horses were harnessed to the stagecoach. Do you know of whom I speak?"

"Not Dr. Herff?" exclaimed Jacob.

"Ja, it was he. We were both surprised to see each other. Of course he asked about you and sent his best wishes for yours and Christine's happiness. We only had moments to talk before his stagecoach would be leaving. He was glad to see me hale and hearty. He asked about the progress on your air machine and I told him what I knew. Before he left, he sat down and wrote this short note for you and put it inside this envelope for me to give to you." Johann handed the envelope to Jacob.

Jacob hurriedly opened the envelope and read the note inside aloud to Johann.

> Greetings, my dear friend,
>
> Please accept my congratulations on your recent marriage and give my regards to your bride.
>
> I may have means for room and board for you; you could work on your air machine here at my ranch in Boerne. It might mean staying away from your home and wife for a few months. I regret the arrangements can accommodate only one.

Saturday next, I will be joining my family here at our home in Boerne which should be only a few hours away from you by horseback. Please come and dine with me.

I shall hope you can accept. Note, I have crudely drawn a map for you on the back of this page.

Regards,
Ferdinand Herff

Jacob looked over at Johann, "Does that mean when I come, I should plan on staying that day?"

"Ja, the letter is not very clear about that. Of course, Dr. Herff was in a hurry. But in my opinion, he surely meant that you should come and be prepared to stay a few months."

Christine came out the door to hear Johann's last few words. "Where would Jacob be prepared to stay for a few months?" she asked with misgiving in her voice.

Chapter 30
A Time Apart

Dr. Herff stood on the balcony of his two-story country home. Spying a lone rider in the distance, he scurried downstairs onto the porch to wave a welcome to his good friend, Jacob.

As Jacob came riding on the part trail and part road from Luckenbach, the first things he noticed were two tall white colonial posts which supported the railed balcony of the modest-sized stone house. Then he caught sight of Dr. Herff waving him onto the premises.

Once the greetings took place and a servant led Jacob's horse to the barn, the two men retired to the drawing room.

"Great news I have for you, Jacob. In San Antonio, a family wants you to give their children piano lessons. They provide room and board for you in exchange. In your spare time, you can complete your plans for your models. When you are ready to build them, you come to the ranch here where you will have plenty of room for experimenting with their flight. That is agreeable with you, ja?"

"Ja, but maybe not so agreeable with my wife. However, before I rode over here, she resigned herself to the fact that I might not be back for a while."

Dr. Herff placed a hand on Jacob's shoulder while he took another puff on his cigar. "Sometimes, difficult it is for men of science to have wives and families. But both your wife, Christine, and my wife, Mathilde, knew before they married us, it would be so. Now let us not tarry. The dinner hour approaches when we have more than enough family talk and questions from Matilde."

With the cigar in mouth, he clapped his hands together in anticipation and declared, "Let us have a look at your latest drawings."

Surprise registered on Dr. Herff's face as he noticed the drawing of a boat attached to the bottom of the aircraft. He read the title of the plans out loud.

"Air ship!" So unlike your toy models, your man-sized craft will have a boat attached?"

"Ja, do you not remember my concern when the air machine flies over water? If it needs to land, it will be able to do so."

Shaking his head in disbelief, Dr. Herff said earnestly, "Jacob, either you have a Gott-given vision or you are somewhat crazy in the head."

"Ja, my neighbors all say, "Er hat grosse Rosinen im Kopf!" ("He has big raisins in his head.")

Both men enjoyed a hearty laugh over the old German saying.

*****

During the next year, Jacob devoted most of his spare time at the Herff ranch where he built many models and experimented with their flight. As of yet, none of them were large enough to hold an aeronaut.

Afterwards, he would ride the two-hour ride over to Luckenbach to be with Christine. By this time, their first son, Henry had been born and another baby was on its way. In order for Johann to be closer to help Christine when Jacob was away, Johann bought a tract of land adjoining Jacob's. On this tract, Johann built a log cabin.

Later, whenever Jacob was home, he and Johann added a two-story rock house which consisted of two rooms over a cellar and a large double room upstairs.

Before the rock house was started, Johann suggested to Jacob, "Bruder, your growing family gets too big for your small cabin, ja? Why not move your family into this house? That way, I could help watch over Christine and the babies."

So with the help of neighbors, the house was finished that same year. Knowing his family was more comfortable, Jacob felt not as anxious about them when he was gone for weeks at a time. By the end of the year, their second son, Edward was born.

In 1865, Jacob needed more money for his experiments. By then, two more children, Hilmar and Matilda, were added to their family, one in 1863 and the other 1865. Jacob and Christine were now the parents of four small children. Jacob could not spend much money on his experiments as he needed the money for his family.

He still had the shares that he and Dr. Herff had created. He felt he was ready to go before the public with his idea of an air ship and shares. He wrote an article about his plans and took it to the San Antonio News. They printed his article; and it was printed again in August of that same year by the Galveston Tri-Weekly News with this introduction by the editor:

We find in the San Antonio News, a call made by Mr. J. Brodbeck of that place, upon the people of the United States to aid by stock subscription in the construction of an "Air ship" constructed on new principles.

As Texas inventions are novelties in the world of art and science, we hasten to lay the call before our readers and the world at large.

The article:

> For more than twenty years, I have labored to construct a machine which should enable man to use, like a bird, the atmospheric region as the medium of his travels. First trying empirical experiments without a guiding idea, I soon satisfied myself that the means heretofore used were hopeless.
>
> I left this barren field and took up the way which had been so successfully followed in modern times by natural science. I studied the flight of birds, examined into the mechanical laws governing these wonderful structures and observed the various peculiarities of the air, and never with the same celerity in every direction, with the wind and against it, not resembling, however in form, a bird; but being constructed like a ship, which has caused me to call it "Air Ship".
>
> A small model constructed in that year proved by successful experiments with some improvements in the model, resulted still more favorably.
>
> The blockade, and the state of the country during the war prevented me from progressing in the invention and from opening a new era in

intercommunication by a larger ship, arranged for practical purposes, but now I hold it to be my duty, after those impediments do no longer exist, to follow without hesitation the path shown me by Providence and the spirit of progress.

The construction of a large "Air Ship" requires more means than I possess by this surely should not be an insupportable difficulty.

Should I not be justified to call upon the aid of my fellowmen who will be all, directly or indirectly, benefited by the result of my invention?

I have therefore concluded to collect subscriptions, in order to build, under the protection of a United States caveat a large "Air Ship" and then to take out a patent. These subscriptions I shall not ask as donations, but as shares, to be refunded together with a part of the proceeds of the sale of "Air Ships", as the case may be, I have put the price of one share at five dollars.

Every shareholder will receive a certificate, securing to him a proportionate interest in the proceeds of the enterprise.

I will give a few ideas indicating generally the character of the airship, and what it will be able to accomplish.

The airship consists of three main parts:

1. The lower suspended portion, formed like a ship with a short prow to cut the air; it serves to hold the aeronaut, as also the power of producing engine with all the steering apparatus. This portion

is shut up all around to prevent the rapid motion from affecting the breathing of the man within.

In this, as low as possible, lies the center of gravity of the whole structure, so as to steady the motion.

At the back end of the ship, there is a propeller screw which will make it possible to navigate in the water, in case, that by any accident the aeronaut should have to descend while he is above water. In this case, the ship can be detached from the flying apparatus.

2. The upper portion, or flying apparatus, which makes use of the resistance of the air, consists of a system of wings, partly movable, partly immovable, presenting the appearance of horizontal sails, but having functions entirely different from sails of vessels.

3. The portions producing the forward motion consists either of two screws, which can be revolved with equal or unequal motion, so as to serve the purpose of lateral steering, or of wings of a peculiar construction. The preference to be given to one or the other depends on the nature of the motive power.

Another apparatus regulates the ascending motion. The material is so selected as to combine the greatest strength with the least weight. When the airship is in motion, the aeronaut has in each hand a crank, one to guide the ascending and descending motion, the other the lateral steerage. Immediately before him is the compass, while a barometer with a scale made for the purpose, show him the approximated height. Another apparatus, similar to the ball regulator of a steam engine, shows him the velocity, as well as the distance passed over. It is self-evident that the speed of the airship depends upon the motive power and on the direction of the winds; according to my experiments and calculations it will be from 30 to 100 miles per hour.

Signed:

> *"Where there is no vision, the people perish . . ." Proverbs 29:18*

Chapter 31
Flight Plans

After the article appeared in the papers and posted around town in Fredericksburg, Jacob traveled to different settlements and found growing interest in his air ship. Quite a few friends and neighbors gave Jacob their support and bought shares.

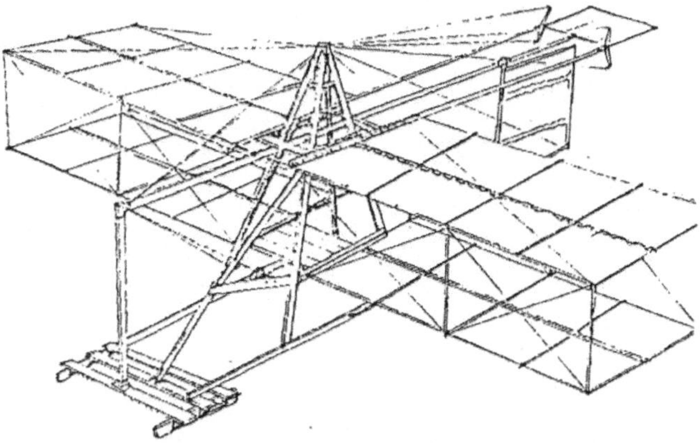

By late August, he had collected enough money to finish his air ship. He knew as soon as possible he needed to give a demonstration to his backers to prove to them his air ship would fly.

The next Saturday, when he was on the Herff ranch working on the last stages of his air ship, he heard a familiar voice behind him.

"Jacob, I join my family for the weekend. Come have a schnapps with me while we talk about your air ship, ja?"

"Ja, that sounds gut to me!" Jacob was glad for a short rest from his work.

After they were settled with their drinks on the Herff's porch, Dr. Herff got down to business.

"Jacob, I hear much talk from my patients and around the communities about your air ship. Das ist gut, ja? Your first flight, it is soon now, ja?"

"Ja, I believe it is ready for flight in about two weeks at the most," answered Jacob.

"Have you thought about where you make your first flight?"

Hesitantly, Jacob replied, "Because it is assembled here, I hoped you might allow it to take place here."

Dr. Herff let out a loud guffaw, "Why, of course, my good fellow. Did you not take that for granted? Nein, I meant where on the ranch did you plan to begin your flight?"

Jacob breathed a sigh of relief for he had not taken this for granted. He did not want to transport his air ship for fear of something happening to it.

"Ja, I thought the meadow just south of your barn is a good place. I plan to have friends and neighbors help me build a structured platform about twenty feet high. The air ship would be hoisted on the platform to give it extra lift for take-off. Would this meet with your approval?"

"Ja, that is fine with me. Speaking of lift makes me think of thrust. Months ago we talked about power. Too heavy the steam engine is . . . did you ever locate any other power for your large model other than the spring power you used in your toy models?"

"Nein, I have studied flight for the past twenty years. Long have I studied George Cayley's aerodynamic ideas. Recently he used a human to engineer the power for a plane, but that would only give short spurts of flight. One day, someone will invent a lighter power source, this I know . . . perhaps even I will. I hope that my aerodynamic ideas will hasten that invention. Until then, I use only what I have . . . a coiled spring which I will endeavor to rewind myself in air or discover yet some way for it to rewind itself. You know that I invented a self-winding clock. I want to be able to use the same principle in flight. That, however, takes time and money— two things that are not in abundance for me."

"Ach, my friend . . . science is not a benevolent master. But my support and prayers go out to you!"

"Danke, I need both of them."

*****

Warm, but slightly dry air settled over the hills of the Texas Hill Country the week before September 20, 1865, the date chosen by Jacob and Dr. Herff for the first flight of the air ship. Jacob, having left the employee of the Hearst family after their children were too old for more piano lessons, was between jobs. Having done all he could to the air ship, he decided that he wanted to spend the week with Christine and the children. Needing to mend a few fences with his wife over his long absences, he also wanted to reassure her about the upcoming flight.

Arriving home just at suppertime, he was met with the usual exuberance from his wife and children. Christine was always so happy to see him—at first. It was only later when her anger and frustration from his absence surfaced to torment both of them.

After the children were down for the night, the adults sat on the porch for dessert and coffee. Knowing the two of them needed to talk, Johann soon excused himself for an early bedtime.

Christine began, "My Mutter comes for a visit this next week. Her husband and my Bruders go to San Antonio for supplies for her husband's store."

Jacob's eyes lit up. "How wunderbar! She can help you travel with the children to see my flight on Saturday. This allows Johann to go with me early instead of with you."

Christine looked away from Jacob's relieved face to hide her own dejected one. "Always you must rely on someone to be with me and the children. What a burden we must be to you, my husband."

"Ach, Liebchen, I did not mean it that way," soothed Jacob.

"Nein, perhaps you did not. But the reality is your children often call your Bruder, Papa, instead of you or have you not noticed?"

Jacob confessed, "Ja, I notice. That is why I am here for this week . . . to spend more time with you and with them. But what about Saturday? I want you by my side for this most important event of my life."

Again Christine turned her head away from Jacob's enthusiastic face to hide her own resolute one. "Jacob, you have not needed me by your side all these months of trial and error, success and failure . . . why now?"

"Ach, Liebchen, please try to understand. It was not that I did not need you, but a situation of practicality. You know that. But this! This is a time when you can be there—when I need you and the children there to see what I have done—to be proud of me!"

"Nein, if indeed you do soar up in the air as you predict you will, I cannot take the chance of the children watching you fall from the air and break into bits and pieces. Nor can I watch it! It is too much you ask of us this time, Jacob, too much!"

Jacob could feel the heat of anger rising up his neck into his cheeks. He took several deep breaths to calm himself and then waited until he found an even voice.

"Perhaps I have been wrong for not allowing you to know more about the inner workings of my air ship. It would allow you to trust that I will fly and trust that I know what I am doing."

"Ja, trust is the right word, Jacob. You could not trust me to help you and be by your side during these past months and I cannot trust you know what you are doing. Nein, your wife stays here. I stay to pray for your safety and I stay to pray after this is done, you come home to us where you belong."

With that final word, Christine rose and went into the house. Jacob knew better than to follow her and try to change her mind. He knew Christine's mind was set. He knew when Christine set her mind to something, wild horses could not change it.

The rest of the week, Jacob did his best to be a good husband and father. Christine, for her part, did the same. It was as if the first night on the porch never happened. But Jacob knew Christine, no matter how jovial and fun-loving she was playing games with the children, would not change her mind.

Jacob and Johann rode off before dawn on Friday morning while the children still slept. Christine had requested it that way. She did not want the children to see them leave. She did not come out to say good-bye or wish them well. Instead, she kneeled down beside their empty bed, and allowed herself to cry her heart out as the bed covering muffled her sobs.

Chapter 32
First Flight

Until daylight, both men rode along in silence. Jacob, struggling with two diverse emotions, needed time to process them. He felt devastated by the sadness he left behind, and at the same time, he felt exuberant for what lie ahead. Johann, for his part, sensed his brother's confusion and decided it prudent to let Jacob speak when he felt ready.

As the first rays of a brilliant sunrise streaked through the spreading branches of the old oaks along the trail, Jacob spoke, "Ach, my Bruder, what I feared if I married Christine has happened. I am not a good husband to her, nor a good father to our children. She is very unhappy with me."

Johann chose not to speak right away. Instead, he let some moments pass as he gathered appropriate words that might both ease his brother's conscience and clear his mind for the upcoming event.

"Mein Bruder, a decision to marry is not a decision by one party, but by two." Raising his hand to cut off Jacob's denial before he uttered it, Johann went on, "Ach, do not tell me she was too young to make that decision. Old for her years, Christine was then and is now, and besides, you asked her Mutter before you asked Christine. Anyway, you would have had to ride off into Indian country to escape Christine's dogged determination for you two to marry.

Nein, mein Bruder, love chose you and Christine. You had little choice, so let the past be the past. For today,

Christine is safe with her Mutter and her children. And I believe that was the best choice for all of you. Your mind must be focused on your flight in the sky and not on your family on the ground. Today keep your mind on operating your machinery with skill so that when you do come back to earth, you can go to Christine and improve your skills as a husband and a father."

Jacob smiled at his brother and said, "How is it that my younger Bruder knows better how to put problems into perspective than I do?"

"Because your Bruder has the benefit of seeing it from two vantage points."

"Meaning yours and mine?"

"Nein, meaning yours and Christine's."

"Then, that would be three, counting you," teased Jacob.

"Ja, I suppose so," Johann agreed.

"So, Christine discusses her troubles with you?" continued Jacob.

"Ja, what do you think? She has no one else when you are not there."

"And do you sympathize with her and guide her while trying to remain neutral?" prompted Jacob.

"Ja, of course, what do you think?" defended Johann again.

"Ach, mein Bruder, why did Christine not choose you instead of me? You are so much better suited for each other than we are," sighed Jacob.

"Because she saw you first and from that first moment, there was no one for her except you. Surely, you know that," answered Johann.

"Ach, well I do . . . well I do," Jacob admitted. "But you are right about today. Today I must concentrate solely on my experiment for tomorrow."

The two men rode along in silence for some time. Then Jacob opened up the conversation again.

"The thing that concerns me most about tomorrow is will I be able to rewind the giant coiled spring fast enough once it has been unwound? The apparatus I have constructed takes me about ten minutes to rewind the spring on the ground. I am hoping like a bird glides on the wind currents, my air ship's wing designs will glide on the currents and give me the time I need to rewind the spring for more power to stay aloft. Does this make sense to you, mein Bruder?"

"Ja, it makes sense, but it is a big chance you take, mein Bruder. We shall pray to our heavenly Vater you fly like a dove, ja?" encouraged Johann.

"Ja, for sure, for a dove flies straight ahead and glides on the wind currents."

*****

As planned, friends and neighbors arrived early on the day of September 20, 1865, to help Jacob and Johann hoist the air ship on top of the twenty-foot platform they had constructed.

When the air ship was mounted on the structure, Jacob and Johann slipped off to the side. They took a brief moment to bow their heads and ask Gott to be with him and keep him safe.

The rather large crowd that had now gathered amazed both Jacob and Johann. Johann slapped Jacob on his shoulder and said, “From the looks of all the horses, buggies and wagons, people have come from miles around to see the wonder of your flight, Bruder. Ja, they want to see history in the making."

"Ja, they are curious to see if Schoolmaster Brodbeck can make his man-sized machine fly like his toy models. Many have seen me demonstrate my small models at fairs and community events. But they are wondering if it is possible for this large contraption of wires and wings to actually fly from the twenty- high platform and into the air?"

Jacob noticed the anticipation shining on the many faces in the crowd. But he also felt the nervous tension filtering through the air as well. He could only wonder what his air machine looked like to them—probably like some kind of giant insect resting on a platform.

He saw how the children not knowing what to do, ran too close to the platform. Their mothers had to steer them back to what they hoped was a safe distance.

None of them knew exactly what to expect. Like Johann said, would they see history being made in front of their own eyes? Or would they witness a public disaster?

Jacob had invited his friend, Charles Nimitz, and other military men to come and observe. Nimitz, the proprietor of the Nimitz Boarding House and a Civil War border officer of the Confederate Army, wanted to give a speech in Jacob's honor before the flight took place.

Nimitz spoke mainly to the backers who had bought shares in the air machine. He emphasized the importance of such an invention as Herr Brobeck's air ship to mankind but moreover, to the military.

The tension in the crowd was alleviated somewhat

when Dr. Herff gave his short, but passionate speech explaining Jacob's research and past experiments.

"Herr Brodbeck's air ship has an aeronaut's chamber where he will sit and work the controls. When the craft is in motion, the aeronaut has in each hand a crank, one to guide the ascending and descending motion, the other the lateral steerage. Immediately before him is the compass, while a barometer with a scale made for that purpose, shows him the approximate height. Another apparatus, similar to the ball regulator of a steam engine, shows him the velocity, as well as the distance passed over."

After stopping to catch his breath, Dr. Herff announced, "Now step back. Let us watch and see Herr Brodbeck fly like a bird!"

Jacob had dreamed and planned for this day for over twenty years. Now the time had come. He shook hands with his friends and hugged Johann.

An eerie silence swept over the spectators as Jacob climbed the platform and walked over to the machine. With unusual composure, he eased himself inside the aeronaut's chamber.

Taking a few seconds to adjust himself, he took a deep breath. He reached over to cut the rope loose and release the lever for take-off. As the propeller started turning—the machine wobbled and began to move. With the spring driving the propeller, the crazed creature took flight!

Expressions of wonder spread over the crowd as they watched it rise off the platform and into the air. It was hard to believe what they were seeing. Then, like the suddenness of the flight itself, they erupted with cheers and applause.

Jacob, up in the aircraft, was too frantic to hear the roar of the crowd below. The aircraft was treetop high and its coil power was running out fast. He had to wait for it to completely unwind before he could rewind it. Now came the moment of truth: would the aircraft glide on the wind currents as he hoped while he rewound the coil spring? With all his might, he worked at the apparatus to rewind the spring coil. He needed to work faster. He could feel the machine gliding all right, but gliding downward. Almost before he realized it, the propeller fluttered to a stop. Steering it the best he could, he braced himself for the crash.

The machine plowed into the ground leaving a jumble of twisted wires and splintered wood.

The crowd rushed forward. Would the fallen schoolmaster be crushed and mangled . . . or even dead?

Jacob surprised everyone. Crawling to find a way to extract himself from under the crumbled air ship, he pushed aside the broken metal, dangling wires, and shards of wood until he surfaced all in one piece—except for a few bruises and abrasions.

> *"And I said, Oh that I had wings like a dove!*
> *For then would I fly away and be at rest."*
> *Psalm 55:6*

Chapter 33
A Change of Direction

Dr. Herff advised Jacob to remain at the Herff country home to recuperate so Johann rode the two-hour horseback ride back to their Luckenbach farm to let Christine know what had happened.

Jacob laid on the bed in the guest bedroom as Dr. Herff examined him.

"Jacob, look at my hand. How many fingers do you see?" Dr. Herff held up two fingers in front of Jacob's face.

Jacob, a little irritated, sat up and grumbled, "Two! Dr. Herff! Bitte, I am fine. What I want to know is how far did I fly? How high did I go? Are there any backers left to give me another chance? What did they say to you after the crash?"

"Whoa . . . Jacob, there is time for all your questions when I finish your examination. A fall like that could cause a concussion. You fell from about 25 to 30 feet!"

Jacob moaned, "Is that all . . . it felt much higher," then wincing with pain, he grabbed his head.

"Ach du lieber, Jacob! Lie back down. You must lie still and let me finish what I am doing," demanded Dr. Herff.

When the examination was over, Dr. Herff felt satisfied there were no serious consequences. He instructed Jacob to rest the remainder of the afternoon before he could ask any more questions. Jacob relented, and much to his surprise, fell asleep almost immediately.

*****

Johann rode onto the Brodbeck farm and dismounted as Henry and Edward came running up to greet him.

"Where is Papa? Did he die?" Six year old Henry looked up at his uncle anxiously while four year old Edward looked on with huge inquiring eyes.

Johann kneeled down to be at the boys' level. "Nein, your Papa is fine. He is resting back at the Herff ranch." Johann gathered the two young boys in his arms.

Christine waited on the porch holding baby Mathilda on one hip and holding two-year- old Hilmar by his hand on her other side.

The older boys ran back to the porch with Henry hollering, "Papa did not die!"

Four-year-old Edward ran after him repeating, "Nein, Papa did not die!"

"Of course, he did not die! What made you think that?" Christine was alarmed at what her boys were yelling.

Henry said slyly, "Sometimes we sit on the stairs in the dark and listen to you and Uncle Johann talk."

Christine and Johann gave each other exasperated looks. Then Christine assailed Johann with her questions.

*****

Jacob woke up to a heavenly aroma. There across his lap was a tray full of steaming hot potato soup along with slices of fresh baked bread lathered with butter and dewberry preserves.

Dr. Herff sat across from him and said, "I thought a light supper might be in order. Are you hungry?"

"Ja, I am, indeed. Danke shörn for all your care." As Jacob sat up to partake of his meal, he suddenly felt sore all over and just a little light-headed.

"Ach, be careful. Take it slowly. You have lacerations and bruises on your head, arms, and chest. One of your ankles is swollen and may be sprained, but other than that, you are one lucky fellow." Dr. Herff finished his assessment.

After he ate, Dr. Herff began answering Jacob's earlier questions. "Jacob, your air ship, as you like to call it, rose about twelve feet, traveled about a hundred feet and was up in the air for about sixty seconds. Quite an accomplishment for your first flight! I am sad to say, that it did not impress any of your backers and they all withdrew their support."

"Ach, Dr. Herff, I just know that if I could increase my speed at take-off, I would get more lift. If I get more lift, I will have more time aloft to rewind my coil spring."

"And how do you plan to increase your speed, Jacob?" Dr. Herff asked earnestly.

"I am not sure, yet. But I know it can be done," insisted Jacob.

"But you must have more money to rebuild another airship and even then, it may crash as well, ja?" Dr. Herff reasoned.

"Ja, that is true. And right now, I am between jobs," Jacob admitted.

"What about the idea you had for an ice making machine?" Dr. Herff paused, "I have recently become associated with the La Costa Ice Company and we would be interested in such an invention.

"In a few days when you are better able to travel, why not go home and get started on your idea? Your wife and family will be happy to have you home for a while and I will be happy to give you an advance on your machine to get you started. Perhaps switching your mind from one invention to another, might actually give rise to a surprise solution you had not even imagined. That often happens to me. Sometimes when I am not thinking about a medical problem I am experiencing, out of nowhere, a possibility comes to my mind."

"Ach, Dr. Herff . . . you are a wise man. And ja, my Christine truly aches to have me home again. Danke, I accept," agreed Jacob gratefully.

The two men worked out terms agreeable to both of them. In two days, Jacob rode home with money in his pocket. He smiled as he imagined the pleasure he would see on his wife's face when she learned that his work would take him no farther than the backyard shed. For a while, at least, Jacob must be satisfied to look out his window and watch the doves fly instead of being up in the clouds flying beside them.

> *"Who are these that fly as a cloud and as the doves to their windows?" Isaiah 60:8*

Chapter 34
Hopeful Anticipation

As soon as Jacob got settled, he started working on the idea for the ice making machine. Soon he knew the small shed would not house his tools for the ice making machine and even less, his plans to rebuild his air ship.

It was not long before he and Johann began building a workshop for Jacob. They built a story and a half building, which would serve as a storage building for the air ship when it was repaired. The higher roof would also provide a launching pad for the air ship. Even though the workshop was close to the house, Jacob and Johann built a rock wall in back of it which offered some protection against a possible renegade Indian raid.

When the building was completed, Jacob and Johann took a flatbed wagon and went to Dr. Herff's ranch to get the damaged air machine. When they returned, some of the neighbors came over and helped them lift the structure from the wagon into the workshop.

*****

That winter, Jacob came down with a siege of arthritis and took to his bed for several weeks. Christine had her hands full tending to him and her four small children.

Early one morning, Christine woke Jacob to ask, "Jacob, I need a few things from town. Do you think you could manage to watch the boys while the baby and I ride into town?"

The mornings being the worst times for his arthritic pain, Jacob requested, "Could you wait until Johann can get them for you tomorrow after his work?"

"Nein, he is staying in town for a meeting tomorrow night. Besides, I need to select some material to make more pants for Henry—he grows too fast for me. I will give the children instructions to remain in the front yard. They are good boys and can even bring things to you when you need them."

"Ja, you go along. We will manage," Jacob relented with some reluctance.

An hour or so later, Henry, Edward, and Hilmar were playing out in the front yard. Their laughter and enjoyment of their game kept them from noticing two young Indian braves riding up and encircling the small boys.

Soon the boys' screams alerted Jacob that something was wrong. Limited in motion, Jacob crawled to the door on his all fours. Not knowing what else to do, Jacob rose to his knees with his hands raised high above his head and let out a fierce and threatening scream.

During his illness, Jacob had grown a long white beard. He wondered if the Indians believed they were encountering a great white spirit when they saw and heard him. He was relieved when they decided not to find out and made a hasty departure.

*****

Several years later . . .

Jacob worked alternately on the ice making machine and repairing his air ship. The time seemed to creep by for

Jacob. He would much rather work full time improving his air ship. Even though Jacob took on jobs of teaching music, repairing pianos, and building furniture, his income remained meager.

Things looked up when he and Christine acquired more land. They bought one 500 acre tract for fifty cents an acre. Then Jacob secured an adjoining 320 acre tract which was being sold for back taxes for the nifty sum of $6.00. Their livestock now had ample grazing land. This provided them the extra money needed to support their growing family.

By the summer of 1874, Jacob finished both the ice making machine for Dr. Herff and the repairs on his air ship. He had tinkered with a few designs on the coil-winding apparatus and thought he would be able to rewind it faster than before. Also, he had devised a way to wind the coil tighter, thereby, giving the airship more thrust. He felt he was ready for another trial run.

Jacob asked his neighbors to help Johann and him hoist the airship on the roof of the workshop. One such neighbor was Henry Habenicht. He was more than a good neighbor—he had come to have faith in Jacob's inventions after seeing Jacob's ice making machine work. Herr Habenicht thought Jacob a very brave and smart man. Rounding up some townspeople, he wanted more eyewitnesses to see Jacob's next marvel.

This time, however, there were no speeches from famous people. Jacob's reputation suffered from the first event.

Jacob also learned another lesson from the previous flight: he permitted Christine and the children to help where they could in the repairs of the airship. This allowed them better understanding of how it worked. As a result, they seemed less frightened about his safety.

Before taking off, Jacob bowed his head and offered this prayer:

> "Our Heavenly Vater,
> Today, I look forward to flying like a bird again. Help me to fly as one of Your doves and ride the wings of Your wind. Let me glide to earth as one of Your majestic eagles.
> Amen."

With a kiss from Christine, hugs to his children, handshakes to Johann and the neighbors, Jacob climbed to the roof of the one and half story building. With a wave to those below, he climbed into the aeronaut's seat.

Just as before, the airship took off quickly. Jacob felt sure that he went faster than before and higher. He soared over the stately old oak trees on his farm. But again, just as before, he could not rewind the coil fast enough, and the airship did not ride the wind currents as Jacob planned. He soon crashed in his nearby cornfield.

Once more bruised and somewhat battered, Jacob crawled out from under the mass of wires and wings. As he took time to stand up on his own, he saw Johann running as fast as he could toward the crash site. Seeing his brother standing steadily on his own, he shouted to Jacob, "Jacob, I timed your flight. This time you flew two minutes and flew twice as far! What a success!"

Chapter 35
A Matter of Trust

After Jacob's body healed, he began thinking he needed to get his ideas of flight to people in other parts of the United States . . . people who had lived for more time in the United States and no longer had to fight the perils of pioneer life.

He knew his oldest brother Johannes had a son, Michael, who had come to America and settled in Ann Arbor, Michigan, in 1872. He had even written months ago to his family in Germany asking for Michael's address, so he could write to him and inquire about a visit, but as of yet, he had not heard from them. Jacob knew his skills would allow him to find odd jobs along the way to Michigan to pay for his room and board plus train fare.

As for his family, he had managed to save back money over the past nine years just in case he came upon some source of power for his air ship that might cost a sizable sum. He had not made that discovery, and so now, he could leave that money with Christine while he was gone. He knew Johann would see after his family during his absence.

To that end, he approached Johann first with his plan. Expecting to garner Johann's support as usual, he was surprised at Johann's reaction.

"Nein, Jacob, you ask too much this time. Not of me, but of Christine and the children. For the past nine years, you have made good your word to be a good husband and father. Your wife and children depend on your love and guidance. You cannot take it away from them now when they have grown so used to it!" Johann's face grew flushed with exasperation.

"Ach, Johann, that is just the reason I can go away for awhile. They are secure now. Henry is sixteen and the youngest one, Mathilda, is nine. They are old enough to help their mother now."

"Ja, but Jacob . . . your boys approach manhood now. They need you to guide them in their choices for trades and skills. And what about their education? You, who have helped others with their education by establishing schools and teaching our youth, you want to leave your own sons' futures to someone else?"

"Another good point, Johann. Because of these schools, I can leave my sons' education in yours and my wife's hands. Johann, you have always been behind me with my dream. Why not, now?" pleaded Jacob.

Johann realized the two of them stood face to face yelling at each other as if they were one hundred feet apart instead of the two feet separating them. He turned and sat down on a bench in the workshop where this debate was occurring.

Jacob took his brother's cue and sat down as well. He fully comprehended if Johann was set against his plan, he could never win Christine over to it. Instinct and knowledge of his brother's nature told Jacob that given a little time and gentle persuasion, Johann might agree to his plan.

Finally, Johann spoke, but in a much calmer voice than before, "What you have to make me understand, mein Bruder, is how can this venture you want to take mean more to you than the happiness of your lovely wife and beautiful children?"

For the first time in a long while, Jacob looked into his brother's eyes and saw something he had not noticed—loneliness. Why, of course, why had he been so stupid and blind? Jacob had everything Johann longed for and had wanted with his Katarina. And here Jacob was willing to set it aside for awhile in order to follow a dream— a dream that heretofore, led to nothing but hurt and heartache.

Jacob walked over and sat next to Johann on the bench. "Ach, my younger and gentler Bruder. What an ignoramus I am. I am sorry for my thoughtlessness. Do you object so much because you wish you had a family such as mine?"

Johann, a little ashamed of his brother seeing into his soul, hung his head and nodded "Ja . . . at times."

With his arms around his brother's shoulders, Jacob asked earnestly, "Have Christine and I depended on you so much you had no time to have your own family? I suppose Christine and I always assumed you were a confirmed bachelor and never bothered to ask if we imposed upon you with our family needs."

"Nein, I love your children as my own . . . you know that. But ja, at times, when I see you and Christine together, I imagine what it would have been like had Katarina lived. But the love I had for Katarina was so strong, there was never anyone else who came even close to what I felt for her. Finally, I do not even bother to look anymore. And ja, it may be my life is so full with you and your family I do not have a need to fill my life with anything else."

"So help me understand. Do you object to my going away because then you certainly would have no time for a chance at love even if it came to you?"

Johann was about to answer when shrill screams for help came from outdoors.

Both men jumped up at once and ran outside. Face down on the ground under the large oak tree where the children had a tree house, lay Matilda sprawled out and gasping for breath.

Hilmar stood over her and Edward came scrambling down from the tree house.

"Papa," Hilmar cried, "She fell from the tree house. She is dying and I am to blame."

Johann assured Hilmar that Matilda was not dying while Jacob turned Mathilda over.

"There, there . . . my liebchen, just relax. You had the wind knocked out of you. Take slow breaths and it will come back to you," soothed Jacob.

Later that night, when all was well, Johann excused himself to take an early bedtime.

Christine noticed Johann's early bedtime and commented, "Is there something bothering Johann? Quiet he was during supper and early to bed, also."

Jacob looked away from Christine when he answered, "Perhaps he was just tired."

Christine made no further issue of it, saying, "Ja, perhaps so. Ach, Jacob, would you check the hen house? I counted one less hen today and a couple of nests disturbed. There may be a coyote coming to call."

Jacob nodded and grabbed his shotgun, glad for the excuse for some alone time.

Once outside, he let his eyes adjust to the faint light of the half moon. He decided he could see well enough to investigate any unwanted intruders.

Positioning himself near the roosting hens, he settled down to thoughts of his earlier conversation with Johann. The troubled look on Johann's face immediately sprang into his mind's eye. *Why have I not noticed Johann's unhappiness before tonight?* Jacob berated himself.

"O my Gott," he prayed, "Forgive my thoughtlessness towards mein Bruder and help me understand his needs better."

Meanwhile, Johann lay in his bed also thinking about the prior conversation with Jacob. He pondered whether to tell Jacob the whole truth about why he so firmly objected to Jacob leaving on what would surely turn out to be months and months away from home. But he thought, *how do you tell your Bruder you may be in love with his wife? That you are afraid of how strong your feelings are toward her and being left alone with her is pure torture?*

> *"O send out thy light and thy truth; let them lead me . . ." Psalm 43:3*

Chapter 36
Secrets

A quiet, but unsettling mood hung over the Brodbeck home during the next few weeks. Jacob, deciding not to mention his dreams of visiting Michigan again to Johann or at all to Christine, had little to say otherwise. Johann, relieved his brother did not mention his Michigan trip again, said little for fear he might divulge both his own and his brother's secrets.

Christine had a secret of her own; she was with child, again. It had been nine years now since her last baby. She just assumed she was through with childbearing. She had suspected she was carrying a child for a few months now, but for some reason, wanted to get used to her condition before she told anyone.

Frankly, she did not want to give up the freedom she had now. With her children old enough take care of themselves as well as help out with all the chores, she had time to read and write in her journal, her favorite pastimes. She also enjoyed the quilting bees with her neighbors without the responsibility of an infant in tow.

The arrival of a letter soon brought two of the secrets to the surface.

Returning from a shopping trip to town, Christine laid the letter on the kitchen table. Both Jacob and Johann came in from work around the same time that day.

"Jacob, there is a letter waiting for you on the kitchen table. Hurry, it is from your nephew, Michael, in Ann Arbor, Michigan. I am so curious to hear what he has to say," Christine announced.

When Jacob heard this news, he felt a flush creeping up his neck and face. Somehow, he had not received a return letter from his family in Germany, but obviously they had written Michael and given him his address. He desperately wanted to run out to his workshop and read the letter alone, but he knew Christine would have nothing of that; she was already by his side anxiously waiting for him to read the letter. Under his breath, Jacob said a short prayer that somehow Michael would not mention the fact Jacob wanted to come visit him.

Nervously, Jacob began reading the letter aloud to Christine and Johann:

August 10, 1874

Greetings, my Texas German Family:

I send you my warmest wishes. As you may know, for nearly two years now, I live in Ann Arbor, Michigan. I am recently married to a fine local girl, Dorothea, who is also a German immigrant. I work in a factory where pianos and organs are made. It is interesting and I like my work.

Aunt Barbara wrote you desired to come for a visit. You are most welcome to come. Our home is old, but large and comfortable. We encourage you to come and bring your family as well. Indeed, the last two weeks of October is a perfect time for us to have guests; the factory shuts down during those weeks for repairs. I will have the opportunity to show you interesting parts of Ann Arbor and the surrounding areas.

Aunt Barbara wrote of your "air ship." I am most interested in any kind of mechanics; thus, I am deeply curious about your invention. We shall burn the midnight oil going over your designs and sharing news of our families.

Please come! Write back soon to advise me of your plans.

Affectionately,

Your nephew,
Michael

Jacob had not dared to look up during the reading of the letter. Now, he forced himself to look at Christine's bewildered gaze upon him. He waited for her outburst. Surprisingly, quiet and rather resigned, she turned and began preparations for supper.

Both Jacob and Johann exchanged incredulous looks. Then Jacob quickly stepped up behind Christine and put his hands on her shoulders.

"Christine, let the supper wait. We need to talk about this, bitte!" he implored.

Christine only stiffened and said, "Why talk about it now? The time to talk about it was when you wrote to your family in Germany. Your decision was determined then . . . this letter now only confirms it."

Jacob backed up a few steps and looked around to seek help from Johann. But Johann had already slipped out of the room and gone outside.

Forced to face the issue on his own, Jacob again pleaded with Christine, "Nein, Liebchen, the decision is not made . . . only explored. Bitte, let us sit down together and talk about it."

"Jacob, there are four hungry children outside to feed as well as all of us. Mutter always said, 'Big decisions need full stomachs.' There will be time after supper. Now, on with you . . . wash up for supper and tell Johann to do the same. And send Matilda in to set the table, would you, bitte?"

Christine, relieved when Jacob did as she asked, went about her supper duties. But her mind, used to the routine of food preparation, focused itself on this new development in their lives.

She had no choice now but to tell Jacob about the baby. But she had wanted a chance to become happy about it herself before sharing it with Jacob. Now, he would resent the new little life more if it trapped him into staying here with them when wanderlust tugged at his heart. She had known inside it was only a matter of time before Jacob wanted to pursue his dream again. And finally, at last, she had come to accept that part of her husband. For after all, without this huge dream of his, he would not be the Jacob she loved so much.

After supper, Christine asked the children to clear the table and wash the dishes while the adults sat on the porch with their hot coffee. The three of them sat quietly at first, savoring the strong aroma of the coffee as it steamed from their mugs. The hot August sun cast shimmering shadows of heat as it settled behind the tree-lined hills surrounding their Luckenbach farm.

"Jacob, I have an admission to make to you and Johann. As you both know, always, I have resented the times you went away. But over the last nine years, you stayed and became the dearest and sweetest husband to me. You take so much time with our children that it has freed me to pursue some of my interests. Now that the children are older, and can help me so much, I feel the happiest I have been since the day that I met you. I want to thank you for this treasured gift. Ich liebe dich, my husband." Christine leaned over on the swing where she and Jacob sat, and kissed him on the cheek.

Too stunned to speak, Jacob sat for a moment letting Christine's words sink into his psyche. Before he could think of a response, Christine directed her next remarks to Johann.

"And my dear brother-in-law, I do not think I have ever told you just how much you mean to Jacob and the children, but most especially, to me. I want to thank you with my whole heart for all the times your kindness, guidance, and steadiness have helped me to overcome my rash and impulsive nature. Jacob has often teased me that I married the wrong brother," then getting up, Christine walked over to the rocking chair where Johann sat and gave him a hearty hug.

Jacob recovered first, and with a serious face, asked Christine, "My dear, there is something you are not telling us. We already know you appreciate and love us, even though it felt good to be reminded of it just now," then another thought occurred to Jacob and he hurriedly asked, "My dear, you have been quieter than usual lately. Are you ill? Are you coming down with the dreaded cholera?"

Looking down, Christine shook her head quickly, "Oh, nein, I am fine."

"Then what is it?" Jacob persisted.

Still looking down, Christine explained further, "What I was trying to say, my husband, is I am ready for you to follow your dream again. We can manage here just fine . . . of course with Johann willing to help us as always," she looked questioningly at Johann.

Johann smiled that gentle smile of his and answered, "Ja, why not? The horde of women knocking at my door have become frustrated and moved on to better hunting grounds," he joked.

Jacob, ignoring Johann's hint at humor, would not be put off, "Christine, what are you not telling us?"

"My husband, it is very important to me you believe me when I say I want you to go on this trip and I do not want you to feel trapped into staying home with us. Say so and then I will tell you my news."

"Ja, my liebchen, I believe you."

"I am carrying a new life again," Christine said softly.

> *"Charity beareth all things, believeth all things, hopeth all things, endureth all things." 1 Corinthians 13:7*

Chapter 37
A Questionable Journey

Jacob struggled for nearly a fortnight seeking Gott's will for this journey. He had thought having Christine's blessing would bring peace to him; but, it had not. He wanted the peace that passeth all understanding . . . the peace one receives when one knows he is in the will of Gott.

One night as he sat up late by lantern light pondering and praying about his predicament, Johann tiptoed back down the stairs to check on him. Noticing him in the shadows, Jacob whispered, "Ach, did my light keep you awake up there?"

"Nein, but I notice you down here late each night. Why are you not packing? Are you still undecided?" Johann questioned.

"Ja, no matter what Christine says, how could I leave now that she is having another baby?"

"Mein Bruder, may I remind you Hilmar was born while you were in San Antonio?"

"Ja, but I was less than a day away. Over a thousand miles away I would be this time."

"Even so, she had her Mutter and me back then, and she will have both of us again this time. If Christine says for you to go, then she means it."

"Ja, das ist richte. But you, Johann, you say you have changed your mind. Why is that, when you were so against my trip in the beginning?"

"I suppose it is what Christine said . . . she said she loves you for who you are and you are a man with a big dream. You would not be Jacob without that dream.

Neither of us wants to stand in your way of following your heart wherever it leads you."

*****

Jacob left in late September of 1874 and headed for Ann Arbor, Michigan. He left with a heavy heart. Should he have waited until he had the faith soon Gott would lead him in a new discovery or in a different direction?

But he had waited and pondered over his air ship plans patiently at home for nine years. Nothing had materialized. This seemed like such a good opportunity. Surely he needed to take action to make his dream come true. His will to go was stronger than to his patience to wait on Gott's will.

As planned he did many different odd jobs along the way paying for his room and board as well as his train fare.

He arrived in late November of that year. Michael hardly recognized Jacob as he had been only a small boy when Jacob had left Germany for Texas some twenty-eight years ago. They spent most of the next few days catching up on family news. Since Michael had only left Germany two years earlier, he was able to share more recent news about the Brodbeck family.

They talked about the death of Jacob's brother, Johannes (Michael's father) and about the death of both Jacob's Mutter and of late, his Schwester, Barbara.

"Tell me, Michael, do you remember if Mutter spoke of us before she died?" Jacob inquired.

"Ja, Aunt Barbara often said how much your Mutter missed you and Johann. She said she called for both of you three times before she died."

Jacob was not surprised to hear of this. Any number of times in the middle of the night, he would awaken thinking he heard his Mutter's voice calling him. He seemed to remember he had heard her call to him on the night Michael said she died. He could not be sure so he said nothing about it to Michael.

Michael was captivated with the small model of the air ship Jacob brought along as well as the blueprints of the air machine's design. He agreed with Jacob that his invention needed the proper publication and support.

In Michael's spare time, he helped Jacob research and locate important businessmen who might be interested in backing Jacob's invention. But with the Yuletide season approaching, they had little or no luck with any responses.

*****

On the Brodbeck farm in Luckenbach, the hum of activity and excitement ushered in the Christmas season. Christine, now some seven months pregnant, lumbered along determined to get the Christmas baking done as early as possible. She was slower than usual so she needed to allow extra time. She pulled out her baking tins to store the cookies and other sweets until Christmas Eve. With the children in school, and Johann at work, she planned to bake all day. A fresh norther had blown in earlier that morning, helping her decide this was a good day to remain inside and heat up the house with her baking. She planned to bake their favorite German cookies, Lebkuchen and Pfeffernüsse.

Towards mid-afternoon when she stepped outside to get more wood for the cook stove, she happened to notice the horses coming back to the barn. *Ach, the horses come home early today. That must mean much colder weather is coming tonight.* Then looking up, she noticed a clearing sky: signaling a frigid night ahead. She walked out to the corral to count the horses . . . only four of their six horses stood drinking from the horse trough.

She pulled the gate to and fastened its horseshoe latch to the gate post. Guessing at the sun's placement in the western sky, she surmised there were only a couple of hours of daylight left. She worried if she did not go right away to try and find them, Indians might decide to capture them. If she waited until the boys or Johann came home, it might be too late.

Hurrying back inside, she grabbed a coat as well as a heavy blanket to wrap over her shoulders. She also located two ropes; one to use on the horse she would ride back and the other rope to tie around the second horse's neck to lead him.

She figured the horses would be easy to locate because of the bells tied around their necks . . . thus, not bothering to take time to leave a note.

She also did not take into account the north wind blew at her back, blowing the sounds away from her. She walked to every conceivable place the horses might be, but saw and heard no sound of them. Realizing they may already be stolen by the Indians, and aware of the approaching darkness, she decided she better head back home. She had no doubt she knew her way back, but the more she walked and the darker it became, she was not so sure anymore.

The wind picked up; the setting sun took its warmth with it. She stood still trying to find her center.

Taking several deep breaths, she looked around but the deepening shadows played tricks on her sense of direction. Then, barely making out a hollowed-out crevice in the limestone cliff to the leeward side of her, she knew what she must do.

She walked over to investigate the slight overhanging cliff. Shuffling through the piled-up leaves to find her a nesting place, she felt satisfied that instead of using all her stamina searching for her way home, this was a good place for her to spend the night. At least she was protected from the wind.

Suddenly feeling very tired and cumbersome, she snuggled up inside the warm blanket the best she could. She went to sleep within moments.

*****

On cold blustery days, Johann often took his buggy to work in order to drop the children at school in the mornings and pick them up in the evenings on his way home.

Riding up to a dark farmhouse, Johann suspected right away something was wrong. The lanterns were always lit by now welcoming them home.

He tried not to show any concern to the children as they got out. He instructed the two older boys to tend to the horse and buggy as he and the younger ones went inside. He quickly lit a lantern as Matilda was already calling for her Momma.

Soon it became evident Christine was not home. The baking goods were left a sprawl all over the kitchen table; very much unlike Christine. Could she have been abducted by a stray Indian party? And yet, no reports of

Indians capturing white women had been heard of in many years. And there were no signs of a struggle. No, it must be something else, he concluded.

About that time, Edward came running in from the barn. "Uncle Johann, Henry and I noticed two of our horses are missing from the corral."

"Ach, that is where your Momma has gone . . . looking for the horses and on a night like this. Is Henry still tending to the horses?"

"Ja, after we unhitched Ol' Mae and began feeding the others, we discovered the two missing," Edward answered.

Johann was already securing a lantern, and getting a heavy blanket while he gave orders to the children. "Edward, you go out and saddle up the roan for me. Matilda, put on the coffee and get some ready for me to take in a jug. Put some cheese and bread in a grub sack as well. Then you scurry up some supper for you and the boys. Hilmar, do you have any homework?"

"Ja, I do, but Momma always helps me. Why is she not here?" questioned the young lad.

"I think she may be out looking for the missing horses, but I will find her. In the meantime, you get Edward to help you with your homework. Can you do that for me?"

"Ja, I can," Hilmar said rather unconvincingly, but Johann was already out the door not hearing the lament in the young boy's voice.

When Johann got to the barn, Edward was just finishing girding up the saddle and Henry had pitched the last fork load of hay into the horses' stalls.

"Henry, while I go look for your Momma, you are in charge here. If I do not return by daylight with your Momma, go to the nearest neighbors and get them to organize a search party. And one more thing, it is getting colder by the minute. Take more wood into the house and keep the fire going in the fireplace."

"Ja, but would I not be more help coming with you?"

"Nein, under no circumstances, should you leave your post at the house. There is no sense in the two of us freezing out there. You are needed here to calm the children."

"Ach, I hope Momma is alright . . . you know, with the baby and all," worried Henry.

"Ja, I know . . . but you also know how strong your Momma is. Think on that and pray some prayers for all three of us," urged Johann.

*****

Sitting back in a rocker in the parlor of the old, two story stone home of Michael's, Jacob pulled the sheer lace curtain aside to watch the gently falling snowflakes outside. Michael walked in with two cups of steaming coffee.

"Dorothea begs your pardon. She decided to read and has retired early for the evening," Michael announced.

"Ach, that sounds nice. It is a good night for reading." Admiring the falling snow, he observed, "I have not seen snow this deep since leaving Germany. We rarely get snowfall in Texas and when we do, it is gone in a day or so."

"Well, if I might interrupt your reverie," Michael said, "I have some interesting news for you. Upon seeing one of your pamphlets about your "air ship," a business associate of my father-in-law tells me he believes you should share your "air ship" ideas with a civil engineer by the name of Octave Chanute. He is a brilliant man who is interested in new ideas of inventions."

For the first time since arriving at Michael's, Jacob felt a sudden stirring of hope form in his chest. Thumbing through some of Michael's recently gathered newspaper articles about Mr. Chanute's inventions for the railroad, Jacob began thinking here was a man already interested in transportation.

Surveying the rest of the articles, Jacob lost no time in saying, "When can I meet Mr. Chanute?"

"Unfortunately, he is planning a trip to Europe right now and will not be home for three or four months. I know you are worried about getting back to Christine before the baby arrives at the end of January, but this is the best opportunity you have had so far to place your plans into the hands of the right man."

"Ja, but how will Christine react when I write her I am going to stay months longer?"

*****

A strong gust of icy wind woke Christine from her exhausted sleep. The wind, changing directions and coming from the south, had a damp feel to it now. Was there freezing rain in store for her? Half of her senses were still back in the lovely dream she was having. She dreamed she and Jacob were sitting by the warm glow of a fire and watching through their window as their children played outside in the snow.

Strange, she thought, it rarely snowed in this part

of Texas.

Tonight, the air seemed as laden with chilling moisture as she was with child. Only instead of being in a warm and cozy house with her husband by her side, she was alone out in the middle of a pasture struggling to keep her and her unborn baby shielded from the freezing and fiercely biting wind.

She managed to pile some brush and more leaves around her to better shelter herself from the cold. Settling back down in her nest, she shivered as she rewrapped the blanket around her. How could she have been so foolish to leave without writing a note? She knew she could find her way back in daylight, still she worried about the welfare of her baby through this long cold night and she also felt terrible about upsetting her children and Johann with her absence.

She hung her head and whispered an urgent plea, "O mein Gott, please forgive this foolish woman. Ease the minds and hearts of my children and Johann back home. O, mein Gott, I pray thou art with me . . . to protect my child and me . . ."

No sooner had she uttered those few fervent words of prayer, than exhaustion overcame her again.

> *"Fear thou not; for I am with thee: be not dismayed; for I am thy God: I will strengthen thee; yea, I will help thee; yea, I will uphold thee with the right hand of my righteousness." Isaiah 41:10*

Chapter 38
Love Unwanted

When a chill awoke her again, she raised her head and noticed the changing sky. In between the swiftly moving clouds, the full winter's moon shining directly overhead told her it was about midnight. The clouds, churning across the nighttime expanse, obliterated most of the stars except for one, the bright and twinkling North Star.

As she gazed upon the star, glistening even amidst the swirling clouds, a picture of that long ago Christmas Eve night formed in her mind. Like the shining star breaking through the clouds above, Mary's faith brought her through that perilous journey to Bethlehem where her baby Son was to be born.

A sense of calmness settled over her. She closed her eyes and blessed sleep came again.

Some time later somewhere between sleep and lucidness, she heard a far away voice calling her name. In her semi-conscience state, she called out, "Jacob, Jacob . . . I'm here. Jacob, please help me."

Though her words came out faint and fuzzy, Johann, intent upon hearing Christine's voice, recognized something. Swinging the lantern around, he spied the limestone cliff. Figuring Christine would have had the sense to choose that for shelter, he made his way toward it. The weak words came again, "Jacob, please help me. Jacob, where are you?"

Pinpointing the voice, Johann cleared away the brush and leaves that sheltered Christine. Suddenly she was in his arms and he was crooning her voice over and over,

"Christine, Christine, Mein lieber Schatz! I have you. You are safe. You are safe, my darling Christine!"

"Oh, Jacob, you came! You really came," she responded to his arms by lifting her face up to kiss him.

Johann's emotions came upon him with such fierceness he had no time to think. His instincts took control. He returned her kiss with all the pent-up passion bottled up in his soul from decades of loneliness.

Johann's scent alerted Christine's senses even before his touch did. It was a familiar scent— but not her husband's.

"Johann! I thought you were Jacob! Oh, Johann, what just happened? Why did you kiss me?" Christine's previous illusion now turned to confusion.

"Ach, Christine, please forgive me. I did not plan it. It just happened. I have been so worried about you . . . we all have." Then as he grabbed the lantern to shine it on Christine, he implored, "Are you hurt in any way? How is the baby?"

"We are both fine. I am just very tired, cold, and hungry . . . but Johann . . ." and then before Christine could unravel the meaning of Johann's kiss, they both heard the tinkling of the horse bells.

"Did you hear that? The horses must be close by," Christine said in a rush and tried to get up . . . only to sink back in place.

"Christine, are you sure you are all right?" Johann asked again.

"Ja, I am fine, just weaker than I thought," she said with a little surprise.

"You are weak from your overnight ordeal. Here, I had Matilda pack some hot coffee and food for you." Giving Christine the hot jug and tin of cheese and bread, Johann said, "That should give you some strength. I go to get the horses. Here, let me cover you up with another blanket. I will be back as soon as I can."

"Ach, danke shörn! But here, Johann, take the ropes for the horses."

In the minutes that Johann was gone, Christine's mind raced over the earlier incident as she sipped the hot coffee and consumed the cheese and bread.

That was not a brotherly kiss!

It was too full of emotion and passion. Ach du lieber! Could Johann be in love with her? She racked her mind of any instances that might have given her warning that this could happen. But of course, it could happen—Johann never got out to socialize on his own—he was too busy taking care of Jacob's family! She was the only woman he was ever around for any length of time.

Pulling the blanket tighter around her, she shivered not only from the cold, but from the grief she felt for Johann. She and Jacob had presumed on Johann for too long. Ja, she knew all about Johann's lost love, Katarina. Johann had talked about her many times. Many times Johann had said that he could love none other than Katarina. She and Jacob had both believed him. But now! Now, things must change.

The sound of horse bells alerted her of Johann's return. She decided she would act as if nothing happened right now. Later, once she had time to compose her thoughts and feelings, she must talk to Johann.

Finding both horses drawn together alongside a strand of brushy cedars, Johann tried to keep his hands from shaking as he tied the ropes around the horses' necks to lead them back. He could not quit trembling. He felt the icy cold; but more than that, he felt his raw emotions. Stung with shame and regret, he was also moved by the tender moment he and Christine had just shared. Ach, but he knew that her lovely response was not for him, but for his Bruder. And well, it should be! He felt envy for his own brother. In der Tinte sitzen! What a mess he was in!

Riding back to the place where Christine was, Johann knew he must keep the subject of what happened between them closed. To speak of that moment in time would give it life; it must fade and die in both their memories as if it never happened. The Holy Scriptures instructs one to flee from temptation and that he must do. But how do you flee when you must live day in and day out with the temptation in your home?

The ride back to the farmhouse was chilly and silent. Johann let Christine ride his saddled horse while he rode bareback on one and led the other one behind.

The ensuing days rushed by with Christmas activities. Amid the preparations, both Christine and Johann maintained a mask of politeness in each other's presence—each hoping to hide their thoughts from the other.

The unsaid words hung in the air between them like a wispy veil—floating back and forth between reality and imagination. Christine could not muster up the courage to talk to Johann about what happened and Johann was glad she had not. If it were not for the spirit of the season, the strain of keeping their thoughts to themselves would have been difficult indeed, given that the two of them—as old friends usually do— shared without any restraint their daily thoughts and concerns with one another.

*****

Jacob, too, was beset by wariness. Sitting by the fire, Jacob felt the old familiar tug between his duty and his dream. Why must he always have the same struggle? In the end, he just could not give up on his dream when there was even a glimmer of hope visible. He located pen and paper and composed a letter to Christine; he would be staying months later than the end of January so he could meet with Octave Chanute.

Jacob's letter arrived three days before Christmas. It was not apparent which person was more disappointed by its news—Christine or Johann. Actually, Johann was more angry than disappointed. He wanted to find the first train to Ann Arbor, Michigan, and haul his brother back to where he belonged. After Christine read the letter to him, he made no comment at all. Instead, he told Christine that their wood supply was low and he went out to chop wood.

Christine knew better, of course. The boys had chopped a whole mound of wood the day before wanting to be free of that chore during the coming holidays. But she sensed Johann needed to let off some steam. She noticed the muscles in his face tightening when she read the news of Jacob's delay.

Johann was angry. She wished she felt anger. Then she could let off tension as well in a legitimate fashion. Instead, she stuffed back her sobs of sadness, not wanting to deprive her whole family of a happy Christmas. In doing so, she was reminded of a plaque hanging on her Oma's kitchen wall: "Man's strong muscle it is that chops the logs and builds the house, but the woman's strong will is the mortar that holds the home together."

With that resolute reminder, she put away the letter and put on her apron.

Chapter 39
Illness

Later . . . May, 1875 . . .

According to newspaper accounts, Octave Chanute was back from Europe. Also in the articles, Jacob read Chanute had attended the 10th Annual meeting of the Royal Aeronautical Society in London. Jacob lost no time, with the help of some of Michael's influential business friends, in finding a time when he and Chanute could meet. It turned out Chanute would be in Chicago briefly during the month of May. Since Chanute was more than just a little interested in the challenge of flying, he readily agreed to meet Jacob while in Chicago.

Fortunately, with Michael's help, Jacob booked a second class passage on the Michigan Central Railway from Ann Arbor to Chicago. Second class was all they could afford. The trip would take a little over twenty hours and since he had little money for food, Michael suggested they pack some food for the overnight train ride to Chicago.

"I am sorry Dorothea is feeling so poorly or she would be packing you a real feast,' Michael commented.

"Ach, what did the doctor say this morning when he came, Michael?"

"He says she has a case of the influenza and must stay in bed until she recovers. I take off work not only to see you to the train depot this afternoon but also to see she takes in plenty of hot broth, liquids, and try to keep her warm from the chills. It is so unusual to have these symptoms with the spring weather."

"Ja, but we have a late spring this year, you said so yourself. It does not feel like spring to me. I am accustomed to Texas springtime! But does the doctor say it is serious?" questioned Jacob.

"Nein, not if she gets plenty of rest and liquids, which is my job to see she does."

"Well, take care of yourself, so you do not come down with it as well," cautioned Jacob.

Jacob finished his packing by carefully seeing that his blueprints and plans were secure in the new black leather briefcase Michael gave him just for the trip. He wondered about Michael's choice. This new briefcase seemed so ordinary and looked like every other businessman's briefcase. He rather preferred his old brown and tattered one. But he did not want to offend Michael's generosity.

His train left the Ann Arbor depot at 1:20 p.m. and would arrive in Chicago the next morning at 9:20 a.m. His meeting with Chanute was scheduled for dinner that evening in the lavish dining room of the Palmer House Hotel.

Once on the train, Jacob sat back to enjoy the lovely landscapes of Michigan passing by his window. Languid lakes and streams lined the sloping hills and valleys along the tracks. The dark green of the tall white pine mingled with the new yellow green leaves of the deciduous hemlock, beach, sugar maple, and tamarack. Jacob loved the spring, always had. The rebirth of old to new always amazed him and gave him encouragement his old trials and failures with his air ship were about to receive rebirth as well.

As the hours passed, so did the towns and stops along the way. He enjoyed the conductor's robust voice calling out the town names. "Next stop, Chelsea . . . Next stop, Jackson . . . Next stop, Marshall." All the towns along the Michigan Central Railroad line.

Right between the stops of Marshall and Battle Creek, Jacob knew he was getting sick. He felt very woozy and weak. He thought maybe he had not eaten enough as he was trying to make his food last. He ate some bread and cheese, but instead of feeling better, he became nauseous. He discretely asked the porter for a pail in case he vomited. The porter was quick to furnish him with one.

By the time the train left Battle Creek, Jacob was having chills and asked for a blanket. The porter was becoming alarmed for Jacob's well being. He knew of a doctor on board and went to seek his help.

When the doctor arrived, Jacob was shivering so much that he was barely able to speak. As the doctor was getting off at the next town of Kalamazoo, he advised Jacob that he must go with him and be admitted into the hospital. Jacob had the influenza.

With all the determination he had, Jacob objected, "I cannot get off here!" Then a series of coughs overtook him and before he could object further, several porters placed him onto a narrow stretcher. With a raspy voice, he cried out as loud as he could, "My briefcase . . . I must have my briefcase. I must get to Chicago with my briefcase . . . important papers inside." Then another round of coughs overcame him.

The doctor calmly placed his hands on Jacob's shoulders and pushed him gently back onto the stretcher. Then he leaned down and quietly said to Jacob, "My good man, you are contagious to the other passengers . . . we have no choice but to remove you from the train. And here, is this your briefcase? I have it here with mine. We will take good care of it for you . . . do not worry. But now, we must get you some help . . . you are running a very high temperature."

Jacob was so weak by now all he could do was close his eyes and hope for the best.

Two days later, Jacob woke up to sunlight streaming in on his face. He looked around. Nothing familiar. Then just as he began getting his bearings, a short and stout woman in her mid fifties entered the room.

"And a good mornin' to ye," she said in a brisk Irish brogue, "I see the sunlight brought ye around. Nothing like God's smilin' rays to heal what ails ye." Then placing her hand on Jacob's brow, she continued, "Well, saints alive, I do believe the fever has passed. How are ye a feelin'?

"Confused. I am not quite sure where I am." Jacob answered.

"Ye're in a hospital in Kalamazoo, Michigan. Ye've got influenza and ye've been in a delirium, mostly caused from the fever ye've had from the influenza. But ye are one lucky fellow . . . looks like ye are going to be fine and dandy real soon."

"How long have I been here?" Jacob asked with great anxiety.

"Two days. Yes, sir, ye've . . . ," but Jacob did not let her finish her sentence.

Sitting up straight with his eyes wide open, Jacob implored the nurse, "Not two days. I have missed the most important appointment of my life." Then suddenly remembering his briefcase, he looked around wildly, "Where is my briefcase? I must have my briefcase."

"Now, just lie back down, Mr. Brodbeck. Not to worry . . . I placed it right here in ye night table drawer." Bending down, the nurse opened the drawer, pulled out the briefcase and handed it to Jacob.

With great haste, Jacob fiddled with the snap and flung the briefcase case open. Staring down at its contents, Jacob started sobbing with uncontrollable despair.

Leaning closer, the nurse curiously looked inside the briefcase to see what could cause her patient's reaction. All she saw were ledgers of business records . . . no doubt belonging to an accountant or such.

> *"And we know that all things work together for good to them that love God, to them who are the called according to his purpose."*
> *Romans 8:28*

Chapter 40
Acceptance

Summer, 1875 . . .

On the trip back to Texas, Jacob pondered his life. Nearly fifty-four years old now, did he have the will to start all over again redrawing his plans and rebuilding his airship? All he had now was a broken-down dream and empty pockets. Where would he find the money to rebuild the air ship? And encouragement? Where would it come from? Surely not from his disappointed wife and beleaguered Bruder. That is, if he had a family left. Perhaps Christine would not take him back.

So many whys and what ifs. What if he had first gone to Washington, D.C. to secure a patent for his airship before going to see Chanute. Then he would have had proof. Why could he not reach Chanute when he finally was able to get to Chicago? Out of money, and still half sick, he did not have the resources to stay and locate Chanute. He had felt immensely discouraged, alone and depressed. He must go home and stop chasing this useless dream.

Looking out the train window as the summer landscapes passed by, Jacob wondered, *had it been Gott's will leaving his family to pursue his dream?* He never felt peace by going so far away. He had become impatient with Gott's timing. Nine years was such a long time to wait for Gott to show him the next step.

He was reminded of the story of Abraham and Sarah in the Bible. They waited twenty-five years for

Gott's promise of a child to be born to them. They, too, tried to speed the promise and disobeyed Gott. It only brought heartache.

Seeking comfort from the Scriptures, Jacob opened his Bible. As he meditated upon what scripture he should read, he felt led to read in Numbers. Perusing the pages of the book, he came upon Numbers 20:12. "And the Lord spake unto Moses and Aaron, Because ye believed me not, therefore ye shall not bring this congregation into the land which I have given them."

Another much younger man, Joshua would lead Gott's people to their promised land. So Mose's dream was fulfilled, but by another man. Not putting *all* his trust in Gott hindered Moses from entering the promised land.

Understanding began to come upon Jacob.

He had believed Gott placed the dream of manned flight in his heart. But now he realized he had not trusted Gott with *all* his heart and waited for Gott's timing in directing his path. He lost patience and relied on his own understanding instead. Because of this, he encountered many hardships—not only for himself—but for his whole family.

He took in a deep breath and let out a huge sigh. The tension between his shoulder blades was still there, but no longer sending sharp daggers of pain down his back. Ja, he felt his body relaxing. With each succeeding breath, he felt a quiet assurance; Gott was in control even now, when all seemed at loss. The dream of human flight surely came to him from his Heavenly Vater. But would he be the one to make it happen?

Perhaps, like Moses, his life's work had blazed a trail for a Joshua and a Caleb to accomplish the miraculous feat of manned flight. He could only hope and pray that like Moses, he would live to see it.

If only he knew what happened to the briefcase with his blueprints in it! Would it somehow get into the hands of someone who would know what the blueprints were for and how much they meant?

A thought occurred to him. He must pray the contents of his briefcase be forwarded to the ones who could deliver the dream. Peace began growing within him—the kind of peace only Gott gives. With peace, came insight. His dream of manned flight was bigger than one person and much, much bigger than his pride.

*****

The hills of central Texas beckoned him home as he rode the stage into Fredericksburg. It was near the end of the work day and Jacob dearly hoped Johann might be at the Nimitz Boarding House having a beer with his friends. To his disappointment, he was not there. As he said hello to many of his friends and neighbors, one of them said . . .

"Jacob, if you hurry, you might catch Johann at the blacksmith getting a wheel from his buggy repaired."

"Ach, danke schörn!" Jacob gratefully replied.

When Jacob found Johann, he was bent over examining his repaired wheel.

With some caution, Jacob began, "If you can repair an old wheel, can you take back an old Bruder?"

Johann jumped up quickly when he heard that familiar voice.

“Mein Bruder! Mein Bruder!” Wrapping his arms around Jacob, Johann gave Jacob no concern that he was not joyous to see him.

On the buggy ride home, Johann listened to Jacob's disheartening experiences and Johann filled Jacob in on all that had happened in his absence.

Surprising, thought Johann to himself, *now that he is here, joy replaces the anger I have felt for so long.* And he said as much.

"The joy of seeing you alive and well, my Bruder, crowds out the anger I have felt for you since you have been gone." Johann confessed.

"Ach, for that I am grateful. Do you think Christine will feel that same way?"

"Christine and I have not mentioned your name since your letter arrived telling us of your delay. Then when you did not write again, it gave us more reason not to speak of the fears we might each have in your regard."

"Ja, I understand. But do you understand, mein Bruder, how I could not force myself to write what was happening to me? It would only cause more worry for the two of you." Jacob pleaded.

"I understand now, but I did not then," Johann conceded.

When the two men arrived at the Brodbeck farm, Christine was out digging in the garden while six month old, Lena, happily played in an obviously homemade wooden enclosure near-by.

Jacob was unsure of the welcome he would receive. He felt almost bashful again . . . much like the times he courted Christine.

Just after the buggy pulled up, Christine looked up from her digging with one arm shading her eyes from the afternoon sun. She saw another figure in the buggy with Johann and wondered if Johann had brought a neighbor or friend home for supper. She got up to dust off her hands and straighten her garments. As she was doing so, Jacob climbed down from the buggy and took off his hat. He slowly began walking toward Christine . . . not wanting to force himself on her if she was unwilling to talk to him.

Just as Jacob was taking measured steps toward her, it began to dawn on her who it was. She had wondered what her response would be when he finally came home. She had not planned it and was surprised she could not look at him and turned away from him.

Seeing her turn away stopped Jacob in his tracks. He felt completely inept in all ways and had no idea of what to do next. Fortunately, little Lena piped up with two syllables . . . "pa-pa." Instinctively, he responded.

"Little Lena, your pa-pa is home! Come to your Papa." Jacob reached down to lift Lena up in his arms. When he did so, she let out a hair-raising yell and reached her little arms toward Johann who stood a few feet back from Jacob.

Johann stepped forward and gently took Lena in his arms all the while explaining, "We tell her over and over that I am Uncle Johann, but she has not learned to say Uncle, yet."

The sound of Lena's screams brought the other four children running from their various chores to see what was happening.

Christine allowed the children to gather around their Papa asking him question after question. Still not looking at her husband, she gathered her things together and started walking toward the house. As she did so, she turned her face slightly to say to all of them, "I will be getting supper ready and setting an extra plate at the table."

*****

As the days passed, life at the Brodbeck farm started to ease back to normal. Little Lena adjusted to Jacob and soon began calling him Papa as the other children did. Christine seemed constantly busy to Jacob. Household chores, tending to the baby, gardening, and helping out the neighbors occupied so much of her time and energy that she went directly to sleep as soon as she went to bed. Jacob felt her distance from him both physically and emotionally.

When he brought up the subject with his Bruder, he sensed the same kind of distancing from him.

"Ach, why do you ask me, Jacob? Ask your own wife," was Johann's somewhat curt reply.

"I ask you because you and I always talk to each other about our concerns. Why is this time so different?" Jacob wanted to know.

"It just is. Talk to your wife, Jacob." Without realizing it, Johann put an emphasis on the word "wife."

Before Jacob could comment on this, Johann was out the door without saying where he was going. Jacob felt the unsaid words between them and that bothered him. He must try and mend fences with both his wife and his Bruder. He would start with his wife.

Noticing all the wild mustang grapes on the vines this year, Jacob thought about making wine in their cellar.

He wanted to get Christine away from the house in order for them to be alone and do some talking before she wore herself out doing chores. It took some persuading to get her to go and then managing the older kids to take care of the younger ones while they were gone. But finally they were riding out in the buggy, a picnic lunch on board, in the search of grapes.

After a good morning's work of gathering Mustang grapes, Christine spread the picnic lunch out under an oak tree near their creek. As they ate, Jacob teased her that she might find a large rock near the creek from which to dangle her feet. For the first time, Christine looked up into Jacob's eyes and smiled as she remembered how he and Johann had brought her a rock for their creek when she and Jacob were first married.

"Ach, miene liber schatz, it is so good to see you smile and to know that smile is just for me." He placed his arm around her shoulders hoping she would lean her head on his chest as she always did.

Instead she countered with "I have not had many smiles for you, das ist wahr."

"Have you not forgiven me for not being here for Lena's birth?"

"Forgiving you is easy, but trusting you will not leave us in Johann's care again is not so easy."

"Christine, I have already told you I am at peace about letting go of my plans to build my airship. And what do you mean 'Johann's care?' Was he not good to you and the children?"

"Ja, of course he was. He is too good, Jacob. You take advantage of his generosity and so do I. Have you ever wondered why he does not have a family of his own? In your heart, you know why. He is too busy taking care of yours while you drift from place to place in search of this folly of yours."

"Ach, Christine! You and Jacob both encouraged me to follow my dream. Now you call it my folly. What has changed?"

"We all have changed, Jacob. Can you not see that? Enough is enough. Now that your blueprints are gone, it is time to give up on this "air ship" of yours and ja, perhaps folly is a better word for it."

Jacob hung his head and said, "Does Johann feel the same way as you do?"

"You will have to ask Johann about that."

"I shall. But right now, I am with you. What can I do to help you believe I am home to stay?"

Christine paused and breathed out a deep sigh.

"You can talk to Johann and encourage him to seek a wife and start his own family. And may I remind you, we live in Johann's house. It seems only right we either find a place of our own or offer to buy his house."

"Ach, but Christine . . . you seem to forget Johann and I built the house together as if it were ours together. He would think we were trying to get rid of him if I suggested such a thing."

"Perhaps right now he would. I am talking about the future. You asked me what would make me feel secure. I would like for you to encourage him to get out more. Then when he meets someone, it will be the time to offer to move or pay him for what part of the house is his."

"I am not as sure as you are. Johann is fifty years old and has been a bachelor all his life. I am not sure Johann even wants a wife. Besides, it is not easy to find an available woman, much less a good one." Jacob argued.

"Still, I ask you, Jacob, for me, to do this. And I ask for your brother as well."

With a good bit of trepidation, Jacob consented, "If it pleases you, mein liebchen, then the first time we are alone, I will have a talk with him."

Chapter 41
A Promise Kept

Jacob could not possibly know Christine's request was two-fold. It was true giving Johann the chance to move on with his life elsewhere would cause Jacob to remain at home. But what Christine dare not share with Jacob was how concerned she was Johann might still be in love with her.

To be sure, since that eventful night in the cave when he kissed her, there had been no such other encounters. Nonetheless, it seemed they were always uncomfortable in each other's presence. She wanted Johann to find his own happiness. He deserved it. She knew Jacob wanted the same for him.

After supper one night, Jacob asked Johann to join him on the porch for a glass of his homemade wine. Christine shared one glass with them and then she excused herself to go to bed early with the children.

As the two men casually enjoyed another glass, Jacob brought up the subject of the future.

"Johann, what do you see for yourself in the next five years?"

Johann, a little taken back, said in all earnestness, "I have not thought much about it. Why do you ask? Are you planning on leaving again?"

"Oh, nein," Jacob was quick to answer, "I have assured Christine and now I assure you . . . I am home to stay. Nein, my question is not about me. But I am not surprised you think so. I am sad to say this, but I think your life has usually been about me. I urged you come to Texas with me. I needed you to help me build my air ship and I needed you to stay with my family all the times I was gone. I have not been fair to you and now I want you to know, it is your turn. I want to help you make a life for yourself. Christine and I have burdened you too long with ours."

"Jawohl! Am I being booted out the door?" Johann asked half in jest and half in earnest.

"Nein, of course not. We are family. You know that. But as family, perhaps we have taken advantage of your generosity." Jacob tried to explain.

"Well, then, mein Bruder, let me assure you as well. I have not given or done anything I did not want to do as far as you and Christine are concerned. This questioning does not sound like you, Jacob. Is Christine unhappy I am around?"

"Nein! Nein! Do not even think of such a thing. But it was Christine who suggested you might be unhappy here and want a life of your own."

"Ja, but I have made a life of my own here, Jacob, in many ways. I help carry on the traditions from our Vaterland of marksmen's festivals and singing festivals, but we still call them by their German names— Schuetzenfests und Saengerfests. I play my harmonica at dances quite often.

"Please do not concern yourself about my happiness. I could not bear to leave the children, nor you and Christine. Even if I found a woman willing to marry a fifty-year old bachelor, which seems very unlikely, she would have to live here with us because I would miss all of you too much. Nein, mein Bruder, your family is my family. And ja, you made it so, but I also let you. What is done is done. I have no regrets and neither should you and Christine."

"Ja, well then, I am so relieved and pleased, mein Bruder. For as much as you say you would miss us, we all would miss you more."

Later that night Jacob shared their conversation with Christine. She told Jacob she felt relieved.

But as she lay in the darkness of their bed listening to her husband's heavy sleep beside her, she pondered the situation to herself.

Had Johann put the incident in the cave long behind him and never thought of it anymore? Did she just imagine he was uncomfortable around her simply because she still felt uncomfortable around him? She wanted to talk to him about it, but if she did, it might only serve to bring it all to the surface again. Perhaps, as the saying goes, she would "just let sleeping dogs lie."

Johann also lay thinking about their conversation. He knew his Bruder. He felt sure it was Christine's idea for Jacob to talk to him. He wondered if Christine still thought about that kiss which took place many months ago. Was she worried it might happen again or Jacob would somehow find out about it? Ever since that night, Johann kept a special distance from Christine. He deprived himself of her friendship in order to "flee from temptation" as scripture commanded.

And to his surprise, it had worked. He found other activities and friends to fill in that void. He especially loved his Saengerfests and Schuetzenfests where he made many new friends. One friend, August, loved to fish and persuaded Johann to go fishing with him. Johann had never thought of fishing as recreation, but only a means to put food on the table.

Johann smiled as he thought, *I was "hooked" on fishing the moment I caught that monster of a catfish.* He wondered why he had found nothing that could fill the hole in his heart left by Katarina. Nothing could, but fishing came close to satisfying a man's soul.

*****

As the following years passed, Jacob made good on his promise to Christine and Johann to stay home.

After returning to Texas from Michigan, Jacob and Christine found a joint project with the wild Mustang grapes they picked. They made wine to sell. There were ready markets for good wine and their cellar became a perfect place to store it for aging. This common endeavor brought them closer as a couple. It helped make up for the many times over the years he was gone from home.

Jacob found different jobs to earn their keep as well by offering his skills to community service. He ran for County Commissioner and won that bid in 1876.

The next year a daughter, Otillia, their sixth child, was born. During that year, he helped raise money to organize and to build a school in their district—the Grape Hill School. He made furniture, was a land surveyor and continued to be involved in the building of schools around the area.

Jacob stayed busy as the years rolled by. But he often thought of the times he flew like a bird and still dreamed about a way to make it happen again.

*****

It was February in the new year of 1897. *Not too cold. Could be a fair day for fishing*, Johann thought. Around four o'clock, he walked down to the creek to go fishing. He cast his pole one time and then pulled it back in. He gathered his things and walked back to the house. He set his fishing gear down next to the front door. He went straight to his room and crawled into bed.

When Jacob came home that afternoon, he noticed Johann's fishing gear standing by the front door. That was strange. Johann was always very careful to put away his things and keep them organized.

"Christine, is Johann home? His fishing gear is out here by the front door."

"Ja, I thought I heard him come in, but he did not come to the kitchen for coffee as he usually does. Did you look in his room?"

Jacob thought it was odd for Johann's door to be closed this time of day—not even supper time. He tapped lightly on the door in case Johann was taking a nap, which he rarely did this time of the day.

No answer. By this time, Christine had come from the kitchen and was by the door, too.

"Just crack the door a little and peep in," Christine suggested.

Johann did so and they both looked into the bedroom. There was Johann lying with the covers pulled up to his shoulders.

"That's odd," said Jacob.

They looked at each other and at the same time, ran over to his bed— saying his name.

"Johann! Johann! Are you okay?"

*****

On a frosty February morning, family and friends gathered round the Brodbeck Family Cemetery on their Luckenbach homestead to lay Johann Georg Brodbeck to rest. His death, so unexpected, left Jacob bereft and shaken. Numb with shock, he heard only the first few words the minister spoke at the service—that Johann was seventy years old at the time of his death.

From that point on, Jacob's mind flashed back to the day twenty-one year old Johann stood beside him on the wharf at Antwerp eager to sail to Texas. Major events in their lives from that day on passed before his eyes—one after another. Together, they shared them all.

The service ended. People were leaving. Jacob perceived there was someone trying to get his attention. But he did not want to be taken away from the images playing before his eyes.

Christine managed to get him to walk back to the house and into their bedroom. She closed the door. Wetting a washcloth from the bowl of water on their nightstand, she wiped Jacob's brow and face.

When he realized Christine was by him, his sobs came in gulps of pent-up breaths.

As he let it all out, he said in spurts, "I wanted him to live and let me die first."

Christine comforted him, "Oh, mein Schatz . . . Your mind was keeping Johann alive until you could face the reality of his death."

"Ja, I suppose so. I did not hear any of the minister's message. There were many wonderful things to say about Johann. Ach, did the minister talk about what Johann mentioned to us just the other day, after all these years, that he had been a Texas Ranger when he lived in San Antonio?

"Ja, ja, he did. He told how Johann was employed as a stone mason at Fort Inge some eighty-eight miles west of San Antonio. It was during this time he spent about three months as a Texas Mounted Volunteer."

"I never got to ask Johann why he never told us that before. Somehow you think you have another day to share these things with each other. But the next day, Johann was gone without any warning."

> *"He healeth the broken in heart, and bindeth up their wounds." Psalm 147:3*

Chapter 42
A Dream Revisited

1909 . . . Twelve years later

Jacob and Christine sat on their porch in their rocking chairs enjoying the Indian summer afternoon. Their last child to leave home, Arthur, having turned eighteen, left the day before to find his calling in life.

Ever since Jacob's return from Michigan back in 1875, he remained true to his word—he let go of his plans to build an "air ship." Oh, he still dreamed about it. He believed one day someone would invent an energy supply light enough to be airborne . . . such as a gasoline combustible engine.

They had added five more children to their family since the birth of Lena: Otillia in 1877, Edwin in 1879, Emma in 1883, Amalia in 1884, and Arthur in 1886.

Ja, Jacob made good on his promise to Christine to stay at home.

As Christine rocked in her rocking chair, thinking about their last child leaving home, she looked over at Jacob beside her. She wondered how much Jacob's promise to stay at home had cost him.

And what about her own promise to her mother back when she was thirteen and determined to marry Herr Brodbeck? Her mother asked her to meditate on *Psalm 37:4 "Delight thyself in the Lord and He will give thee the desires of thine heart."*

Did she ever come to understand the significance of that scripture as it applied to her? No, not for a long time.

Not for many years. But often now, when she found times to be alone and meditate, she delighted in the Lord's presence above all else. Above any personal desire she might have. And with these sacred moments, she found joy and freedom.

She had finally come to know what her Mutter wanted her to grasp: when she was so strong-willed and wouldn't surrender her deep desires, life had its own way of teaching her those spiritual truths through many hardships and sufferings.

Jacob interrupted her thoughts when he said, "Well, mein lieber schatz, it is just the two of us now. It seems so strange not to have any family here in the house with us," Jacob mused as he watched the last rays of a brilliant sunset let go of the day. "We are like this sunset, letting go of the day and passing into the twilight hours."

"Why, Jacob Brodbeck, are you telling me you are getting ready to die on me?"

"Nein, but one never knows. Johann went so fast. He was here alive one day and it seemed the very next day he was gone."

"That has been nearly twelve years ago, Jacob, and I believe you grieve for your Bruder just as if it were yesterday." Christine commented.

"It still feels as if it were yesterday. I loved him so. He was more than a Bruder to me. He was my friend and often my conscience as well."

"Ach, and now you only have me for your friend and your conscience." Christine soothed him as she patted his knee.

Jacob was about to answer when a hoot and holler came from a distance. Around the corner of the road, came Arthur, his horse galloping at high speed.

Both Christine and Jacob rose to their feet as quickly as their-not-so young bodies allowed.

"What the blazes is Arthur yelling about?" Jacob wondered out loud.

“Papa . . . Papa,” Arthur continued to yell with excitement as he tumbled from his horse. “It has happened! Just as you said it would happen. Papa, you were right all along.” Then handing his father a newspaper, he said, “Look at the headline, Papa, just look!”

Jacob took the newspaper from his son, and saw the headline, “Wrights Fly First Airplane!”

Before he could comment, Christine was by his side urging him, “Jacob, read it out loud to us, bitte!” she implored.

“Ach du lieber! Just a moment, bitte!” Jacob adjusted his reading glasses and began reading aloud:

> “Daytonians Wilbur and Orville Wright made the world’s first powered, sustained, and controlled manned flight in their heavier-than–air flyng machine on December 17, 1903, thereby achieving one of mankind’s oldest and most persistent dreams. On the morning of December 17, 1903, the Wright Brothers took turns piloting and monitoring their flying machine near Kitty Hawk, North Carolina. Orville piloted the first flight that lasted just twelve seconds. On the fourth and final flight of the day, Wilbur traveled 852 feet,

> remaining airborne for fifty-seven seconds. That morning the brothers became the first people to demonstrate sustained flight of a heavier-than-air machine under the complete control of the pilot. They had built the 1903 Flyer in sections in the back room of their Dayton, Ohio, bicycle shop. Through their own research and experimentation, and by studying the attempts of other would-be pilots, the Wright brothers knew that heavier-than-air flight was possible. They corresponded frequently with engineer Octave Chanute, friend and supporter of their work.

At this juncture, Jacob paused, looked out into the brilliant crimson sky and said, "So, Octave Chanute really was the right man for me to see. I wonder if my blueprints ever made their way to him and if he was able to share them with these Wright brothers."

Both Christine and Arthur stood mute as they, too, realized how stunning this was that the very same man Jacob struggled and sacrificed so much to see . . . eventually was the very one to aid the Wright Brothers in achieving manned flight.

Breaking the spell, Christine wanted to know, "It is also so odd that like you and Johann, they were brothers who worked so closely together. Does it tell anything else about their lives?"

Jacob skimmed on down the page and said, "Ja, here's more about the brothers." He continued to read aloud:

"Born in 1871, Orville and his older brother, Wilbur (born in 1867) are sons of a minister and live most proper lives. They neither smoke, drink, or have ever married. They always wear conventional business suits even when tinkering in a machine shop. Neither has more than part of a high school education, but have used their instinct, intuition and endless intelligent effort to make new theory.

"Orville was a champion bicyclist and so the brothers went into the bicycle business, which gave full vent to their mechanical aptitude. Another hobby was gliding, which, in the last decade of the nineteenth century became a most daring, yet, practical sport thanks to Otto Lilienthal. The Wright brothers followed Lilienthal's career, read his publications and those of Langley and felt the stirring hope of manned flight grow. It was Lilienthal's death in 1896 that inspired them to begin their own experimentation, for they thought they could correct the errors that had led the German to his end."

Jacob finally sat back down in his rocker as did Christine while Arthur sat on a wooden stool nearby.

Again, Christine was the first to break their silence, "It said neither ever married."

Jacob knew what was in Christine's mind and tenderly reached over to pat her knee. "Ja, mein Liebchen, I know what you are thinking. But put it out of your mind. My dreams of flight— and the efforts and sacrifices made by Johann, you and me to carry them out—*have* served our fellow man.

"Like the article said, men have dreamed of flying for centuries and many others than I have tried it. It was a dream whose time had come and the Wright Brothers were the right men in the right place and in the right time in history to make use of many of the ideas and failures of those before them." Then he chuckled, "Gott always has a sense of humor. Their names are even Wright!"

Both Christine and Arthur grinned at that as well.

"Papa, you can also take comfort in the fact that another German, Otto Lilienthal, was instrumental in making flight possible," added Arthur.

"More than that, my son, I take comfort that at last flight is possible and that other Germans who want to immigrate to this great land of Texas will soon have the chance to fly over the oftentimes treacherous ocean instead of having to endure the storms at sea. It is a wonderful day for mankind," saying that, Jacob looked at the name and date of the newspaper.

"Jawohl, this is a Dayton, Ohio, newspaper and it is from 1909. But it said in the article that the Wright Brothers first flew in 1903. Where did you get this newspaper, son?"

"Why, a traveler from Ohio staying at the Nimitz Boarding House left it lying on the dining table. Herr Nimitz said that the gentleman had gone and that I should take this paper home to you. At first, I did not see why until I read the headline. Strange that it reads like it just happened instead of six years ago."

"Ach, not so strange. It might have taken that long for the Wright Brothers to convince anyone that they had actually flown. This I know from experience." Jacob related. Then looking at continued pages, Jacob continued, "Listen to this," he said.

> "The Wright Brothers filed an application for a patent for their flying machine on March 23, 1903 and were granted the patent on May 22, 1906. But the world was not really convinced of man flying until Wilbur Wright flew around the Statue of Liberty in New York Harbor on September 29, 1909. Here is an account of the event:
>
> Nearly a million people crowded along the docks, parks, streets and rooftops. Some forty warships from many nations filled the harbor.
>
> Leveling out at 200 feet, the Wright Flyer circled the island once and headed out to sea in the direction of the Statue of Liberty. As Wilbur reached the Statue, he passed over the outward-bound Lusitania, the pride of the oceans. Passengers crowded the decks to watch him.
>
> Wilbur pointed the Flyer directly at the Statue; then banked sharply and circled behind and passed within 20 feet of the metal drapery that makes up the waist. Spectators in New York thought he was going to crash as he passed out of their sight behind the statue.
>
> On he continued, banking the Flyer as he passed under the upraised arm. Then he leveled the wings and turned toward Governor's Island. As he

> passed over the Lusitania again, people were waving hats, coats and anything else they could find. There was a deafening blast in salute from the ship's foghorn.
>
> Two minutes later he landed back at Governor's Island and was mobbed by reporters. Wilbur, as usual, showed little emotion. Some thought they saw a slight smile."

"Ach du lieber, what a great story," mused Jacob.

All three stood there in silence letting their minds absorb the significance of what Jacob had read. Before anyone could make a comment, Arthur's horse whinnied.

Arthur stood up and said, "Gus wants to be fed. I think I will bed him down and go back to Fredericksburg in the morning."

"Good decision, son," Christine agreed as Arthur walked the horse towards the barn.

The two of them lingered on the porch rocking quietly in their rockers. Finally, Christine placed her hand on Jacob's knee and softly asked, "My husband, you worked hundreds of hours and traveled thousands of miles in order to build your air ship. Do you not wish it could have been you?"

Jacob took his time in answering her question. He gazed again at the sky as the night closed in on the day.

"Ah, but in some ways, I was there. Just as there are many stars that make up the nighttime firmament, Gott placed the dream of flight in many men's hearts. I would like to believe my dream of flight, and the dreams of many others, flew beside the Wright Brothers. I feel their joy and triumph because I have flown, even if only for brief periods. I know their fears and frustrations, their difficulties and disappointments. Should I not know, then, their success?

"Nein, instead of envy in my heart for the Wright Brothers, Gott has placed kinship . . . Ja, ja, das ist richtig!" Jacob said with recognition dawning in his mind and then, with a gleam in his eye, went on to repeat, "I feel kinship. I feel kinship for those who went before, and for those who are yet to come."

Christine let out a sigh of relief which eased into contentment. The two of them continued rocking in the stillness of the unfolding darkness. Soon, above them, there appeared a multitude of stars glittering across the clear sky. In the midst of the bountiful array, as if to accentuate Jacob's last words, a shooting star blazed across the heavens.

"Ach, there you see? Gott affirms my feelings." Jacob proclaimed.

Christine, looking up, smiled as she said, "And maybe Johann does, too."

Jacob took her hand as they both peered up at the star-studded sky, and said, "Ja, mein Schatz, da haben Sie recht . . . Ja, I believe he does . . . Ja, I believe my Bruder smiles through the starry night."

> *"To every thing there is a season, and a time to every purpose under the heaven . . ."*
> *Ecclesiastes 3:1*

Epilogue

Jacob Brodbeck lived to be 89 years of age. Many mysteries surround his memory. Did he ever file a patent for his "air ship" and if so, why are there no records of it? What happened to his wrecked aircraft? What happened to his blueprints? Did he ever get to meet with Octave Chanute? Could any of his blueprints have accidentally landed in the hands of Octave Chanute and could Mr. Chanute with his many communications with the Wright Brothers unknowingly shared Brodbeck's plans or blueprints with them?

If any reader knows of any leads that might uncover more details in this story, please send me an email at **texasiris9@gmail.com**. Perhaps, someone has a piece to the puzzle.

Jacob Brodbeck died on January 8, 1910, and is buried in the Brodbeck Family Cemetery near Luckenbach, Texas. A bust of Jacob Brodbeck can be found in San Pedro Park in San Antonio, Texas. Another bust, for which my father, Hugo Brodbeck posed, stands on the grounds of the Vereins Kirche Museum on Main Street, Fredericksburg, Texas.

On April 15, 2018, Brodbeck descendants gathered near the Brodbeck Family Cemetery where an Official Texas Historical Person Marker Dedication was held in honor of Jacob Brodbeck. It was presented by The Texas Historical Commission, The Gillespie County Historical Commission, and The Descendents of Jacob and Christine Brodbeck.

Each year, from across Texas and beyond, Brodbeck descendants come together for the Family Reunion. Visiting and reminiscing, they enjoy a wonderful meal of Texas-style barbeque and a variety of delicious homemade dishes. In this way, the legacy of Jacob Brodbeck and his air ship are preserved for future generations.

Much gratitude goes to the members of the Brodbeck Reunion Committee and the members of the Jacob and Christine Brodbeck Foundation for their tireless work in making all these projects and events possible.

For information on current projects of the Jacob and Christine Brodbeck Foundation, visit the website of brodbeckfoundation.org.

Jacob Brodbeck may not have achieved in his lifetime his goal of providing flight for mankind, but the drawings at the end of this book show his aeronautical ideas reached into the future even if his blueprints were lost.

*****

In closing, the story of air travel is an ever unfolding quest for knowledge.

Like Jacob Brodbeck, another schoolteacher dreamed of sharing her experiences of flight with her students. On January 28, 1986, Krista McCauliff lost her life in such a pursuit when the space shuttle, Challenger—of which she was aboard—exploded as it was leaving the earth's atmosphere.

What makes men and women dare to travel higher and higher despite the dangers of flight?

Perhaps the words of John Gillespie McGee, Jr., a World War II fighter pilot and poet, say it best. After the Challenger tragedy, in his eloquent speech, President Reagan quoted the first and last lines of Gillespie's poem to a grieving nation.

High Flight
by John Gillespie McGee, Jr. (1922-1941)

Oh, I have slipped the surly bonds of Earth
And danced the skies on laughter-silvered wings;
Sunward I've climbed, and joined the tumbling
mirth
of sun-split clouds—and done a hundred things
You have not dreamed of—and wheeled and soared and
swung
High in sunlit silence. Hov'ring there,
I've chased the shouting wind along, and flung
My eager craft through footless halls of air . . .

Up, up the long, delirious, burning blue
I've topped the wind-swept heights with easy grace
Where never lark, or even eagle flew—
And, while with silent, lifting mind I've trod
The high untrespassed sanctity of space,
Put out my hand, and touched the face of God

(The poet's original writing of *High Flight* is on display
at the Library of Congress, Washington, D.C.)

Drawings and Photographs

Copies of drawings, the stock share and a photograph of the crashed aircraft were available to Brodbeck descendants during the Jacob Brodbeck Day, May 16, 1986, at Randolph Air Force Base, San Antonio, Texas,

The drawings that follow are an artist's concept of Brodbeck's "Air Ship" taken from the inventor's description in his article appearing in the Galveston Tri-Weekly News, August 7, 1865. Currently, there are no blueprints found to illustrate a more accurate view.

The photograph of Brodbeck's crashed aircraft on page 226 of this book (shown again below) is an official photograph of the United States Air Force.

Brodbeck's Crashed Aircraft: Approximate Date, September 20, 1865

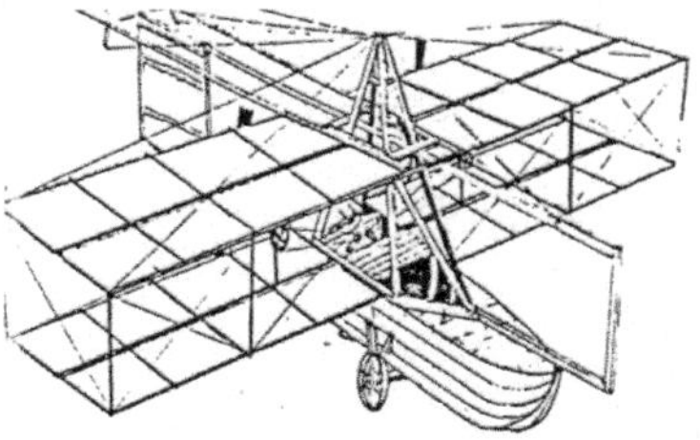

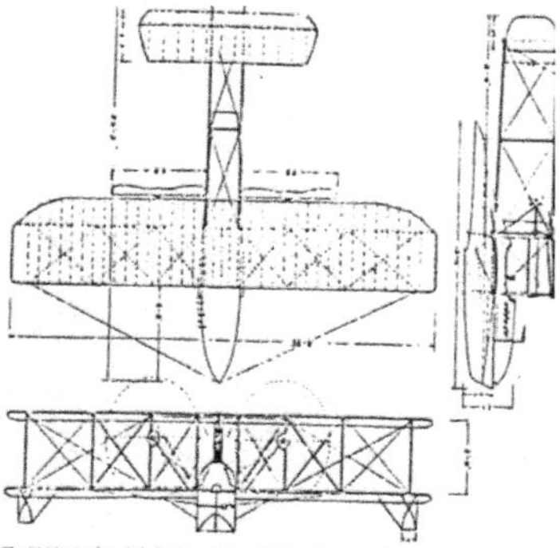

The Wright Aeroboat. It had twin propellers with chain drives.

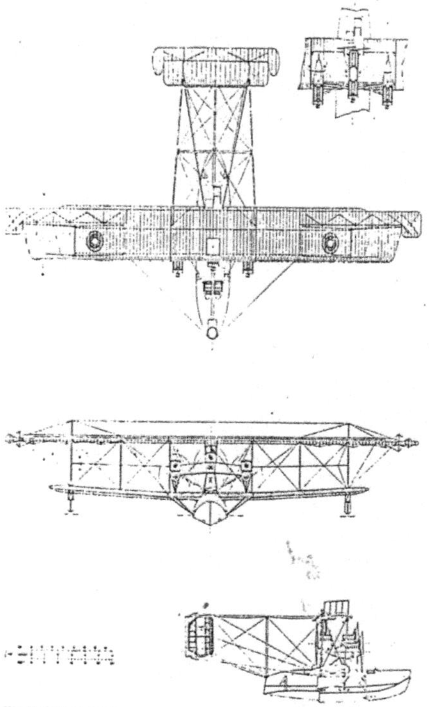

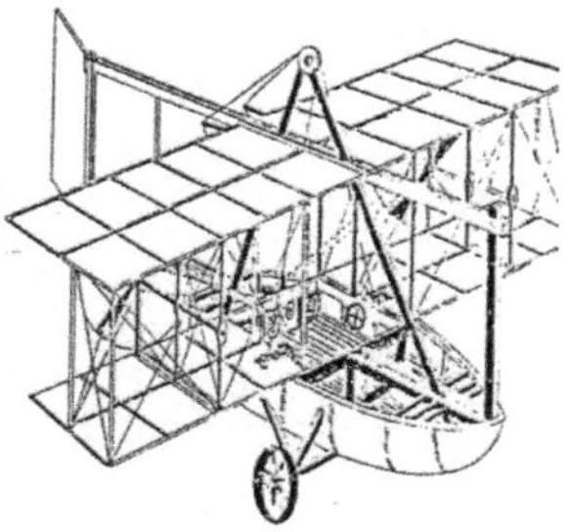

NC-4. (Smithsonian Institution)

The two drawings, above left corner and lower right corner, demonstrate the advanced thinking of Brodbeck's plans for a flying boat. His designs and innovation were incorporated in the aeronautical designs that spanned 100 years, most of which are fundamentally unchanged from his designs in a stock offering in 1865. The Wright Aeroboat, shown above, had twin propellers with chain drives.

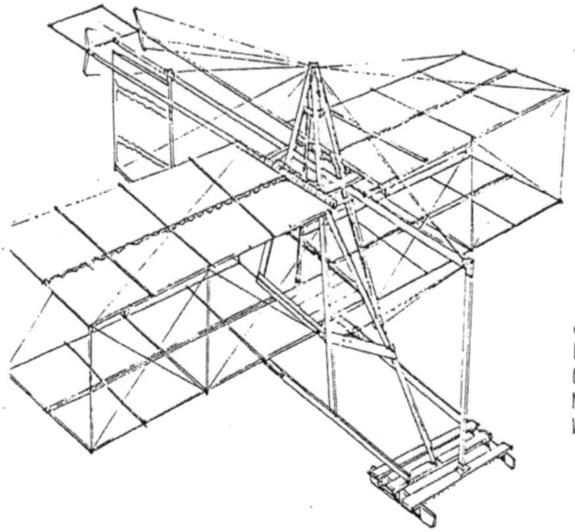

JACOB BRODBECK'S EARLY EXPERIMENTAL GLIDER (BEFORE THE MOTOR & PROPELLERS WERE ADDED 1864)

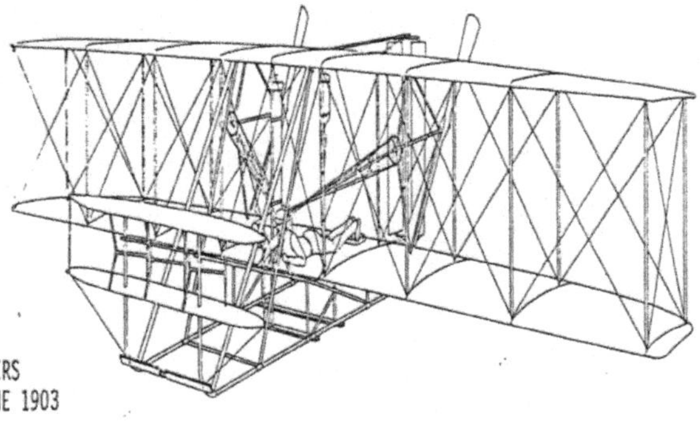

THE WRIGHT BROTHERS "KITTY HAWK" PLANE 1903

There is a remarkable similarity between Jacob Brodbeck's early designs and the Wright's "Kitty Hawk" Flyer.

Portrait of Jacob and Chistine Brodbeck

Picture of Jacob Brodbeck's family taken about 1896

Bibliography

Scripture references from the King James Bible.

Source Books

Allen, Oliver E., Time-Life Books, *The Windjammers.* Time-Life Books, 1978

Colby, C.B., *Sailing Ships.* Coward-McCann, 1970

Gurasich, Marj, *Letters to Oma.* Texas Christian University Press, 1989

Langenscheidt's *German – English - English – German Dictionary.* Simon & Schuster, 1970

Lasky, Kathryn, *Tall Ships.* Charles Scribner's Sons, 1978

Lich, Glen E., *The German Texans,* The University of Texas Institute of Texan Cultures at San Antonio, 1981

Roemer, Dr. Ferdinand Roemer, *Roemer's Texas-1845-1847.* Eakin Press, 1995

Rogers, Lisa Waller, *A Texas Sampler-Historical Collections,* Texas Tech University Press, 1998

Rosenberg, Joseph, *German - How To Speak and Write It.* Dover Publications, Inc.

Shefelman, Janice Jordan, *A Paradise Called Texas.* Eakin Press, 1983

Struve, Walter, *Germans & Texans- Commerce, Migration, and Culture in the Days of the Lone Star Republic. University of Texas Press, 1996*

Tatsch, Anita, *Jacob Brodbeck "REACHED for the SKY" in Texas.* TXU 227301, 1986

Tunis, Edwin, *Oars, Sails, and Steam.* Thomas Y. Crowell Company, 1952

William, Chester, and Geue, Ethel Hander, *A New Land Beckoned-German Immigration to Texas, 1844-1847.* Texian Press, 1966

Magazines, Pamphlets, Online Research

The Handbook of Texas Online Articles: *Adelsverein; Aviation; Brodbeck, Jacob Friedrich; Herff, Dr. Ferdinand Ludwig; Indian Point, Indianola; Meusebach, John O.;* Fredericksburg, Texas; *Adelsvereins-Kirche; Victoria, Texas*

Historynet.com/ahi/bljbrodbeck, Harris, Janet W., *Jacob Brodbeck: Early Flier?*

The German Texans, Principal researcher; James Patrick McGuire, *Jacob Brodbeck 1865*. The University of Texas Institute of Texan Cultures at San Antonio 1970

Century of Flight, *Wright Brothers*

Smithsonian National Air and Space Museum, *Wright 1903 Flyer*

Texas Highways, November 1992, *Speaking of Texas.*

Texas Co-op Power, March 2009, *Flights of Fancy*

Petersen's Materia Medica and Therapeutics, *Ether*

Countway Medical Library – Records Management – Image of the Month, August 2000, Art and Artifacts – Ether inhaler, ca. 1840's

The Overland Trail: *A Stage Coach Vocabulary*

Texas Talk, *Lexicon*

TexasRanger.org/halloffame/*Wallace, William A. A. "Big Foot" 1817-1899*

Wells Fargo, Stagecoach Holdups, Overland Stage Line

Octave Chanute's Glider Experiments of 1896

Bernoulli's Principle of Flight

Texas Newspapers

Austin American Statesman, October 13, 1968; also May 31, 2003

Blanco County News, May 13, 1982

Fredericksburg Standard-Radio Post, December 17, 1986; also August 15, 1990; and March 31, 1993

The Record-Courier, May 6, 1982; also December 18, 1986

San Antonio Express-News, December14, 2003

Colorado Newspaper

The Denver Post, September 12, 1971, Maguire, Jack, *The Man Who Flew Before the Wright Brothers*

Made in the USA
Middletown, DE
08 March 2020

86046728R00169